A Holiday Romance

Seth Sjostrom

TreeFarmPress.com
wolfprint, LLC
Hernando Beach, FL 34607

Trade Paperback
ISBN-13: 978-1-960501-16-5

First wolfprintMedia edition 2024. wolfprintMedia is a trademark of wolfprintMedia, LLC.

For information regarding bulk purchases, please contact wolfprintMedia, LLC, at wolfprint@hotmail.com.

United States of America

To Kathi, for sharing my dreams and my nutty stories with me.
To Hayden, my son, forever my love.
To Mom who has always been my biggest supporter.

That's 4 Entertainment and their real-world Christmas Con magic. While my convention is fictional, theirs is inspirational.

To Christmas is Not Cancelled, Jen Lilley, Ale Boggiano, and head elf Mandi Kinninger for providing a real-world vehicle to give back and support foster children.

To Jessica Reel, Nicole Clatterbuck, Vanessa Senni, Raquel Baez, Michelle Goss, Makayla Jude, Rhonda Jude and Michelle Heidt for being drawing winners and allowing their namesakes to adorn a few characters scattered throughout the pages.

To my extraordinary writer friend Nancy Naigle, your heart-warming stories are inspiring.

To my friends at Jewels for Hope, Merry Christmas, Stevie Lynn and Sandy. Yes, their jewelry is worn by stars and they do give back to charity.

Thank you, Jen Boles editor extraordinaire, a friendly voice who whispers sage corrections into many of my titles, including Love at the Christmas Con.

Thank you, Bryn Donovan, for your deft hand at ensuring this story flows from pages to hearts.

Love at the ChristmasCon

One

Abby Wells sat staring out the window of the coffee shop, tapping her caffeinated toes nervously. Half listening, she nodded even though her friend Michelle, on the other end of the phone call, couldn't see her.

With a heavy, trepid sigh, Abby said, "I know I am doing this for Mom. Still, I didn't think it would be so hard."

"I know. It's been a tough year. We all miss her," Michelle said.

"It's a bit more than that..." Abby said.

"You can't predict the future, Abby. You had no idea."

"There's no excuse. I should have spent more time with her," Abby said. Straightening in her seat, she added, "What did I get myself into, taking on the con?"

"It sounds like help is on the way," Michelle said.

"You really think he knows how to put on a Christmas convention?" Abby asked.

"Not a Christmas convention, *the* Christmas convention," Michelle pressed. "People from all over the country, all over the world, come to it."

Abby's chest felt only heavier, "Right. Thanks for reminding me how big this is."

"How *important* it is. You've got this. I'll be there every step of the way with you," Michelle said.

"I know. Thank you," Abby said. Her throat tightened. "I was thinking, this will probably be the last."

"Well, if it is, let's make it the best ever. For your mom," Michelle said. "So, is he there yet? I thought you were meeting at ten. It's like, twenty after."

"Yeah," Abby said, her eyes scanning the parking lot of the coffee shop. Absently, she began packing up her meeting materials. "Like I said, how much help do you think this will be?"

"For publicity? It will be huge," Michelle said.

Pausing, Abby held her folder in midair. Her eyes fell on a man climbing out of a gleaming SUV. Dressed to the nines in a tailored suit cloaked by a wool overcoat and scarf that danced in the breeze, he held a phone clamped to his ear as he made his way toward the cafe.

"Ooh. He's here. I've got to go," Abby blurted into the phone.

"How does he look…?" Michelle's question would go unanswered as the line went dead.

Abby straightened in her seat as the undeniably handsome man approached. He paused before entering the coffee shop, intent on finishing what appeared to be a rather animated conversation.

The man's voice carried through the glass, causing Abby to look away and shuffle in her seat.

"Are you sure I need to do this? I mean, can't I just donate some signed scripts and photos or something?" Brett Walker asked as he gave the little coffee shop a once over. Pausing just outside the door, he paced on the sidewalk.

"Need I remind you of your situation?" his agent, Liza Accorsi, asked on the other end of the call. "I am pretty sure it was you and not me who said that Christmas romances were a joke, in front of a crowd of people. And, if I recall, that was your face in the video that went viral after speaking those words."

"You know I was talking about Jessica!" Brett argued.

"I know that. The million viewers, however, don't know that. Nor do the studio executives who would normally be lining up to cast you for, oh, that's right, Christmas romances," Liza said.

"I was going through a break-up," Brett moaned.

"A bad, very public breakup with one of your romance movie co-stars," Liza said. "Which I warned you about."

"We hit it off," Brett said.

"Until you didn't," Liza said. "Your vast dating history prior to Jessica doesn't help, either."

Brett cracked a grin and shrugged, "What am I supposed to do?"

"Listen to your agent and get your career back on track," Liza said. "The studio wants you to prove yourself. Get yourself in there, and their audience's good graces. Or, they are threatening to cut you loose."

"I have three more movies under contract," Brett said.

"A contract that has very wide-ranging clauses about personal behavior fitting the studio's virtues," Liza said. "Which your smash hit follow-up video clearly violated."

Brett sighed, "I punched *one* paparazzi photographer… who had it coming, by the way…"

"And now you get to serve a little community service while hopefully improving your image with the studio, as well as with their fans," Liza said.

Brett stared at his phone, somewhat oblivious to the fact that his conversation had drawn some attention in the coffee shop. "But, this is embarrassing. Kowtowing to some event planner while the rest of my fellow co-stars get to hang out in the green room."

"This will be good for you. Don't be a grinch, Brett."

"The only grinch is this event planner who made me come all the way to Pigeon Forge for this meeting. I mean, a phone call or video chat would have worked," Brett complained.

"Behave!" Liza demanded. "Besides, the event center there is gorgeous. You'll love it."

"Fine. I'll check in with you as soon as this is over," Brett said.

Hanging up the call, Brett pushed into the cafe, suddenly very aware that his conversation had drawn on too long just outside the coffee shop.

Looking sheepishly at an expectant woman with a large binder and stack of flyers in front of her, he called out, "Abigail?"

"Abby, yes. And I know you are Brett Walker," Abby said. Her face delivering few clues as to her mindset.

"In the flesh!" Brett grinned.

Abby looked at his broad smile, thinking it was only missing that gleam you would see in a cartoon when the hero flashes their knee-wobbling smile. For her, the look only intensified her squirming.

Brett wrinkled his face as he slipped his phone in his pocket, "Sorry about that. How much of that… did you hear?"

"I'm a grinch. You feel pretty good about decking a guy with a camera. You consider yourself to be a bit more regal than the roles that I might have planned for you at the Christmas Con," Abby recounted the conversation as she heard it through the cafe window.

"So, yeah, just about everything," Brett sighed. With a frown, he asked, "Catch the 'too many girlfriends' and off-handed statement about Christmas romances being stupid?"

"Missed those, but I've got them now," Abby said.

"Yeah," Brett sunk in his seat across from Abby. "On social media much?"

"Oh, I have seen your antics. I was planning on giving you the benefit of the doubt," Abby said.

"Was?" Brett scowled.

"If the green fur fits," Abby shrugged.

"Maybe my shoes are a bit too tight," Brett said.

"Or your heart just isn't right," Abby said.

"Ouch!" Brett winced. "But probably true. And a bit too soon."

"Sorry, just going with the story," Abby said.

"Right," Brett nodded. Pointing toward the counter, he asked, "Do you mind if I grab a cup of coffee? You want one?"

"I'm good. I had time to enjoy my share of caffeine for the day. And yours, too, while I waited," Abby said, playing with the cups in front of her.

Brett glanced at the empty coffee mugs on the table, "Yeah, I ran a little late, didn't I?"

"A bit," Abby nodded.

"I'm sorry." Brett's chin fell.

"It's all right. Go on. Grab a cup. I'll wait," Abby said.

The words stung like little jagged icicles stabbing Brett in the chest. With a quiet nod, he excused himself.

Settling back at the table with his cup, Brett leaned in, "So, what is it you'd like me to do? A promo spot, some extra photo ops?"

Abby wrinkled her nose into a frown. "I was told you wanted to sign on as a volunteer."

"Well, yeah," Brett leaned back, his coffee failing to hide his movie star smile.

Abby wondered how often that award-winning grin bailed him out. "As in like, you'd be helping with the convention staff."

"Yeah, sure. What's that?" Brett began to squirm in his seat.

"You know, convention prep. Like setting up tables, helping the vendors load in, things like that. I'll take the promos, though, as a bonus. They'll help with the charity drive," Abby said.

"Oh." Brett's face fell.

"What? Manual labor an issue?" Abby asked.

"No, I can do manual labor. I think," Brett said, his voice trailing off.

"Look, if your heart isn't in this, it's all right. I'll sign off on whatever you need. But the truth is, this is a big deal. It means a lot to a lot of people and my… mother," Abby said, once more gathering her things.

"Your mother? Is she a fan?" Brett asked.

"She was," Abby nodded. "She started the Christmas Con. Christmas movies touched her like so many people. She wanted to create an event that drew the stars, writers, creators and the fans together. Create a sense that, just for a moment, those idyllic Christmas towns and shops and experiences could be real. But it was more than that. She, uh, she had a passion for caring for foster children."

"You said she *had* a passion?" Brett leaned forward.

"She passed this last year. That is why I had to pick up the reins," Abby said.

Brett's eyes widened, "You are Maggie Wells' daughter. I should have known. She is… was… a gem. I'm sorry for your loss. Her passing was a loss for all of us."

Abby was taken aback by the movie star's reaction, "Thank you."

"How about you… a fan?" Brett asked.

"I like the escape. I like the sweetness, the sense of community and family that they offer. But not the romance. You said it. Those types of romances are silly and unrealistic. A waste of time," Abby said.

"That isn't, well, it *was* what I said, but it was out of context," Brett said.

"I'm sure it was," Abby said, her voice reeking insincerity.

Brett leaned across the table, "I have made some mistakes and said some things that I wish I could have taken back. My agent thinks, *I* think, the idea of embracing the spirit of Christmas Con might do me some good. What do you think?"

"I think we have a lot of work to do and I need all the help I can get. Are you in or are you out?" Abby asked.

Brett was almost taken aback by the matter-of-fact tone.

He softened for a moment. "I'm in."

Two

Abby watched Brett Walker head out of the restaurant, offering a smile and waving at a group of giggling women who peered at him over their coffee cups.

Her mind drifted back to a moment before the previous year's Christmas Con.

"Abby, come join me," her mother sang into the phone. "It's been years since we shared the convention together."

"Trust me, I would have preferred being at the con instead of cramming for exams," Abby said as she paced around her apartment.

"I was hoping once you graduated, you'd start coming again," Maggie said.

"I have a job, Mom. It seems this time of year is always busy for us. It's tough to get away," Abby said.

"We always had such fun together. It hasn't been the same without you. Remember walking the floor together before anyone got there?" Maggie asked.

"Of course, Mom," Abby said. "I loved the Christmas scenes and playing on the stage sets. It was like being in a movie. That was my favorite part."

"Yes," Maggie Wells laughed. "It always was. You liked the magic and the wonder."

"You liked the people and the movie stars," Abby said.

"I liked the stories and the impact that stories had on those who watched them. I enjoyed the convention fans see the movies from their televisions become living, breathing realities at Christmas Con," Maggie said.

Abby laughed, "You were made for the limelight, Mom. You captivate the audience as much as any of the stars do."

"You can help me. I have a special project I could use your help with," Maggie said.

"Mom, I'd love to. But if I am going to take time off for Christmas to come visit you, I can't take time off for the convention," Abby said.

"Then come for the weekend. I'll buy you a plane ticket. Have you back home for work by Sunday night," Maggie pressed.

Abby sighed, pulling away from the phone for a moment.

"Abby?" Maggie called softly into the phone.

"I'd like to. Things are crazy at work right now. It's like we're all fighting for our jobs. I don't think I could handle the distraction right now," Abby said.

"Think of it as a welcome respite. A weekend to refresh. Go back to work stronger and revitalized," Maggie said.

"Mom! You are so… persistent. No wonder you were able to convince movie stars to attend a convention in Tennessee just weeks before Christmas," Abby said.

Maggie laughed, "The stars were easier to get to come to Christmas Con than my daughter."

"They made better career choices," Abby said.

"I just want to spend time with you, too," Maggie said, her voice softening.

"I know, Mom. I want to spend time with you. And we will. I'll be home for Christmas," Abby said. Sensing the disappointment on the other end of the call, she added, "Christmas Con is your event. You thrive in the bustle of it all. Mingling with the stars, bringing Christmas cheer to the crowd. I like my space in my tidy little cubicle."

"I guess, I had always hoped it would be *our* event. That's why…" Maggie started before a beep cut her off.

"That's work. Mom, I have to go. We'll talk later," Abby said.

"Promise me you'll think about coming?" Maggie asked.

"I'll think about it, Mom," Abby said, reservation clear in her voice.

"I love you, Abby."

"Love you, too, Mom."

As her memory of the phone call ended, Abby was brought back to her seat in the diner. Her chin propped on her hand as she stared blankly out the window. Squeezing her eyes shut, a tear pressed through her eyelids and wet her cheek.

Swiping at the tear with her hand, Abby shook herself. Her eyes scanned the diner self-consciously. Relieved to see her check returned at the end of the table, she put her credit card away. Clearing her throat, she sat up, pulled her coat tight and hurried out of the diner.

The crisp air urged her to pull her collar up. Abby appreciated having the wool fabric as a veil to hide from others as much as for its warmth.

Climbing into her car, she shielded herself from the diner's customers, but she couldn't shield herself from her memories. Staring at her phone, she winced at the decisions she had made.

She pictured her mother on the other end of that call- phone in hand, pleading with her daughter. She pictured herself- promising to weigh joining her mother at the con while knowing that her mind was already made up. The priorities that now seemed so superfluous and silly made her ache. The image of her glibly hanging up the phone to focus on her work call sent icicles into Abby's heart.

Safe in the confines of her car, she let the tears flow.

With a heavy sigh, she said, "The stage sets weren't my favorite part, Mom. My favorite part was being with you. Watching you be a light for so many people. Those were my favorite parts."

Closing her eyes, her hands draped on the steering wheel, Abby choked through a cough, "I miss you, Mom. I want to spend Christmas Con with you."

Abby wiped a tear and started her car.

Three

Abby Wells waited outside the doors of the Pigeon Forge convention center. Her heart fluttered as the sound of footsteps echoed from the other side of the large double doors.

A smiling face peered through the skinny convention center windows. A hefty set of keys jangled as the lock was twisted and the steel door was pushed open for Abby to walk through.

"Thank you," Abby said.

"You must be Ms. Wells. Your mother… she was a very special lady. No matter who you were, she treated you like were… *someone*," the man said. "Even the janitor. Welcome to Pigeon Forge."

"Thank you," Abby repeated as the man sauntered away, his keys clanging in rhythm with his footsteps, bouncing off the empty center's walls.

Abby wrapped her arms around her chest as she stepped into the massive convention center. The building was cold and sterile in its vacant form.

Walking deep into the center of the convention space, she did a slow pirouette with her toes, her eyes sweeping the vast building. Abby could barely believe that the concrete landscape could somehow transform into a winter wonderland. Neither could she further believe that the center would be packed with Christmas movie lovers.

It had been a while since Abby had played any major role in the convention. This was her mother's world. It was fun and exciting when it launched. It was a lot smaller then, too. The original space was much smaller. The list of stars who made an appearance held fewer names. Everything was on a much quainter scale. Abby liked that cozy, intimate environment.

The magnitude of the event did have one very big upside. The larger it grew, the more foster children the convention could buy toys for. An idea that had Abby swinging for the fences with a lofty goal for this year's convention.

Walking through the space, she tried to visualize the layout of the Christmas convention as detailed in the giant binder that her mother had left her. The echo of her footsteps followed her as she paced out of the convention space.

With a heavy sigh, she breathed to herself, "I don't know how I am going to do this."

Even her soft voice echoed in the empty space.

"Mom, what am I doing here?" Abby asked.

Abby could picture being there with her mother. Entering the space much like it was at that moment - a vast empty canvas. She could feel her mother holding her hand, her eyes glistening as she shared her vision with Abby. Her mother bent down, her hands on Abby's shoulders, "This is for you, my dearest Abby."

Leaning in, they wrapped in a hug.

Her memory of the first convention spun through her mind like fast-forwarded mini-video clips scrolling past in her mind. Suddenly, the space was filled with vendors. Massive decoration sets turned the space into a magical Christmas village. Attendees milled about in awe, as Abby had when she was younger. Seeing stars from their favorite Christmas movies stop to smile and chat with them as though they were just another attendee made the entire experience special.

She pictured the children, some with their parents, some in a group. Wide-eyed, they got a helping of Christmas beyond their imaginations. Only Santa's workshop itself could have been more magical.

Abby jumped as a loud noise brought her out of her daydream. Steady pounding on the door drew her toward the front of the convention center. Her friend Michelle's face peered through the small slits of windows as she bounced up and down, calling for Abby to let her in.

Crossing the convention center, Abby pushed the bar that opened the door.

"It's about time!" Michelle gasped, slipping into the building. Rubbing her arms, she said, "It's freezing outside."

"It's not too much better in here. They won't turn the heat on until the day before the event," Abby said.

"Make sense since the doors will be open most of the time during load-in," Michelle said.

A low rumble gently shook the foundation of the convention center.

"The trucks are here! It's time to get to work!" Michelle clapped her hands. "Are you ready for this?"

Abby choked, "I need my binder."

Her palms began to sweat, and her neck felt hot. The reality of what she was about to embark on suddenly overwhelmed her.

"You've got this, and I've got your back," Michelle assured, a comforting hand on her friend's shoulder.

Abby nodded.

Michelle looked around, "Maggie is here with us. You know that, right?"

Abby looked at her friend, a thin smile across her lips, "Yeah."

Retrieving her enormous binder, Abby feigned a confident expression and followed her friend to the loading dock.

The giant doors rumbled open, revealing a growing pool of convention staff. They smiled and waved at the ladies as more helpers filtered in behind them.

Stepping into the convention center, they gathered.

Michelle nudged Abby, "I think it's time to rally the troops."

"Rally the troops?" Abby asked, peering nervously over her binder.

"Yeah. You know, like your mom did," Michelle said.

Abby sighed, "I am not anything like my mother. She was… so full of life. When she walked into the room, everyone stopped to listen to her. I was very comfortable in the shadows, thank you very much."

"Abby," Michelle looked directly at her friend. "You are every bit as vibrant and brilliant as your mother. Even if you have very different styles. Trust in yourself. Be yourself. You've got this."

Abby chewed her lip nervously.

"Just one more thing," Michelle said. Wrestling the binder out of Abby's hands, she said, "I'll hold this. Now… go!"

Abby looked at the crew, a little perturbed at being forced to relinquish the binder. It had become her safety blanket as the convention neared.

Taking a deep breath, she walked to the center of the loading dock where the volunteers had gathered to begin unloading the trucks.

Scanning the group, Abby recognized a few faces. As the conversations stopped and all eyes fell on her, she forced a nervous smile.

"Thank you all for coming. Most of you have worked with my mother, who started the convention almost two decades ago. Some of you have been there since the beginning when it was a small fundraiser to buy foster children Christmas presents. Her dreams were as large as her heart. She was an amazing woman. If she had a goal in mind, nothing would stand in her way. Christmas Con started as a small tribute to Christmas, Christmas movies and the fans who love them. That is what Christmas Con still is today, but way, way bigger, touching more lives than I could have ever imagined. This three-day event with dozens of stars and thousands of attendees was her vision all along."

"Speaking of her vision, this year's theme comes straight out of her playbook. In addition to her love of uplifting Christmas movies, she had a big heart for children. Her sketchbook had this year listed as Winter Wonderland. A portion of the convention proceeds will go to ensuring foster children receive Christmas presents along with a toy drive during the event. Last year, we served over twenty-five thousand presents. I must have channeled Mom, because this year, our goal is thirty thousand. With all of you, we can make this big open space of concrete floors and steel beams into her vision of creating a winter wonderland under this roof. I need you. I need your help… to keep Mom's vision alive!"

The crew collapsed around Abby in an impossibly large group hug. The emotions she had fought to hold in streamed down her cheeks.

Catching her breath, she wiped her eyes and called out, "All right, all right. We have work to do!"

Following a diagram that Abby taped to the wall, the crew began setting out to deliver the trailer loads of décor, props and event merchandise to their marked locations.

The crew moved so fast, it was difficult for Abby to keep up with her mental checklist.

Abby's heart warmed as the cold, empty convention space burst to life with activity. Retrieving her binder from Michele, she clutched it to her chest. Deciding she needed a place to organize her notes and her thoughts, she headed to the event office.

Relieved to find a few moments alone, she plopped the binder onto a desk with a notable thud. Overstuffed, it nearly opened on itself. Abby cocked her head to the side as she eyed a little note card with a swoopy letter 'A' on it. Her mother used to leave her little note cards. Sometimes she would find the cards in her luggage before a trip, on her car window before an important event or simply placed on her kitchen counter after a visit. Whether inspirational during a time of stress or a note "just because" they were always filled with love.

Abby slowly pulled the card from the binder. Holding the note with both hands, Abby chewed her lip in an attempt to avoid a torrent of tears. Sliding the note out of the envelope, Abby flipped the card open with trembling hands.

My Dearest Abby,

Bringing joy into the world has always been my passion, sharing the world with you has always been my greatest joy.

It is my wish that the ribbon of joy may spread through you to others, as you have given to me since I first laid eyes on you.

You have filled my heart with the wonder of a child experiencing the world and embracing everything it had to throw at you.

You have made me so proud of the young woman you are who has forged her own path and found new and wonderful ways to touch the world.

If just for a weekend, I hope our two worlds can collide as a united force to bring goodwill and cheer to those who need a little Christmas magic.

Forever my love,

Mom.

Abby took a deep breath as tears rolled down her face. Bittersweet tears swirled the gift of her mother's words with the stinging pain that it couldn't be from her mother's voice to her ears.

Guilt, sorrow, sadness and anger engulfed her all at once.

The last place she wanted to be was Christmas Con. The only place she wanted to be was Christmas Con with her mother.

A rap on the office door broke her moment. Seeing her friend Michelle's face lean into the room, Abby wiped her cheeks and smiled. "Yes?"

Michelle frowned, "Are you okay?"

"I found a note from Mom," Abby said. With a nod, she added, "I'm good. It's hard, that's all. This was Mom's big thing. I see her in… all of it."

"That's a good thing, right? You are keeping a part of her with us. And I promise you, that woman is an angel looking down on us right now," Michelle said.

"An angel on earth, she is most assuredly one in heaven," Abby nodded.

Michelle glanced at her watch, "I believe Mr. Wonderful is supposed to be arriving. We should greet him."

Abby frowned, "I don't know. I'm not sure what to make of him."

"What would your mom do?" Michelle asked.

"Treat him like family and welcome him," Abby said.

Michelle smiled, "Well, there you have it. Come on, I'll wait with you. Make sure he doesn't bite."

Reluctantly, Abby rose from the desk and her work. Following Michelle to the volunteer entrance, they dodged the busy crew working hard to transform the space.

"So, what's your plan?" Michelle asked.

"What do you mean?" Abby frowned.

"With Brett," Michelle said.

Abby shrugged, "Treat him like any of the volunteer crew."

"Hmm," Michelle said.

"Hmm?" Abby asked.

"Well, it just seems like maybe he could serve as something special, like a Christmas ambassador," Michelle suggested.

Abby looked blankly at her friend.

"Just think about it. What would Maggie do?" Michelle grinned.

"I think that might just become a poster on the office wall," Abby said. "What would Maggie do?"

Glancing at her watch, she danced, "Shouldn't he be here by now?"

Michelle shrugged, "Give him a few more minutes."

Abby turned on her heel and watched the buzz of activity in the center. Little by little, the space was blossoming from blank canvas into a crude painting of a Christmas scene. "What would Mom do," she whispered to herself.

After another glance at her watch, she huffed, "We have way too much work to do to wait on the glamor boy."

Without another word, she stormed off, leaving Michelle to watch her.

Taking a final glance out toward the parking lot, Michelle nodded and continued with their preparations.

Four

Brett Walker slipped out of his ride share. With a nod to the driver, he held his phone to his ear as he eyed the convention center.

"I know I'm late. I thought there would be an executive car pickup. It didn't come, so I called a ride," Brett said into his phone.

His agent Liza said, "There are executive cars set up for the convention days, but not for set up."

"Well, I'm here now," he said.

"Remember, this is to get your career back on track. Plus, it is for a good cause. Dig in and find your Christmas spirit," Liza said.

"Yeah, yeah. I know," Brett said.

"Have fun!" Liza sang.

"Hmph!" Brett grunted. Hanging up the call and slipping the phone in his pocket, he thought, "Reminder to myself, get a new agent when all this is over."

Whipping off his sunglasses, he walked toward the bustling convention center. Seeing his reflection in the windows, he straightened his collar and stepped into the building.

His Italian dress shoes echoed loudly off the concrete floors. With the bay doors open wide for the crews to continue loading the event props, he was happy to have kept the wool overcoat on.

Standing in the middle of the convention space, he quickly drew the attention of the work crew. Whispers of "It's Brett Walker" were followed by a procession of crew members surrounding him.

With a broad smile, Brett welcomed the hard-working crew. As he began shaking hands, receiving hugs, taking photos and signing crew shirts, most of the work in the building came to a screeching halt.

Abby walked the row where the actors' stations were being set up. Confirming all the participating stars had booths, she checked that off her list. Seeing the posters of the Christmas movie stars, she pictured the scenes from her favorite movies. While she wondered whether the "happy-ever-after" was a real thing, she had to admit that the movies still filled her with a sense of hope.

That is what her mother loved about the movies. That is what compelled her to start the Christmas Con in the first place. She wanted to instill hope and a little Christmas cheer in those who needed it. A thin smile creased Abby's lips.

Abby pictured wandering these very corridors with her mother. Holding hands, they would spy their favorite actors and actresses. They would swap lines from their favorite movies. Posing together in front of the props, they would create a photo album full of memories together.

Swallowing hard, Abby wondered where they lost the connection. Squeezing her eyes tight, she knew it wasn't "they" who lost their way, but "she". She was too busy to join her mother for Christmas Con. But it was more than that.

Rounding the corner, she felt something was amiss. The scurrying of activity had come to a stop. Cocking her head, she peered toward the center of the space that would soon become the vendor area. She saw a large crowd. In the center of the crowd was Brett Walker. His movie star smile was on full display as he worked the crowd.

"Abbs!" Michelle's voice called through the center. "I think he's here!"

"You think?" Abby scoffed.

Reluctantly, Abby put away her checklist and made her way into the crowd. "All right, everyone. You will all have your time to visit with Mr. Walker. In the meantime, we have a Winter Wonderland to create!"

The crowd reluctantly dispersed, leaving Abby and Brett squaring off in the middle of the convention center. "Mr. Walker, you are late!"

"Brett," he smiled.

"Mr. *Brett* Walker, you're late!" Abby repeated.

Brett splashed a smile, "There must have been a mix-up with the car service."

"What car service?" Abby frowned.

"Exactly!" Brett beamed.

"Well, you're here. We might as well put you to work," Abby said, her tone flat.

Brett raised a brow as he tried to interpret the woman in front of him.

Abby paused, returning the once over, "You came dressed like that?"

"What?" Brett straightened his lapel and offered a smirk laden smile, "I thought I looked nice."

"Your clothes are lovely. But you're not exactly set up for convention prep work, though," Abby said.

Brett stared back blankly.

"Come with me," Abby sighed.

Abby led Brett to the convention center event office, handing him a lanyard and a badge, "You can set your coat over there," she said, pointing to an unoccupied chair.

Complying, Brett laid his overcoat gently on the back of the chair. Turning to Abby, he asked, "So, you want me to do some photo ops or roll some tape around the setup?"

Abby shot Brett a perturbed look, "No. I want you to actually *help* with setup."

Brett returned a blank look.

"Move tables, position sets, stuff VIP bags. You know, get ready for a convention," Abby said.

"Oh," Brett said. Patting his clothes, he surveyed his attire. "I *am* a bit overdressed for all that, I suppose."

Removing his suit jacket, Brett laid it carefully on top of his overcoat. Surveying his perfectly pressed dress shirt, he hesitated before shrugging and undoing the buttons.

Abby winced and turned away.

"Hey, Abbs … oh!" Michelle's head peered into the office. Her eyes swept over the movie star removing his nice dress shirt.

Abby followed her friend's eyes to see Brett Walker tucking the bits of his T-shirt back in that got yanked out with the dress shirt.

Abby shook herself away from the t-shirt clad actor.

"Well, you look… more comfortable," Michelle said.

Brett smiled, his well-toned arms spread wide, "I'm ready to help."

"Uhm, yeah. Let's… let's get to work, then," Abby said, trying to look unaffected by Brett's wardrobe change. "Did you need something, Michelle?"

"I… was coming to tell you that the tree truck is here," Michelle said.

"Well, there is your first task, Mr. Brett Walker. Come on," Abby said, giving Brett a wave of her hand that he should follow her.

"I'll help, too!" Michelle said excitedly. "It is going to be *such* a fun weekend!"

Abby cast a stern glare at her friend and whispered, "Behave!"

Slipping past, Abby led Brett to the truck on the loading dock. Turning back, she smiled, "Are you ready for this?"

With a nod from Abby, a convention crew member unlatched the truck and flung the doors open.

Brett's mouth fell open, "That is all trees?"

Inside the large trailer, dozens of trees stood in stands.

"It's like a spruce and fir forest," Brett said.

"Or we just opened the wardrobe to Narnia," Michelle said. Pushing her way into the truck, she began swimming through the trees. "This is amazing!"

"What do we do with them all?" Brett asked.

"Each tree has a number on its base. The number corresponds to a number on the map. Your job will be to move them to the right location. I will follow…” Abby started.

“*We* will follow!” Michelle squealed, popping out of the trailer.

“Sure, *we* will follow with the tree skirts,” Abby laughed.

“All right! Let’s do it!” Brett reached over and hoisted a tree in each hand.

Michelle glanced at the stands, “One and twelve.”

Abby glanced at the map, “One goes right by check-in. Twelve is at the entrance to Artist Alley. I’ll grab the skirts.”

Pushing a container of decorated tree skirts on a handcart, Abby caught up to Brett and Michelle as they placed the first tree.

“This good, boss?” Brett asked as Abby walked up.

“Looks great, thank you,” Abby said.

“I’ll find the next spot,” Brett said, picking up the other tree.

Michelle started to follow before Abby cut her off.

"You can fluff the limbs- they got all squished while traveling," Abby said as she dropped to a knee and spread the skirt around the base of the tree. "One down, about thirty-five to go."

Abby's eyes scanned the convention center. No one part of the convention was completely put together.

Michelle noticed her friend's look, "We've got this. Come on, let's catch up with Brett and the next tree."

Hurrying through the center, they found Brett just as he set the second tree down. "Off to a second load," he said, walking away.

Michelle quickly ruffled the limbs until the tree looked even. Abby tossed the skirt into place, and they raced off to meet Brett for the next tree.

Soon, the trio found a rhythm. With each successive tree placed, the makings of a winter wonderland began to take shape.

Placing the final tree from the trailer, Brett swiped at his forehead with the back of his hand. "What do we do now?"

"Now, we put up the big one!" Abby's eyes gleamed.

"The big one?" Brett asked.

"You'll see," Michelle grinned.

Following Abby to the main stage, they watched as several crew members hauled a tall tree and placed it in front of them.

Abby smiled at Brett, "This is *the* tree."

"The tree?" Brett asked.

"The tree. The big one. The town square tree!" Michelle said.

"Just like in the movies. We almost always have one," Brett nodded.

"It is where the community gathers," Abby said. "Same is true here at the con."

Brett looked at the expanse of the tree, his eyes creased into a frown.

Abby laughed, "It's okay. We'll have help putting this one up."

A rumble announced the arrival of a cherry picker. Rolling on big rubber wheels, it made its way to the tree. The crew members tethered the top of the tree to the rail of the cherry picker. Strapped inside, one of the crew steadied the tree as the machine lofted the tree to its full height.

"Thanks, guys! You can leave the cherry picker there. We'll need it for decorating," Abby said.

"The big tree…" Brett mumbled to himself as he studied the tall fir.

Abby bounced a bit on her heels. Decorating the big tree was always her favorite part of working with her mother on preparing for the convention.

"What do we do now?" Brett asked.

"How are your decorating skills?" Abby asked.

"I am a Christmas movie star, I have a lot of experience around Christmas trees," Brett said, smiling.

"Well, we'll see what you've got," Abby said as several boxes were wheeled in.

Brett frowned with his hands on his hips.

"What's wrong?" Abby asked.

"It seems like we're missing something," Brett said.

"What's that?" Abby asked.

"Music. How can we decorate a tree, especially one as grand as this, without music?" Brett asked.

"Hmm, not a bad idea," Abby admitted. "John, do we have the DJ booth set up yet?"

"Not yet, Abby. But we can get the basics going for you in about five minutes," one of the crew said.

"Thank you, John," Abby said. As she turned back to Brett and Michelle, a line had formed for Brett to take photos and sign items. With a roll of her eyes, Abby said, "And then maybe we can get back to work. Uh, five-minute break, I guess?"

Realizing no one was listening to her, she retreated to find her binder and comb through it. She wanted to see where they were in terms of the schedule.

Flipping over to the proposed timeline for setup, another envelope with an ornate scripted letter 'A' fell out. Slipping the notecard out of the envelope, Abby sat on the stage and read.

My dearest Abby,

The journey, no matter how long, can be the path to multiple destinations. Embrace each possible path and let your heart lead you to the one that is right for you.

Don't be afraid or surprised if the path you find yourself on wasn't the one you imagined. Life can be full of wonderful surprises.

Enjoy each step, even the difficult ones, for you never know what light it may bring into your life.

I know that you will make something amazing out of everything you touch.

Forever my love,

Mom.

Abby held the note close to her heart as she watched the procession gather around Brett. Biting her lip, she nearly jumped when the large speakers from the DJ stand came to life, belting out Dean Martin crooning a Christmas tune. Putting the card away, Abby hopped off the stage and clapped her hands together.

"All right, everyone! We have a lot of work left to do. We have the music playing. Let's get back to it, please! Thank you," Abby said.

Michelle nudged, "You okay? You seem a little Scroogey."

Abby looked at Michelle, "I don't want to let Mom down."

"You won't," Michelle said.

"I might if every time I turn around it has turned into a selfie moment," Abby said. "We'll never get this place ready in time."

"The crew knows what they're doing. Brett's doing a great job, even if he is a bit… distracting," Michelle grinned.

"Do I need to switch up your assignment?" Abby scowled.

"Oh, no. I'm decorating this tree with you and I will hardly notice Brett Walker reaching up for that tall branch next to me. You think he can lift me up for the really high branches?" Michelle asked.

"That is why the cherry picker is parked there. But I give you credit for the effort," Abby said.

"A girl's gotta try," Michelle giggled.

Brett bounced over to them, "Ready to go, boss?"

Abby nodded, "Yes, let's do it."

Opening the first box of ornaments, she began passing them out. Stepping back, she provided direction to ensure they had the boughs covered evenly.

With the music cheering them on, they worked from the bottom of the tree up. Using the cherry picker, they reached the branches on the upper third of the tree. When it began to gleam, they stepped back.

"It's beautiful," Abby breathed.

"It is," Michelle said, grabbing her hand.

"There's just one piece missing. It should be your honor," Brett said as he nodded toward the star.

"The star. Mom looked for just the right one for so long. It had to be just the right size. It had to have the right look - elegant, bright, fitting for the King of kings," Abby said.

"She did good," Brett said, admiring the star. Made of glass crystal, its edges created a brilliant prism of light that shone like ethereal lasers bouncing throughout the convention center.

"The only question is, who places it?" Michelle asked, looking up at the top of the thirty-five foot tall tree.

Abby looked at Brett, "Our resident star places the star. Besides, it will make a great photo. Right, Brett?"

"I might star in Christmas movies, but at Christmas Con, you, my dear, are the real star," Brett bowed graciously.

Abby scrunched her face at the thought.

"He's right, Abby. Your mom was the queen of Christmas Con," Michelle encouraged her.

"I always wanted to place the star as a kid. I thought it would feel like flying. But now, as an adult, I realize exactly how high that really is," Abby said.

"We've got you. What do you think everybody?" Brett called to the crew. "Let's have Abby set the star, in honor of Maggie."

"In honor of Mom. All right, I'll do it," Abby smiled.

Abby grabbed the star and climbed up onto the cherry picker. As she did, the cord of the star caught between the rail and the floor of the machine. When Abby's climb reached the length of it, it snapped taut, yanking Abby and the star backward.

Abby's hands reached desperately for the crystal ornament while bracing for the hard concrete floor below. To her surprise, and relief, her body and the concrete never made impact. Instead, a pair of strong arms cradled her.

Closing her eyes for a moment as she caught her breath, she slowly opened them to find Brett Walker staring at her.

"Are you okay?" he asked.

"I'm… I'm fine," Abby said her cheeks flushed crimson red.

"I told you we've got you," Brett smiled, setting her gently on her feet.

Abby clutched the star tight to her chest while Michelle carefully removed the cord from the angle between the rail and the floor of the cherry picker.

"Should we try again?" Brett asked.

"Maybe I should let you do it, after all," Abby held the star out in front of her.

"Nah. Don't let a little snag stop you. Climb back up there and show it that Abby Wells, Maggie Wells' daughter, is the new queen of Christmas Con," Brett said, supporting her toward the cherry picker once again.

"But this time, let's tuck the cord in," Michelle wrapped the cord over the star so the plug wouldn't dangle.

Abby looked over her shoulder one more time before taking a second attempt on the cherry picker. This time, she and the star made it up without difficulty.

With a deep breath, she called, "All right, let's do this."

The machine chugged to life and slowly raised her to the top of the tree. Reaching out over the rail, Abby placed the star at the peak of the tall tree to the applause of the event staff and crew.

Taking a precarious bow, she declared, "Thank you, thank you… now get me down from here!"

Back on solid ground, she looked at the group, "We should light it up, right? I mean, I know we have the tree lighting ceremony, but we should at least make sure it works, right?"

Michelle offered a smile and a "why-not" shrug.

"Hit it, John!" Abby called.

Soon, the tall tree was ablaze with lights. Reflecting off each glass ball and bauble, the light made its way up the tree to the crystal star at the very top. Light shone out from the tree, arms of illumination stretching like a beacon across the convention center.

The crowd cheered.

Abby took in the sight. "It's beautiful," she said through a broad smile.

She pictured her mother standing there admiring the tree alongside her. As the event grew, so did the tree. The first tree, nearly two decades ago, was half as tall, and every bit as beautiful. Over the years, the tree grew larger, it wasn't out of audacity, her mother would say. It was the lighthouse of the convention. It was a gathering place for community.

Unlike her mother, Abby didn't have a carefully crafted rallying speech or profound sentiment to share. She just had a memory.

"Mom would have loved this. The ultimate symbol of Christmas. The beckoning to open our hearts and share. Thank you all for being a part of this," Abby choked.

Unable to hold back the tears, Abby bowed her head. The event workers collapsed around her in a very large group hug.

Brett watched as he leaned against the stage. He was, for a moment, appreciative of being made to work as part of the Christmas Con family.

Leaving them to their moment, he retreated to the main convention space, past the bundled pallets of décor, props and set pieces that were still wrapped in cellophane. Past the forest of bare trees that still needed to be decorated.

Seeing the stack of light sets, he carried them to the first tree and finished wrapping it before proceeding to the next. Working his way around the event center and finally to a stand of trees for a yet to be built set, he began stringing lights on those trees.

As he circled a tree with lights, he nearly collided with another crew member, who clearly had a similar idea. "Abby."

"I was curious where you had run off to. I thought maybe you slipped off after nearly getting me killed on the cherry picker," Abby said, a string of lights held taut in her hands.

"I saved you from that cherry picker, as I recall," Brett said.

Abby nodded, "You did. I didn't have a chance to thank you."

"No thanks necessary. I mean, you are the queen of Christmas Con, after all. Just doing my duty," Brett said, smiling his screen-melting smile.

Abby did her best to remain immune, "I will leave that title to any of the actresses in star alley. I mean, Donna McCall is dubbed the "Queen of Christmas" by fans, anyway."

"She is worthy of the title," Brett nodded. "But don't sell yourself short. I see how all these people are working so hard for you."

"They are working hard for my mother. I just get to represent her, that's all," Abby blushed.

"I don't think anyone expects you to be your mother. I think they expect you to be the Abby that your mother raised. Aside from being a little clumsy on cherry pickers, I think you are special enough in your own right," Brett said.

Abby cocked her head, her eyes narrow slits as though trying to see through the words as if Brett was playing a part.

"I'm not sure where that comes from, but thank you just the same, Mr. Walker," Abby said. Shaking her lights, she said through even eyes, "I've got this. Thank you for your help today."

Brett studied Abby for a moment before nodding and starting to walk away.

"Oh," Abby called out.

Brett spun on his heels.

"Don't be late tomorrow. We still have lots to do!" Abby said as she returned to stringing the final tree for the evening.

Giving a wave over his shoulder, Brett left the convention center.

Abby completed her tree, taking a step back to admire it.

Her field of view grew as her eyes swept the convention center. Her team had accomplished a lot. Clutching her binder close to her chest, they had a lot left to finish.

She wandered the space. The only sound was the echoing clip-clop of her own footsteps.

Set pieces were still sitting on pallets, wrapped in cellophane. Trees were strung with lights waiting for ornaments, garland, and bows. Entire sections remained bare, waiting for their role in the con to be established.

Abby breathed deep and looked up at the ceiling. "I wish you were here, Mom."

Five

As she walked, Abby's fingers ran lightly over the boughs of the trees. She could almost feel her mother's hand slip into hers. Suddenly, Abby was a child, looking up at her mother, the Christmas lights reflecting off her eyes as they toured the convention space hand in hand.

To Abby, it seemed like a giant puzzle. The box cover was a beautiful Christmas postcard. The convention floor was only fragments of pieces placed together, waiting for the next piece to be completed.

Looking up at her mother, Abby admired Maggie Wells' confident smile. It never wavered no matter what challenges life threw at them.

"What do you think?" Maggie asked.

Young Abby's eyes swept over the décor that was scattered across the convention space. Oversized ornaments and a dozen trees with shining lights making them sparkle dotted the space. Abby's eyes moved to her mother's, "It's beautiful. I'd like to live here!"

Maggie laughed, "Careful what you wish for. Over the next few days, we practically will."

Abby danced in the light as her mother watched her soak in the colorful display.

Maggie smiled, "Come on. I have one more thing to show you."

With a tug on Abby's hand, Maggie led her across the floor. A white cloth cut in a flowy, curvy shape had been placed on the floor. Sitting atop the cloth was a gleaming red sleigh. It was a grand piece fit for a noble driver. The red paint was adorned with gold lines and flourishes of holly and ivy.

Abby looked up at her mother, "Is this…?"

Maggie smiled, "Santa's? It is exactly like his, but no. He needs his to prepare for Christmas. This is his backup sleigh, on loan for the convention."

"What's a convention?" Abby asked.

"It is where people with similar interests gather. In this case, it is people who love Christmas," Maggie said.

"Everyone loves Christmas," Abby said, frowning. "We're gonna have a lot of people here."

Maggie laughed, "I hope so. The people coming here also have a love of Christmas stories."

"Like the ones you read me?" Abby asked.

"Yes. And like the movies you watch with me," Maggie said.

Abby's eyes studied the room at the sets that were still coming together, "This is just like one of the movies."

"Sort of. As close as I could get it, at least," Maggie said.

"We have always wanted to visit one of those towns," Abby said.

Maggie nodded, "We did. And then, I decided to make one, and have a few friends from the movies you might recognize come join us."

"That's nice," Abby said. "We'll have a big family Christmas in our special Christmas town."

"That is the plan," Maggie said, her own eyes sweeping across the vast space, calculating how much work was still left to be done.

Abby looked past the sleigh. Following a red carpet laid down atop more white covering, her eyes led to a magnificent chair flanked by Christmas trees. At the base of a small set of stairs leading to the giant chair, a pair of life-size nutcrackers holding candy canes stood sentry.

"Is that… for Santa?" Abby gasped.

"It is. He doesn't have a lot of time, what with Christmas only a few weeks away, but he said he'd drop in for a visit," Maggie said.

"For our friends?" Abby asked.

"For a group of very *special* friends," Maggie said.

"The ones from the movies?"

Maggie smiled, "Even more special than them."

Pulling Abby's hand as they walked, she said, "Some children need a bit of help during Christmastime. I thought we could do something about it."

"What kind of help?" Abby asked.

"Christmas cheer," Maggie said.

"They need Christmas cheer?"

Maggie nodded, "Some of them, yes. You think you could help them find some Christmas cheer?"

Abby's eyes brightened, "Oh, yes! We can have cocoa and see Santa and sing Christmas carols. We can read stories about Christmas and baby Jesus."

"Yes, we can do all of that," Maggie said. "Speaking of... we have one last thing. Want to help me?"

Abby nodded.

Leading her daughter to a pair of pallets still wrapped in cellophane, Maggie stopped. Looking at Abby, she grinned, "I'm pretty excited about this."

Reaching up, Maggie found an edge in the plastic wrap and pulled it down to where Abby could reach. "Are you ready?"

Abby nodded, her fingers clutching a handful of plastic.

"Here we go!" Maggie called and led Abby on a parade around the pallet. Like a reverse maypole, they danced until the wrap was completely off the pallet.

"It's a barn!" Abby said, a little confused.

"A stable," Maggie said .

"Oh, like in the Bible!" Abby squealed.

Maggie nodded, "Like in the Nativity scene. Should we see what is hidden under all that plastic in the other one?"

Abby nodded, already prying at the plastic wrap. Finding a hold, she took the lead as her mother followed.

With each progressive loop around the pallet, they revealed several large boxes.

"Are you ready?" Maggie asked, her eyes gleaming.

"It's like Christmas!" Abby said, her own eyes wide.

Carefully opening the large boxes, they revealed statues of Mary, Joseph and baby Jesus.

Placing them in a rough layout of what the manger scene might look like, they stepped back to admire the set.

"It's beautiful!" Abby said.

"It is," Maggie agreed, her hands clasped to her heart.

"What about the animals? There's always animals in the Nativity!" Abby said.

"I have a plan for that, too. A plan, I think you are going to like," Maggie said.

Abby cocked her head at her mother with curiosity.

"I may have lined up a local farm to bring some final pieces to the set," Maggie said, a wry grin poking the corner of her lips.

"Cows and chickens?" Abby asked through a mischievous smile.

"A donkey… maybe it's a mule, I don't really know the difference and some sheep," Maggie said.

"Aww, can I pet them?" Abby asked, her voice rising in excitement.

Maggie smiled, "Of course you can."

Abby paused, a scowl taking over her face, "What about the camel? Aren't there camels?"

Maggie shrugged, "I suppose a camel was too tall of an order for me. Not as tall as say… a giraffe, but pretty tall!"

Abby rolled her eyes as her mother draped her arms around her and pulled her tight.

"This is going to be fun," Abby said.

"Yeah," Maggie choked as her emotions stirred at seeing the event so close to coming to life. "It is."

Taking in a big breath, Maggie whispered, "You may not know it, but you are the inspiration for me to put all of this together."

"I am?" Abby looked up at her mother.

"You are. You and I love each other so much, I wanted to share it with others," Maggie said.

"I *do* love you, Mom," Abby said, her voice fervent.

Maggie pulled Abby tighter, her voice barely audible, "Forever, my love."

Six

Abby arrived at the hotel. Physically and emotionally exhausted, she was ready for a hot shower and a sweet movie. Entering the lobby, she heard a rowdy crowd in the hotel restaurant.

"Great, probably some sales conference or something," Abby muttered to herself. Sighting the room service sign, she nodded to herself and started toward the elevator.

Walking past the entrance to the restaurant, she froze. Turning her head, she frowned. The Christmas Con crew was gathered inside. In the center of them was Brett Walker. They were sharing stories, taking selfies, and in what Abby thought an odd choice, signing restaurant menus.

With a slight nod, Abby was content to continue on her way.

"Abbs!" Michelle's voice called out through the crowd.

Wincing, knowing there was no way she could sneak away at that point, her shoulders slumped, and she turned toward the restaurant.

Michelle ran up and hugged her arm, pulling her in toward the group. "I was wondering when you would turn up. Your mom would be right in the thick of it. She wouldn't be the last to leave, but she loved visiting with the crew at the end of the workday."

"Yep. Mom was great. I'm, uhm, I'm not Mom," Abby said, beginning to put resistance against Michelle's tugging.

"No, no, you're not. You are Abbs-solutely yourself, and I love you for it. See what I did there? Abbs-so…" Michelle grinned.

"Yeah, I got it," Abby nodded. "Fine. Let me get everyone a round and then I have a very large notebook to go through for tomorrow's set up."

Abby tapped the binder and placed it on the bar counter with a thud.

As she waited for the bartender, she swiveled in her seat and watched Brett standing with one foot on a chair while regaling the team with stories from his movies.

"What was your favorite character?" one of the crew asked.

"My favorite character… I'd have to say when I played Luke from The Toy Store. I liked that character and playing opposite a talented actress anytime is a real treat. Or The Tree Farm, I mean, I got to work alongside Jack Mayer who played the farmer. He is a three time Oscar winner. Ooh, Ryan from The Nativity, one because I got to rappel in that one and I think the movie hit some good biblical chords while being mainstream accessible. I guess, I have been blessed to play some pretty good roles," Brett said.

"Which actress was your favorite to kiss?" a question rang out.

"Well, if you believe the tabloids, I'd have to say, Jessica. But, I'll never kiss and tell, even if it was a make believe kiss," Brett said with a grin.

"Smooth," Abby muttered.

"Tell us about your next movie!"

Abby noticed Brett's posture change.

"Oh, yeah, well, we aren't able to talk about projects until the media releases are out. Let's just say, I can't wait for you all to see it," Brett shuffled. "Did you know in The Nativity, I had to rappel over forty feet? The stunt crew couldn't attach the line to the roof of the set, so we had to start on a cherry lift, sort of like the one Ms. Wells was on today, but sort of a giant version. It was cool…"

"You've got to give him credit, he can work a crowd," Michelle said.

"And talk around things he doesn't want to talk about. Silver screen and a sliver tongue," Abby said.

Michelle took her eyes off Brett for a moment, "What is your deal with Brett?"

Abby scrunched her face for a moment as she thought of how to respond, "It isn't just Brett, though the jury is still definitely out on him. We just live in different worlds."

"What worlds are those?" Michelle asked.

"Those with adoring fans and… I guess, the rest of us," Abby winced at her own answer.

"I'm your adoring fan," Michelle said, batting her eyes.

"Ohh, Donna McCall just walked by," Abby pointed out into the hotel corridor.

Michelle's head whipped around and she nearly fell out of her bar stool. Slowly, her head turned back to Abby, a scowl on her face, "She wasn't really there, was she?"

Abby just dropped her head and shot a knowing look at her friend.

"Okay, you have a skeptical view of actors in general… what is it about Brett that irks you?" Michelle pressed.

Abby shot Michelle a serious look, "You know how important this is to me, for Mom."

"I do," Michelle nodded.

"I know he doesn't take it seriously. This is just another photo op for him. He needs good press so that he can get cast for another movie. We are his community service," Abby said.

"I thought he worked hard today," Michelle shrugged.

"He did," Abby admitted.

"He was very gracious about your mom."

"He was."

"He deflected attention from himself and placed it on you instead, which I found respectful," Michelle said.

"He's probably just afraid of heights," Abby replied.

Michelle stifled a laugh, "Come on, give him a break. He's human, just like the rest of us. Only way, way more handsome."

Abby couldn't resist a chuckle despite rolling her eyes at her friend. Turning to the bartender, she said, "Well, I am going to do my duty of kindness and pick up a round for this band of hooligans."

"Tabs already picked up, ma'am. The center of attention there nabbed it. Would you like to add something to it? It's still open," the bartender said, both hands pressed against the bar, ready for his marching orders.

"No, I'm fine. I'm going to get room service in a bit," Abby said.

"Room service?" Michelle gasped.

"You can order it from me. Just let me know when you would like it," the bartender said.

"Why, thank you. I might just do that," Abby said.

"Here's a menu. Just flag me down when you are ready," the bartender said and moved down the bar to take another order.

Michelle shot a knowing grin at Abby, "Well, he's generous."

"It would appear so. Definitely buying some good will," Abby said.

Michelle scowled, "You are suggesting he made a friendly gesture just to win some gold stars? I mean, look around? No producers. No reporters. Just a band of your mother's most faithful crew members and volunteers from over the years."

"Yeah, you're right," Abby nodded.

"Maybe, just maybe, he's a nice guy," Michelle said.

"Maybe," Abby said, her voice noncommittal. Focusing on the menu, she smiled at the bartender, letting him know she was ready to order.

"They don't even know he picked up the bill. He slid me his card quietly. Nice guy," the bartender said as he took Abby's order and went to the register to put it into the kitchen.

"Hey, boss! You made it!" Brett's voice called through the room.

All eyes swiveled in her direction, making her neck grow hot. Abby forced a smile.

"Are you going to join us?" Brett asked, waving her into the midst of the crowd.

"I was going to stop and say 'hi' and thank you everyone before settling down in my hotel room. It has been a busy day," Abby said.

"I can't blame you. I can only imagine how much is on your shoulders. Still, sure you won't join us for one quick toast. A glass of wine while you settle down to watch a good Christmas movie. I could offer a few suggestions, if you like," Brett grinned.

"Thank you, I…" Abby started before the crew chimed in, urging her to stay.

"Okay, one toast," Abby agreed, her eyes locked on Brett's.

"Whataya like? I'll get it for you," Brett said. Before Abby could even speak, the movie star was bar side with the bartender's attention.

"Uhm, a glass of red wine would be great, thank you," Abby said.

With glass in hand, Brett stood by her side, flanked by Michelle awkwardly close at his other side. Abby stood nervously, not sure if she was supposed to say something. For the first time, she was glad for his scene-stealing bravado.

"Everyone, I wasn't sure what I was walking into, but today has been great. I have enjoyed getting to work alongside and getting to know all of you. But one thing I *did* know, was the magic of Christmas Con and the inspiration created by Maggie Wells. So with that, raise your glass to Maggie. She will always be dear to our hearts!" Brett called out, his glass high in the air.

The group chorused, "To Maggie!"

"To Mom," Abby croaked, her voice hoarse.

Looking around the room, Abby forced a smile through quivering lips. Her eyes landed on Brett's, "Thank you. That was sweet. I should go."

Setting her glass down, she cast a glance toward Michelle and walked off.

Brett and Michelle watched Abby make her hasty retreat.

Brett frowned, "Did I say the wrong thing?"

"No, Mr. Walker. You said the right thing," Michelle said as they watched Abby disappear into the hotel lobby toward the elevators.

"Hmm," Brett grunted. His eyes remained pinned on the closing elevator doors as he tried to understand Abby's reaction.

Seven

Abby and Michelle pushed their way through the heavy doors of the convention center. The space still greeted them with haunting echoes, but instead of a vast and empty canvas, it appeared to Abby as a rough sketch of what would be.

Her mother's heavy binder clutched tight to her chest, Abby sighed, "Good progress, but we still have lots to do."

Behind them, the convention crew began filtering into the exhibit hall. Looking over her shoulder, Abby smiled a good morning at those arriving to complete the setup.

Rounding the corner to the event office, Abby quipped, "I'm sure the movie star will roll in whenever he pleases."

Abby slammed on the brakes, dropping her binder to the floor, Michelle colliding with her.

A smiling Brett Walker, clad in jeans and a Henley, stood waiting for them, coffees in hand.

Abby winced as she dropped to a knee to collect her binder, "How much of that did you hear?"

"Just 'the movie star will likely roll in whenever he pleases' bit," Brett grinned.

"So, everything," Abby blushed, standing up in front of him.

"Coffee?" Brett offered.

"Still want to give it to me?" Abby asked, her voice trailing.

Brett nodded, "Of course."

"Thank you," Abby said as she set her binder on the desk. "That was very nice of you."

Taking a sip of the coffee, a brow raised, she asked, "What is this?"

"Almond milk latte with one pump vanilla, one pump peppermint," Brett replied.

"How did you know?" Abby frowned.

"It's what you ordered at the cafe where we met," Brett said.

"Well, thank you," Abby said. Eager to bury herself in work to hide her embarrassment, she looked out at the convention center, "We have lots to do. We better get to it. This will help."

Hoisting her cup in the air, she pushed out into the convention center space.

"We need to complete the trees, set up the ice pond, indoor snow globe and the forest park trail," Abby said.

"What would you like me to do, boss?" Brett asked.

Abby winced at 'boss'.

"Why don't you and Michelle work on lighting in the park? I need to check on the set designers at the pond and the snow globe," Abby said.

"Divide and conquer, excellent plan," Brett said. Turning toward Michelle, he said, "Shall we?"

Michelle's eager nod brought a chuckle to Abby. Her friend was giddy at working with the Christmas movie star. Abby slapped herself on the forehead, still embarrassed by the comment she made walking toward the office.

The morning wore on with the crew spread throughout the convention center, bringing the entire floor to life. Trees were beautifully decorated and lit. Both the main stage and the breakout panel stages were set with chairs waiting to be filled by guests.

The DJ stand fully up and running was churning out vibrant Christmas tunes, keeping the crew in good spirits.

Abby did a tour of the photo ops sets, each with their own distinct charm. It was her mother's favorite part of the convention décor. Each was a tiny movie scene where convention guests could capture a snapshot of the Christmas town experience.

As Abby wandered, she felt like she did when she was a child, watching her mother's event come to life. She shook herself as she remembered it was her doing it this year. Looking up, she whispered, "I hope you like it, Mom."

Staring up into the lights of the convention center, she blinked as a familiar laugh caught her attention.

Following the sounds, she found Brett sitting in Santa's sleigh, reins in hand.

"You guys having fun?" Abby asked.

"Ooh, Abbs. Get in there. Why don't you two climb in the back? There is a blanket. Still have your coffee cup?," Michelle asked.

Abby looked down at her hand, realizing she was coveting the last sip. "Why?"

"Just trust me," Michelle said, nudging her friend along.

Abby started to move with an unsure expression on her face.

"Grab Brett's cup on your way. Good. Now, climb in. Use the blanket… and perfect!" Michelle called behind her camera.

Running up, she turned her phone around so that Brett and Abby could see the shot.

"It reminds me of a scene in *The Christmas Café*. It was a carriage, not a sleigh and it was white, not red, but still… Nice shot. I see why your mother had these designed. It puts people into a movie, for a moment," Brett said.

"It is pretty cool," Abby admitted.

"We were taking photo ops for the social media team. I figured having Brett Walker photos to blast out would be great marketing," Michelle beamed.

"I see," Abby nodded. Looking over Michelle's shoulder, she watched images of Brett in the life-sized gingerbread house, snow globe with artificial snow cascading down in the miniature snow-covered park and the con staple of the logo in vintage Hollywood style lights.

"It looks like you've been at it for a while," Abby said.

"The trail lights didn't take as long as we thought it would," Michelle said.

A loud clatter rang out through the convention center near the loading dock. The trio turn their heads to see.

A vendor, moving their wares, lost a portion of their load off their cart.

Brett jogged over to help, Abby and Michelle close on his heels. As the vendor reached down to pick up a box, her eyes landed on her good Samaritan. Jaw dropping, she stammered, "You're… you're…"

"Here to help," Brett said, lifting a box and placing it on the pile. Ensuring it was centered on the stack. "Let me hold all this together as you push the cart."

Turning her head to Abby and Michelle, who each clutched a box, the vendor said, "He's Brett Walker!"

"Yeah. Brett Walker. He's wonderful," Abby said with a roll of her eyes.

"So, what do we have here?" Brett asked as he walked alongside the cart, ensuring the boxes were stable.

"I, uh, I'm Marla. I sketch caricatures of movie stars and their characters!" the vendor crooned.

"Oh, do you? I'll have to stop by and check them out. Maybe pick up a few Christmas presents," Brett grinned, casting a glance toward Abby who once more rolled her eyes. "Marla, I'm Brett Walker. It is nice to meet you."

"Stop by, I'll give you one," the vendor said, offering a shy smile.

"Nonsense. You're here to sell. Rule number one in business, don't give your stuff away. It becomes an expectation," Brett nodded.

"Good advice, even if it is tough to follow," the vendor said.

"Thank you for being here. It means a lot to us at the con," Abby said.

"It is my favorite event of the year. And now, with Brett, it might be the favorite event of my life!" the vendor squealed.

"Well, you clearly know Mr. Walker. I'm Abby Wells, this is Michelle Heidt. If there is anything you need from us, don't hesitate to ask," Abby said.

"Wells… as in, Maggie Wells?" the vendor asked.

Abby nodded, "Maggie was my mom."

"Oh, dear, we are so sorry for her passing. She was an angel," the woman said.

"She was," Abby breathed.

To her surprise, the vendor rushed in with her shoulder and wrapped her arms around Abby with a great big hug. "She meant so much to us. I am so glad that you are continuing with this wonderful event that she built."

Abby nodded through thin lips, "We should let you get set up."

"Would it be all right if I got a picture?" the woman asked.

Brett quickly stood beside the vendor. The woman looked at Abby and rolled her hand, "All of us."

Abby and Michelle pressed in opposite of Brett.

"It is a pleasure to meet you," the woman danced as the trio left her merchant station.

"I told you. You're a star here as well," Brett said.

Abby just shook her head.

As the day wore on, the Christmas convention rounded into shape. Gone were the bare concrete floors and wide-open space. In its place was a Christmas village. Vendors sat in the center of a festive Christmas bazaar. The Main Stage looked ready to welcome Santa Claus himself. The big tree was dressed and ready for its debut. An ornate lever in the shape of a candy cane sat idly by for the tree lighting event.

Star alley was prepped, ready to receive fans whose hearts had been touched by Christmas movies.

The green room and the fabric corridors that ran behind star alley were ready to welcome the actors and actresses.

Abby's favorite part was the sets. When most of the crew had left, she took the opportunity to explore them before the festivities launched and those areas got too busy.

The snow globe was still churning artificial snow. Abby slipped inside and let the gentle little flakes fall on her shoulders. Holding her hands out, she was a child again, catching the first snow of the season. She liked the gentle landings on her skin and the little pitter patter sound it made as the flakes fell to the ground.

She caught a shiver, making her laugh. Even though the snow was artificial, it was still cold.

Walking past the Hollywood marquee-style Christmas Con sign, Abby ran her fingers along it. It was her mother's pride and joy. Not because it was more beautiful or held greater meaning than the other set pieces, but because it was exclusive to the con.

Not far from the sign was a Nativity scene. Her mother never wanted to forget that before the fun, and the songs and romance, there was the real reason behind the season.

This scene looked straight out of a Hollywood movie film. Mary and Joseph and baby Jesus were crafted by Hollywood artists. They looked like live actors playing the roles. Abby smiled, "Nice touch, Mom."

Abby took a deep breath as she entered the little winter park trail. A path wound through snow-dusted trees. Faux gas lights adorned with red bows stood sentry along the path, their bases sunk in a foot of artificial snow. It looked so real, it almost felt cool to Abby. She instinctively held her arms close, as if to ward off a chill.

The area was so peaceful. The trees closed walkers off to the rest of the event space, making you feel as though you were in a town park. Abby paused. The solitude was welcome, yet it opened her mind to the one thing that was missing.

"Oh, Mom. I wish you were here," Abby cried.

Her head spun. The center looked beautiful. It looked as good as though her mother had been there to oversee the production herself. The notion gave her a bit of solace as she wiped her tear.

"This may be the last year, but I think we are doing it justice, Mom," Abby said softly.

"The last year?" a familiar voice asked from around the bend.

Abby cocked her head. With a raised brow, she slunk around the tree to peer into the center of the little park area.

"You? What are you doing here?" Abby huffed.

Brett Walker sat on the park bench used for photos. One leg cast over a knee, his arms spread wide over the back of the bench.

"I'm, uh, just taking a moment. Reflecting," Brett said.

Abby cast a dubious look, "Of all the places to lurk…"

"Lurk? You're the one lurking. I'm sitting here. *Not* talking to myself, by the way," Brett said. "So, what is this about this being the last year?"

Abby winced, not wanting anyone to hear those words.

Brett scooted down the bench to make room for Abby.

With a sigh, she relented to sit. "This was Mom's thing. This isn't my life. She loved it. The actors, the fans, the crew, the vendors… all of it. I love it, too. It's just, I don't know if I'm cut out for it. You met Mom. She was… special."

"You can be different and special too," Brett said. Holding up a finger, he asked, "If there was one thing you could change about the con, from your mother's design, what would it be?"

Abby leaned back on the bench, "Writers. I would include the writers of the stories. I love the way the actors portray the characters and the way the directors share the story. I want to learn from those who dreamed the stories up in the first place. That is what I would do."

"You know," Brett smiled. "I like that. Coming from an actor, I like to get the perspective of the writer.

What vision did they have in their head when they were creating my character? That's a good one. See? You can not only carry on your mother's legacy, but you can grow it in wonderful new ways."

"Yeah," Abby bobbed her head, staring at the glistening lighted trees.

"This convention means a lot to you, doesn't it?" Brett asked.

Abby twisted, "Of course it does! And it does to a *lot* of people."

"I liked her. Your mother, she treated me like a person. Not an actor. She appreciated that we have the ability to touch a lot of people with our craft, but at the end of the day, we are people, too. I liked that," Brett said.

"Yeah," Abby breathed.

"How about you? You don't seem to like actors all that much," Brett asked.

"I don't dislike *all* actors," Abby teased.

Brett laughed, "I see."

"Just those who stand outside a coffee shop and suggest that I am a grinch," Abby said, her voice flat.

"Never going to live that down, am I?" Brett winced.

"Not hardly, big movie star," Abby said, getting up from the bench. "Got a big day tomorrow. We should probably go get some rest."

Brett nodded, "I'll be right behind you."

Watching Abby leave, Brett's head fell into his hands, "Movie star with no movies."

Eight

Abby and Michelle got to the convention center early. They wanted to give the green room one more sweep before the actors and actresses taking part in star alley arrived. Each location had a gift basket and a card with the actor's name on it.

"There's one missing," Abby squinted as she pulled out her checklist.

Reading off the names on the tags that were placed, she got toward the end when she realized, her chin dropping to her chest, "Can you guess?" Abby asked Michelle who was following in Abby's tracks.

"Brett Walker!" Michelle laughed.

"The peppermint bark was really good. Almost broke into Manny's and got his too, but then I figured, it's Christmas, it wouldn't be right," Brett ginned. Sitting on the floor, in the corner of the green room, the basket between his legs.

"What are you doing in here?" Abby asked.

"I may have sort of slept here. Well, on the park bench. I thought about the snow globe, sounds fun, right? Too cold. Definitely too cold," Brett said. His eyes widened, "Oh! I should probably put the blanket back in the sleigh!"

"You should probably clean up. Doors open in a few hours!" Abby squawked.

Brett nodded, "Yeah, I'm going."

Abby followed him out and to the park where he retrieved the blanket. "What is going on with you?" she asked.

Brett looked at Abby, "You ever find yourself at a crossroads. You have no idea how you got there. You know where you meant to be, but yet…"

"You've lost your way," Abby said softly. "Yeah. I knew exactly where I was and where I was going. Until Mom died. It changed everything."

"You have a very good reason for being knocked off course. I…" Brett shook his head.

Abby sat on the bench and patted the seat next to her, "You want to talk about it?"

Brett looked to contemplate the offer before Michelle's voice called over the trees, "Abbs! They are arriving!"

"You should probably go," Brett said. "And I believe the boss told me to go get 'cleaned up'. You don't want to miss greeting the stars."

Without giving Abby a chance to speak, Brett turned on his heel and disappeared down the winding tree-lined path.

The executive cars began lining up behind the convention center. Abby and Michelle stood at the entrance to Christmas Con to welcome each as they arrived.

Michelle danced in place as she recognized the actors stepping out of their passenger seats. "That's Dylan McGrew! Erin Cahill, I love her movies! Ooh, The Queen of Christmas, Donna McCall! There's Jen Lilley! Her last movie was so sweet!"

"See, I told you there was a queen of Christmas," Abby hissed.

"There's Cam Cooper. He's so sweet. He produces a lot of the movies, too. Uh, oh, Jessica Landon," Michelle said.

"Why uh-oh?" Abby frowned.

"Jessica and Brett were a star power couple. Until they weren't," Michelle whispered.

"Ooh," Abby nodded. "She's… stunning."

"She is pretty. Figures she'd be arriving with Marie Claire Downs. There had been reports about her and Brett at one time," Michelle said.

Abby twisted and looked at her friend, "How do you know about all this stuff?"

"Fan forums," Michelle said with a shrug.

"Well, they all seem very nice. And gorgeous. And fit," Abby said.

"Come on, time to give your speech," Michelle tugged at Abby's arm.

"My what?" Abby gasped.

"You know, your mom would pop into the green room, thank everyone for coming, ya da ya da," Michelle said.

With a light shove, Abby stumbled into the middle of the green room. The actors and actresses all gathered, swapping stories and giving hugs. Abby paused; it was like a big family reunion. They all seemed to genuinely care about one another. She felt awkwardly out of place and unimportant.

In the far corner, a freshly showered and shaved Brett Walker stood, his legs crossed, his hands shoved into the pockets of his suit pants. Instead of being in the center of the mix, he seemed to observe the proceedings.

"I guess every family has their black sheep," Abby muttered. She watched as Brett's eyes swept across Jessica Landon and Marie Claire Downs. He occasionally offered a nod as a greeting, seeming to be lost deep in a text conversation on his phone.

The doors opened up behind them, and an energetic young man bounced into the room. Giving quick greetings, he focused on the man in the corner. Running up, he poked Brett in the stomach, making him almost drop his phone. When Brett realized who was there, he broke into a grin and hugged the man.

"Who's that?" Abby asked.

"Manny Vega. He was in this adorable movie called *Christmas Voyage*. It was set on a cruise ship. Very cute," Michelle said.

"Yeah, I think I saw that one," Abby nodded.

"It's that time!" Michelle hissed.

"What?" Abby pretended to not understand.

"It's that time!" Michelle sang out, capturing the room's attention. "Ms. Abby Wells, our gracious hostess, would like to say a few words."

Abby glanced around the room. Her mouth quivered as her eyes swept across the myriad of Christmas movie stars who looked at her.

Taking a step forward, Abby seemed to begin addressing the floor before picking her head up, "So, I am not good at this. I am not good at making speeches or being even a few rows from the center of attention. But, my mom was. Maggie Wells loved Christmas. She loved movies that put her in the mood for Christmas. She wanted to find a way to enter the world of those Christmas movies, even if, for a few hours or better yet, a weekend. She started Christmas Con to share that feeling with others. To allow Christmas movie lovers to take a step through their television screens and feel like they are in one of their favorite movies.

"Now, you can't have a movie without actors. You all bring so much life to stories through the characters that you portray. Those journeys mean so much to people. They might not be able to be with their loved ones during the holidays. They might be struggling to find their Christmas spirit. Your movies open the doors for them to feel. To feel hopeful. To feel joy. To uncover at least a bit of the Christmas spirit they are struggling to find for themselves.

Thank you for being here. Thank you from my mom. This event meant everything to her. Thank you for the fans that are going to burst through those doors in a little over an hour. If you need anything over the next few days, I'm Abby. This is Michelle. We are at your disposal."

Abby's face was beat red as she finished talking. The room was filled with adorations for Abby's mother and how much the stars enjoyed attending the event themselves.

Despite the kind reception, Abby excused herself.

Turning the corner outside the green room, Abby pressed her back against the wall and breathed.

Michelle joined her.

Wrapping her arm around her friend, Michelle said, "For someone who doesn't like to speak, you were wonderful! Maggie would be proud."

Abby tilted her head against her friend's shoulder.

When Abby's rosy cheeks subsided and her temperature returned to normal, Michelle nudged her, "Come on. Let's mingle before the guests arrive."

"I don't know, I'd like to make another pass. Say hello to the last of the vendors…" Abby started.

"There is time for that," Michelle steered Abby back to the entrance of the green room.

Abby's eyes inexplicably scanned the room for Brett. She found the actor in the mix. Side by side with Manny Vega, they drank coffee and laughed with the other actors.

"I don't belong here," Abby whispered.

Jessica Landon and Marie Claire Downs walked up to Brett and Manny. Abby watched as Brett tensed. He looked absolutely petrified. His smiling eyes faded to nervous. She had never seen him like that. Not even in a movie.

Jessica offered a wide grin as she approached. Brett shuffled.

"I really hope this doesn't turn out to be a spectacle," Abby whispered.

Manny looked at Jessica and at Brett. Stepping in, he gave Jessica a hug, neutralizing whatever plan she may have had. As they separated, Jessica and Brett shared an awkward brief hug.

"Those are gorgeous people," Michelle breathed.

"I *really* don't belong here," Abby said, shrinking back outside of the green room.

"What do you mean? They are here for you," Michelle said.

"They are here for my mom… and the fans. Mom was a larger-than-life personality. I'm a cup of tea reading a good book on a windowsill," Abby said.

Michelle laughed, "You *are* that. But you are so much more, too."

Abby watched as Brett's nervous, icy shell melted and the gregarious actor once again emerged.

Checking her watch, she asked, "Should we wrangle our star for his opening duties?"

Michelle took the lead. Without hesitation, she crashed the group, "Hi guys! It is so great to meet you. Manny, that cruise movie, fantastic. Jessica, you were such a gorgeous duchess in *A Castle Christmas*. Marie Claire, I loved watching you in *Family Grace*. Such a wholesome show. You don't see that much anymore."

The actors bobbed their heads as they took in the vibrant woman's interruption.

"I'm afraid we need to borrow Mr. Walker," Abby said.

The actors looked at their friend with curiosity.

Brett swatted the air with his hands, "Oh, it's nothing. Just this P.R. thing my agent is having me do."

The actor's words cut into Abby. She looked at Michelle, "Can you handle this? I need to go greet the last of the vendors and get ready for opening."

"Abby!" Brett extended a hand as Abby made a beeline out of the green room.

Michelle smiled at the other actors before hurrying out behind them.

"Abby!" Brett called again in the hallway.

Abby turned, her head tilted, "You don't have to do this. You can consider your penance served."

"No, no, we agreed. What do you need me to do?" Brett asked.

Abby nodded toward Michelle, "Michelle can help you. I need to check on the vendors and get ready for opening."

Spinning, Abby walked away without a further word.

Brett's shoulders slumped as he watched her walk away.

He looked at Michelle who shrugged, "You know how important this is to her."

"Yeah," Brett nodded. "What can I do to help?"

"Well, VIPs enter in just a few minutes. We need greeters to hand out programs," Michelle said.

"I can do that," Brett smiled, trying to appear chipper.

Michelle nodded, "Follow me."

Nine

Abby walked the convention floor one last time before they would open the doors for the weekend. There was a buzz in the area as the final details were set into place. The sets were all fully functional, the vendors all ready.

Peering into the green room, it was clear the actors were ready. The way they interacted with each other reminded her of a family reunion. They greeted each other with warm hugs and laughter. The love between them resonated, even from Abby's position in the doorway.

She watched the pool of actors praise each other's recent films. Some joked around like siblings. They shared family photos on their phones while some showed clips of their airport antics as they traveled together. Others took a moment and prayed together. The scene both filled and tugged at Abby's heart. Her mother was the only family Abby had ever known. Her mother fit in with the Christmas movie stars and had become a part of their family.

Abby felt very much like an outsider. She wasn't elegant like her mother or the stars. She was more comfortable peering into the room than stepping into it. Begrudgingly thrust into the role of convention party planner, she felt even more disconnected. Abby watched, admittingly, they were kind and genuine- full of love.

She could picture her mother working the room. It was difficult to tell her apart from the stars. Flitting from conversation to conversation, giving and receiving genuine hugs as she did so, she fit right in.

Shrinking away from the green room, Abby turned and faced the convention hall. She took it in as a guest walking through the doors. The show floor looked magnificent. It beckoned Christmas with the big ornaments, a forest of trees and abundant artificial snow. It was sweet. It was romantic. It was nostalgic.

Taking in a deep breath, she knew her mother would be on top of the world if she were there to see it. Looking up, Abby assumed she was.

Abby remembered standing in that very spot with her mother. Their hands clasped together, Abby could almost feel her mother's pulse as the excitement of opening the convention came to a boil.

Young Abby looked up at her mother. Her radiant smile was nearly matched by her flowing Christmas dress. Adorned in sparkling ruby sequins which seemed to radiate light as much as reflect the light from the decorations. Abby's jaw dropped.

Stammering, she said, "Mom… you look like a movie star!"

Maggie's cheeks glowed, "Thank you, my love. I certainly do not feel like one, but I do know one thing. They say the show must go on. So, movie star or not, I have a role to play. Care to join me?"

Abby nodded her head.

Side by side, they walked the floor to the heavy doors of the lobby.

With a smile and a nod, the door attendants opened Maggie Wells' first Christmas convention.

Wide-eyed guests streamed through the door.

Abby's mother bounced on her toes as they watched guests nearly collide with each other as they paused to take in the festive scene. Christmas lights glistened in their eyes as they walked into the room.

As the guests made their way into the convention, the excitement and joy scrawled across their faces, Abby's mother clutched her free hand to her heart as she looked down at Abby. "This… this is what I was hoping for."

Over the Christmas music being played, the sounds of laughter and singing filled the air.

Abby's mother guided her to the actors' booths where guests lined up. Each star greeted the guests and spent time to learn who they were and to share a moment.

"It's beautiful, Mommy," young Abby said.

"It is," Maggie Wells nodded. She choked as her eyes began to water, "It's more than I could hope for."

Abby frowned, "Isn't it exactly what you hoped for?"

Maggie laughed and looked at her daughter. "Yes. And at the same time, it is so much more. It was an idea. Now, it is a beautiful reality. It is stories about people, not just an event."

"I see," Abby nodded, her trailing voice let her mother know that she only partially grasped what her mother was saying.

"I could see the room, the holiday decorations, the vendors all take shape in my head. I could imagine the actors and actresses from our favorite Christmas movies at their booths. I could even imagine the line of attendees, at least, what I hoped would be a line. The reactions as they walked in. As they get to visit with each other… of all of them. *That* is more than I could imagine," Maggie said. "It's lovely."

Abby leaned into her mother and gave her a hug, "You did great, Mom."

"I just had an idea and some hope," Maggie said.

"What gave you the idea, Mommy?" Abby asked as they started to walk through the event.

"You did, baby. You did," Maggie said.

Young Abby scrunched her nose, "I did? How did I do that?"

Maggie laughed and with an outstretched finger booped Abby on the nose, "Just by being you. Being my daughter."

Abby giggled, "If that is what it takes to make big dreams happen, I can't wait until I am bigger."

"Why is that?" Maggie asked.

Abby squeezed her mother's side, "Because I have *you* for a mother."

Maggie smiled, "The two of us can do some great things together."

The pair slowly circulated the aisles, taking in the scene as customers purchased Christmas ornaments from vendors, movie stars posed with fans and staff poured hot cocoas and handed out gingerbread cookies.

Maggie's hand ruffled the back of Abby's head. Her eyebrows danced with promise, "And, the best is yet to come."

A sudden commotion shook Abby from her memory.

Standing in front of the still-closed convention center doors, Abby cocked her head. Voices chattered excitedly in increasing volume on the other side.

"Uh, oh. What is going on out there?" Abby muttered.

Striding toward the doors, hand on her hip, she went to investigate.

Ten

Opening one of the doors, Abby cautiously poked her head out. The VIP line had turned into a mosh pit. Bodies, young and old, pushed into the center of a rough circle. In the center of the circle, was Brett Walker.

Rallying the audience in anticipation of the weekend, Brett had them worked up into an excited lather. Marker in hand, he signed programs as he passed them out. The result was a VIP line in shambles. Instead of clean lines, a large amoebic blob formed around him.

It wasn't frantic. Brett calmly and methodically spoke with each person he handed a program to. He thanked them for coming and said he looked forward to seeing them later. He talked about the vendor with the caricatures and that they had to stop by and visit and reminded them about the charity event.

"You've gotta admit, he can handle a crowd," Michelle said.

"Just another acting gig," Abby shrugged.

"I don't know. He seems sincere," Michelle said.

"Well, you are officially in charge of him now. You are his star escort," Abby said.

Michelle looked wide-eyed, "Okay!"

"Have fun, Michelle," Abby said, disappearing back into the convention center.

Abby took a deep breath as she took in the show space. It was indeed a winter wonderland. The DJ began playing Christmas music. The espresso machine began to whir. The vendors were set. They were just about ready.

Abby felt her chest tighten. Her palms began to sweat. Glancing up, she whispered, "Help me, Mom!"

"It's going to be great," a voice said from behind her.

Spinning, Abby gasped, "What?"

"Sorry to interrupt. I had to get more programs," Brett said and shook a stack of programs in his hands. "I get nervous, too. Before every performance. I was nervous this morning when my costars began arriving. I was nervous when I showed up to help you on the first day. I'm sorry if my nervousness comes out… as sarcasm."

"It's okay," Abby said softly, clutching her arms tight to her chest.

Brett spread his arms out, "This. This is amazing. Everyone is going to feel like they entered a magical Christmas land. You are about to give them a weekend they will never forget."

Abby looked up at Brett, almost as though she were waiting for the other shoe to drop. When he stood patiently, only a kind smile in response, she said, "Thank you."

"Well, I should get back to it. Break a leg, boss. Christmas Con is about to open its curtains!" Brett said.

Abby watched Brett walk away and disappear behind the steel convention doors to the cheers of an exuberant crowd.

"Are we ready for this?" Michelle poked her head through the steel doors, almost startling Abby.

"As ready as I'll ever be," Abby nodded, her voice sharing her uncertainty.

"Hit it, boys!" Michelle called to the security guards posted at each entry door.

The doors opened and fans streamed into the convention center. Many raced to get in line for their favorite star's photo op. Others meandered more slowly, taking in the complex Christmasy scene. Others wasted no time snapping photos of the Christmas vignettes they passed.

Wading through the mass, with a large following himself, Brett Walker strode into the convention center.

Joining Michelle, he handed out VIP bags as attendees streamed by. Sharpie at the ready, he signed bags, programs, convention badges, and even shirts that were worn by fans.

Abby watched from a corner behind the forest trail. It was a little hidden cubby she could observe without feeling overwhelmed.

Brett took his time with each person, giving a woman old enough to be his grandmother a hug. Dropping to a knee, he spoke to a mother being pushed in a wheelchair by her daughter. He didn't say quick hellos, he held conversations.

Abby could see the joy in the fans' eyes as they talked.

Michelle stepped next to Abby, "For someone 'just doing a P.R. thing', he seems to be pretty into it."

A crowd formed waiting to take selfies with Brett, which he gladly obliged. He orchestrated the shots so that they would have a better background with one of the Christmas Con backdrops.

Taking his time to speak with everyone he could, he glanced up to see Abby and Michelle observing him.

The celebrity photo manager stopped and cocked her head as they saw Brett taking free photos with the fans. With a scowl and a stern warning, she stormed off to the star alley photo op area.

Brett looked over at Abby and Michelle who merely shrugged.

"Well, what do you think?" Michelle asked, bouncing on her tiptoes.

"I think you better get your star over to his photo booth before Marcy bursts a blood vessel," Abby laughed.

"I don't know, it's kind of in the spirit of things," Michelle said.

"I don't mind if Brett doesn't mind. It's how he gets compensated for being here," Abby shrugged.

Michelle scanned the crowd, "Everything seems to be working well."

"Mom laid out a good plan," Abby said.

"And you carried it out magnificently," Michelle said. Slapping her pocket, she exclaimed, "Oh, I forgot to give this to you. I found it in a box while rummaging for lanyards in the office."

Handing Abby an envelope with an ornate letter 'A' on it, she scurried off, "I better get Mr. Walker to his post before his stunning smile wears out."

Abby nodded, "He's creating a bit of a traffic flow problem already."

Wandering to the yet-discovered snow-covered tree park, she sat on the bench. Opening the envelope, she pulled out a little card and read.

My dearest Abby,

The moment I first looked into your eyes and your precious lips shared your first giggle, I realized the greatest joy in this world is delivering joy to others. No matter how hard you may search for happiness yourself, you will never find greater warmth in your heart than when watching others, especially those you love, be happy themselves.

Forever my love,

Mom.

Abby quickly stuffed the note in her pocket and sniffed back a tear. Shoving her hands in her pockets, she swayed as she thought of her mother in every element of what the crew had built over the past several days.

Remembering the first convention, which paled both in size and grandeur compared to what it had grown into, Abby was amazed at what the con had become. The audience, eager to get inside, was huge. The mass of people filled Abby with both pride and fear. She was glad they had all come. She was happy about the positive impact to the foster charity linked to Christmas Con would enjoy.

The sheer magnitude of the crowd was overwhelming.

Abby felt that their happiness over the course of the next three days was on her shoulders. It was a badge her mother had worn well. For Abby, it was horrifying. She was happy enough working a job where she was rarely acknowledged never mind being front and center. She didn't need the accolades, and she definitely feared the criticism, especially after witnessing her mother carry out year after year of exceptional Christmas conventions.

A lump had built in her throat and her stomach felt woozy.

Shaking her head, she whispered, "I may not be able to continue this, but this year is for you, Mom."

Smiling as a pair of young women streaked into the park, giggling while preparing for a selfie. Abby took that as her cue to head back onto the main floor.

Eleven

Abby held her breath as the doors opened for the general admission crowd. A couple hundred attendees quickly turned into over a thousand attendees. Her heart fluttered for the millionth time that weekend.

"Relax," Michelle said, handing Abby a latte from the coffee cart.

Abby frowned, "Aren't you supposed to be tending Brett's photo booth?"

"I am. I just slipped out for a quick coffee run," Michelle said. "I'd better get back!"

Abby watched as Michelle darted away, a pair of coffee cups balanced on a tray. As she turned the corner, one of the cups fell out of its holder and spilled onto the floor.

With no time to avoid the spill, an attendee slipped on the coffee. Their arms flailed desperately in the air. Grasping a limb of the large Christmas tree posted on the corner, they tried to steady themselves. A brief look of hope washed to a look of panic as they and the tree teetered and crashed to the floor.

The sound of glass ornaments breaking against the concrete floor was one of the worst sounds Abby had ever heard. Racing to help, she was concerned for the attendee.

Michelle had fought to rebalance the remaining cup while avoiding being hit by the tree. Now she stood in horror at the scene.

Abby grabbed the tree to lift it off the attendee and found it much lighter than she anticipated. Placing the tree properly back up on its stand, she saw a smiling Brett Walker on the other side helping to lift it.

Their eyes locked for a moment before turning in unison to the floor. A wide-eyed convention-goer lay on the ground, looking up to see Brett Walker staring back down at her. Her face went from shock to a broad smile. Through oxygen-depleted lungs, she croaked, "Brett Walker!"

"Are you okay?" Brett asked, extending a hand to help the attendee up.

"I… I think so," the woman said. Scrunching her face, she said apologetically, "The tree helped slow my fall. Sorry!"

"Nonsense, we are sorry," Abby said. "Let's get you checked out."

Eyeing her general admission badge, Abby added, "Let's get you upgraded to VIP, too."

"Oh, you don't have to do that," the woman said, her eyes never leaving Brett's.

"I tell you what, why don't you see about the badge and I will personally escort Ms…" Brett suggested.

"Vanessa," the woman blushed. "Vanessa Senni."

"I will escort Vanessa to visit the nurse," Brett offered.

"I'll… I'll get help to clean this up. I am so, sorry," Michelle said.

"Things happen, it's not your fault," Abby said. She watched as Brett put his arm around the woman and began walking her toward the first aid office.

"This is the best convention *ever!*" she heard Vanessa gasp as she walked away.

Abby arrived at the nurse's station with a VIP pass for Vanessa and her friend. Brett sat across from her as the nurse completed her check.

"I think you are right, the tree slowed your fall just enough to avoid injury. A bit of a Christmas miracle," the nurse said.

Vanessa looked up at Abby with remorseful eyes, "I am so sorry about your tree."

"Nonsense, I'm just glad you're all right," Abby said. Handing over the badges, Abby added, "I put my contact information on there. If there is anything you need…"

"Thank you," Vanessa said. With a glance toward Brett, she asked, "Can I get a photo?"

"Of course! Now that we know you're okay, I kinda wish we had the whole thing on video. You'd go viral!" Brett laughed.

"That would be fun," Vanessa nodded.

"Speaking of trees, the tree lighting is in twenty minutes. Would you like to help?" Abby asked.

Vanessa's eyes lit up, "Yes! Oh, yes! It will be just like in the movies!"

"Just like in the movies," Abby smiled. "We'll see you there."

"I'm going to go find my friend!" Vanessa squealed excitedly. Turning back to Brett and Abby, she said, "Thank you!"

With Vanessa off to find her friend, Abby and Brett looked at each other. Abby said, "Well, that could have gone worse. Thank you."

"Part of the team," Brett shrugged.

"Part of the team with a special power the rest of us don't have," Abby said. Turning to the nurse, she said, "Thank you, Jenny."

Nurse Jenny nodded.

As Brett and Abby walked out of the nurse's station, she asked, "See you at the tree lighting?"

"See you there," Brett nodded.

Michelle bounced up as Brett disappeared, "Abbs, I am so sorry."

Abby reached out and cupped Michelle's hands in hers, "It's okay. Things happen. No broken bones."

"The tree is all cleaned up and put properly back in place. It is a little barer, but it is still a Christmas tree," Michelle said.

"I wonder how many of those types of things Mom had to deal with," Abby asked.

"It's a big convention. I am sure she weathered her share of mishaps," Michelle assured.

The DJ riled the crowd for the big event. Convention goers streamed over to the main stage where the enormous tree stood beautifully decorated though still dark.

Manny Vega appeared on the stage and began leading the crowd in Christmas carols while they gathered. Abby and Michelle found Vanessa and her friend and brought them to the side of the stage.

One by one, the Christmas movie stars joined Manny on the stage, each arriving to their own chorus of cheers. Casting each one with a movie-referenced nickname, he announced "The Queen of Christmas", "The Candy Cane Man", and "Christmas' Most Eligible," which garnered a huge response. When he got to Brett, he smirked at his friend when he called out, "The Snow Brawler"!

While the audience laughed, Brett had no choice but to shrug it off and smile his Hollywood smile as he joined in the final Christmas Carol.

Plucking the microphone from his friend in what turned into a comical struggle for control on stage, Brett said, "and our MC, the most likely to melt Frosty the

Snowman as well as your hearts, Manny Vega. Christmas is such a special time of year and Christmas Con is an amazing event to celebrate the season with new and old friends. Speaking of, I would like to invite up a new friend I made earlier today. Vanessa, would you join us for the tree lighting countdown?"

Abby and Michelle ushered Vanessa up the stage steps to join the movie stars. Finding an enormous candy cane-wrapped lever, she walked up to it and wrapped her hands around it.

Brett flipped the microphone back to Manny who took over the countdown.

When they got to one, Vanessa moved the candy cane lever from one side to the other, triggering the big tree to burst into shimmering lights to the roar of the crowd.

The DJ spun one more song for the stars and crowd to sing together before the actors disappeared through the backstage corridor.

Manny looked over the crowd, "Great job everybody, if you weren't filled with the Christmas spirit before that, I have to believe it is running through you now. See you at Star Alley, an upcoming panel or one of the many events we have scheduled this weekend!"

When Manny ducked backstage, the crowd began to disperse.

Abby and Michelle thanked Vanessa once more.

Looking up at the tree, Abby smiled, "It is a beautiful tree."

"I'll try and keep myself and my coffees far away from that one," Michelle said.

Abby laughed, "Probably a good idea."

Michelle frowned as Abby's face fell, "What's up?"

Shaking her said, Abby said, "Manny picking on Brett in front of the crowd. I think it dug a bit."

"Have you watched those two together? It's kind of their thing," Michelle said with a shrug.

"Maybe," Abby said.

"Speaking of, I should get back to his booth," Michelle said.

Abby nodded, "I'll walk with you."

Maneuvering through the crowd, Michelle leaned in, "Attendance is certainly up. You don't have to worry about that."

"It's good seeing so many people enjoying what Mom built," Abby said.

"It wouldn't be here this year without you," Michelle pressed.

"Yeah," Abby said softly.

As they arrived at Brett's booth, a line had formed but the movie star wasn't to be found. The photographer shrugged.

With a frown, Abby said, "Maybe you shouldn't let your actor out on such a long leash."

"Come on, let's find him," Michelle said.

Wandering through the green room, the vendor aisles and ensuring he didn't get stuck taking selfies at any of the props, they finally found him.

Staring up at the tree that had fallen over, he seemed to be frozen. Holding something in his hands, he deliberated.

"What are you doing?" Abby demanded. "You are supposed to be at your station."

"I know. I'll just be a minute," Brett said.

As Abby and Michelle got closer, they spied a couple of open boxes at Brett's feet. In his hand was an ornament. Finding a blank spot, he stepped forward and placed in on a limb.

"Whatya got there?" Michelle asked.

"I, uh, I grabbed some ornaments from one of the vendors. I mean, they aren't as beautiful as the ones your mom Maggie had selected, but I think they are pretty classy themselves," Brett said, placing another ornament and giving it a spin with his finger.

Abby and Michelle looked closer. The ornaments were images from Christmas movie scenes.

"I'm particularly fond of this one," Brett said. Holding it up, the image was of him looking thoughtful as snow cascaded around him.

"I'll make sure it goes home with you at the end of the event," Abby laughed.

"No, no. Consider it a gift for future Christmas Cons," Brett said with a smile.

"Seriously, thank you. That could have been a disaster," Abby said.

"But it wasn't. And, I think we both made a fan for life," Brett said.

"I'm pretty sure she was already part of the Brett Walker fan club," Michelle said.

Abby picked up the last ornament and held it up, "Find a home for this one and we need to get you back. Keep those people waiting in line and that club might shrink a bit."

Brett looked up at the tree, "It was worth it."

Twelve

Brett more than made up for the wait. When he returned to his booth, he was in full energetic form, welcoming the fans, taking multiple photos, signing anything they wanted signed and all with the gregariousness he was known for. In between conversations with the fans, he and neighboring Manny Vega would trade barbs with one another, much to the delight of the audience.

When his time slot had run well over, Michelle finally called for him to have a break.

"Why don't you spend some time in the green room? You've earned a bit of respite," Michelle said.

"No," Brett shook his head.

Michelle scowled and repeated, "No?"

Following the movie star she was tasked with escorting, they meandered their way to the vendor aisles. Brett walked slowly, he didn't mind the growing mass of fans that collected around him.

Taking his time, he spoke with each vendor. Finding the booth for the sketch artist, he smiled, "Do you do commission work?"

"I do," the artist smiled.

Leaning in, Brett said, "I have a couple I might like to have done."

Whispering his order, he thanked her and moved on to the next booth. Freezing, he cocked his head, "Is that me on a shirt?"

The vendor nodded her head and blushed.

"Hmm. I might need one of those…" Brett considered. Hearing the audience's giggles, he waved, "Not for me. For my buddy Manny. I think he would look good in that. May I?"

Pulling out a few bills, Brett handed them to the vendor in exchange for the shirt. "Best Christmas present idea ever. He's going to love it."

Thanking the vendor, they moved. Seeing a display of gemstones in little boxes, he asked, "What are these?"

The vendor smiled, "Chocolates."

"Chocolates? No way! I have never seen chocolates like this. They belong in a jewelry store." Looking at Michelle, he asked, "You want to try some?"

Michelle went wide-eyed but couldn't muster a response.

"A box for her, one for Abby and ooh, can we have like ten delivered to the green room?" Brett asked.

The vendor nodded her head fervently, "Yes. Yes! Thank you."

Handing two boxes to Michelle, Brett noticed a commotion, "What's going on over here?"

"Snowball fight toy drive," Michelle said.

Brett's eyes went wide, "Ooh, I have to be in on this!"

Michelle scanned through her agenda and frowned, "You aren't signed up for this."

Brett was already streaking down the aisle, "Come on!"

Joining the growing crowd, they slipped their way through to the where the stars had lined up. Across from them was a group of fans who had won the chance to participate.

Brett found a nervous Marie Claire standing behind a basket of snowballs.

"Psst! Marie Claire… you mind if I sub in?" Brett called.

Marie smiled wide, looking at the high heels she had kicked off. Her agent had clearly not prepared her for the event.

"Uhm, yes, please!" Marie Claire quickly scooted back from the basket stuffed with cotton-filled plush snowballs.

Stepping in, Brett grinned at his teammates, including Jessica Landon who had somehow transformed from elegant actress to undeniably attractive, though fierce athlete.

"Well, at least she got the memo," Marie Claire scoffed from the sideline.

The DJ stepped up to a line dividing the stars from the fans in two large rectangles. "So, here's how it works, the music plays and you begin. If you get hit, you are out. If you catch someone's throw, they are out. We play until the last actor or fan is left standing! Are you ready?"

The crowd roared in a loud cheer. With a nod from the DJ, the music began playing and snowballs began flying.

The stars grabbed a quick early lead, catching the fans somewhat hesitant. As their teammates started dropping out, their competitive spirit fired up. They began evening the score.

Brett caught a high throw, eliminating one fan and in an almost singular motion returned the snowball catching a fan in the thigh. In the corner of his eye, he realized it was down to him and Jessica on the star side against a pair of fans on the other side.

Sailing a throw seemingly for the closest fan, it flew by and instead drilled one, retrieving a snowball from the floor behind them.

The first fan winged a shot at Jessica as Brett readied a winning throw of his own. Instead of releasing his shot, he dove in front of his former costar, taking the hit and removing him from the competition. After

Jessica's own throw went wide, the win went to the fans as she was quickly hit on the next volley.

The crowd cheered as the actors stood in a line on their side and offered bows to the victorious fans.

Abby applauded from the sidelines. The event was way more of a hit than she could have ever predicted. Leaning to Michelle, she said, "I had my doubts when I saw this in the playbook."

"Your Mom knew what she was doing," Michelle said.

"So did Brett," Abby nodded.

Both Jessica and Marie Claire collided with Brett, showering him with compliments for his part in the fracas.

Playing to the fans, Jessica covered her heart, "You saved my life, good sir. Perhaps, I misjudged you."

"Your loss, madame. It was his kind gesture that saved me from danger in the first place," Marie Claire said.

Abby hadn't known Brett to blush, but his cheeks glowed a distinct shade of red.

"Like I said, the man knows how to work a crowd," Michelle said.

"Hmm," Abby watched as the scene unfolded.

"I need to get our stars to their next event," Michelle said, excusing herself.

Thirteen

Abby found her way to the main stage. A sizeable crowd had gathered to watch one of several panels that were scheduled over the weekend. Taking a seat in the back, she enjoyed a moment to experience what the attendees experienced.

A pair of comfortable-looking green chairs flanked either side of a red velvet sofa. An additional chair sat askew from the others, where the panel moderator stood ready to address the crowd.

Behind the seating was a large, decorated Christmas tree in one corner of the stage. Behind the sofa hung a massive wreath lit with white lights.

The scheduled actors filtered on stage, the fan-favorite actress, glamorous Donna McCall dubbed "the Queen of Christmas" for her long-running successful Christmas films, gracefully took the first chair closest to the moderator. Brett Walker and Manny Vega frantically jostled for the remaining chair, receiving loud laughter from the audience. They erupted when Jessica Landon stepped by and pushed both of the men onto the couch while calmly sitting in the chair they had their eye on. Crossing her legs, she offered a victorious smile.

Brett and Manny looked at each other awkwardly sitting in close together on the center of the sofa while up and comer actress Maire Claire Downs walked casually onto the stage and eyed the actors.

Both men bounced to either side of the couch, allowing Marie Claire to sit with them, their antics beckoning applause and laughter from the crowd.

The moderator looked at the crowd, "Now that that is over, welcome to the Christmas Movie Memories panel. I'll do my best to corral insightful answers from the panel. Thank you Marie Claire, for separating those two boys. My name is Candace Stewart, and I am the host of Holiday Home on the Cozy Channel. But today, I am all about Christmas, Christmas movies and the stars who make them."

Turning to the panel seated on the sofa and on chairs, Candace Stewart said, "Thank you all for being part of the panel. Let's have some fun!"

Sitting down in her chair, which was perpendicular to the audience and the panel, she pulled out a series of index cards.

"Easy question to start," Candace said, teeing up the first question for the panel. "What is your favorite Christmas movie?"

Donna McCall laughed, "I thought you said this was going to be an easy one. There are so many movies that are special to me. I mean, all the way back to *It's a Wonderful Life*…"

"Oh, no. No cheating. Let me rephrase the question. What is your favorite Christmas movie that *you* starred in?" Candace pressed.

Donna McCall took a deep breath, "Okay, I will say *Holiday Haven* because it was my first."

Candace smiled, "Fair enough. Jessica? What was your favorite Christmas movie that you *starred* in?"

Jessica looked out at the crowd as she thought about her answer, "I am going to go with *The Toy Store*."

"Because that's where you met me?" Brett quipped, his smile quickly fading to a wish to reel those words back in.

"No!" Jessica snapped. "That was most certainly not it. I loved the story. The strong lead character I got to play in Blair Cooper. And the setting… the winery, the vineyard, the snow-covered hills of Washington. It was a treat to go to work every day."

Shooting a playful look toward Brett, she added, "Almost every day."

Brett blushed.

"Well, that is an excellent segue into your favorite filming location," Candace asked the panel.

Manny grinned, "Hawaii. I was never cold on that set!"

The crowd laughed.

"I have to say Tennessee when I starred in *Smoky Mountain Silver Bells*. It was a postcard from a Currier and Ives painting," Marie Claire shared.

"Okay, shifting gears from movies for a moment, let's talk about favorite Christmas memories," Candace said, switching her cue cards.

Not having answered a question yet, all eyes fell on Brett. Taking a breath, he looked out at the audience, but his eyes were really fixed on a blank spot on the wall while memories filtered through his head.

"Christmas Eve. My family would stay up late playing games, singing Christmas carols. A fire would be crackling, candles would be lit. It was a moment of feeling truly together. Before I went to bed, I would step outside. There weren't cars on the road. The world was silent. Peaceful. I felt full of hope at the very moment…

"Of course, only a few hours later, my brother, sister and I would burst into Christmas morning chaos with wrapping paper and toys strewn about," Brett grinned. His voice softened, "But that moment on Christmas Eve…"

Candace looked surprised by Brett's poignant memory. Seeing fit to move on, she said, "And after that genuinely sweet response by Brett, we get a bit spicy. What is it like to 'date' each other on camera?"

The panel looked at one another, seeing who, if anyone, wanted to take the question.

Candace said in a low sidebar voice to the delight of the crowd, "Or in real-life if Brett and Jessica have anything to say about that."

"No comment!" Brett and Jessica shouted in unison.

Donna McCall raised her hand amidst the raucous response from the crowd.

"I'll take that one," Donna McCall said. "We really don't see it that way at all. We are professionals. Our job is to help tell a story. It isn't romantic when we are on set with a hundred eyes, cameras, and microphones jabbed at us. There really isn't a moment where you get lost in the romance. When done well, we get lost in the story. Fortunately, the movies we do are about wholesome relationships where good people get to find each other. Our stories are about family, community all under God's watchful, loving eye -and a bit of romance. At the end of the day, we are actors, we are all friends, and we practically feel like family," Donna McCall said.

"Very well said, Donna," Candace replied. "Anyone else? Anything to add?"

"No!" Brett and Jessica blurted, as they shot each other a look.

The crowd laughed again.

"All right, all right," Candace shifted her questions. "Final question and one that I am sure our audience is eager to hear, "What projects do you all have coming up next?"

Each actor and actress shared movies that were preparing to come out, movies they are working on or were scheduled. When everyone on the stage had spoken, their eyes turned to Brett.

Shifting in his seat, Brett looked sheepish. "I was just looking forward to Christmas Con to meet all of you!"

The crowd roared at the response.

"I get to come here and see all of my co-star friends. It isn't often we are all in the same place. It's fun to share an event… and a stage with them," Brett said, panning his arms across the panel. "I mean, sharing a stage with *the* Donna McCall. Highlight of my career."

Donna dropped her head and looked over at Brett through the top of her eyes.

"But nothing in the works right now, Brett?" Candace pressed.

"No, I took a step back to work a few things out at home, *but* I am back and ready to start work on my next film, and I can't wait to share it with all of my new Christmas Con friends," Brett said.

The crowd cheered.

"Okay, I lied. Truly the last question and I will let you all off this stage. What is your favorite part about Christmas Con?" Candace asked.

"The fans," Manny replied.

"Getting together like family," Donna McCall said.

"Celebrating Christmas with everyone here," Jessica added.

"Yeah, this place is so full of Christmas spirit," Marie Claire nodded.

Brett looked at Candace and then at the crowd, "Making new friends. Like real, genuine friends. I have gotten to know so many of you already. I look forward to getting to know you all more."

Candace stood up from her seat and addressed the crowd, "That is it. Everyone give the panelists a big round of applause!"

The crowd complied.

"And thank you, Candace," Donna said, speaking into her microphone before they were turned off.

Standing up from their seats, the panelists took a bow together and moved in to personally thank Candace before slipping out of the back of the stage.

Abby stared at the emptying stage. She had never taken the time to listen to one of the panels. She was usually busy with one task or another.

She had watched the audience throughout as they gathered hints about what the actors' lives off the screen were like. They seemed to like the connection.

Abby chuckled to herself. She kind of did, too.

Fourteen

At the end of the day, Abby once again closed down the convention and sauntered her weary body toward the hotel and her cozy bathrobe. The lure had kept her going for the past hour.

The lobby was as raucous as ever, a particular voice could be heard above the others.

Moving with her head down, Abby tried to circle around the gathering space and avoid detection from the revelers inside.

Walking past, Abby couldn't resist taking a peek into the restaurant as she peered through the limbs of a Christmas tree just outside the restaurant entrance. There, a few steps from the bar, was Brett Walker, sharing stories with fans. This time, he had help from his friend Manny Vega. The pair had the crowd very entertained, though by Abby's vantage, they could speak gibberish and the crowd would eat the duo up.

Manny looked at his watch. After a quick whisper to Brett, he disappeared. Brett watched him leave for a moment before returning his attention to the crowd.

Abby peeled away from the restaurant entrance. Turning to take a stride toward the elevators and the beckoning respite of her hotel room, Abby spied a lively group of her crew assembled by the elevators. Exhausted, Abby elected to slink down in a cushiony chair just outside the restaurant until the group had boarded their elevator car.

Once comfortable, she might sneak through undetected, Abby rose from her seat to race toward the elevators and bubble bath that was calling her.

Making her way stealthily past the entrance, Abby froze. Brett had made his way through the main throng of convention goers and now kneeled next to a mother and daughter she recognized from earlier in the day. Sinking to a knee, Brett spoke with the women who were resting in thick leather chairs. Their smiles were broad and genuine. The actor took his time, seeming to enjoy the conversation himself.

Realizing she was gawking from the restaurant entrance, Abby snapped her head away and dodged out of sight. Her abrupt movement nearly caused her to collide with Michelle who corralled her in her arms.

"There you are! I was looking for you," Michelle said. "You missed Brett and Manny- they were a riot entertaining the crowd in the bar."

"I caught a glimpse of that," Abby nodded.

Michelle cocked her head. She studied her friend and then her eyes swept along the path Abby had been on, "Were you looking to sneak off to your room again? Abby!"

"I, yeah, I was," Abby admitted. "I'm tired."

"You can be tired on Monday. That's what your mother used to say," Michelle said.

Abby laughed, "I know. I heard that one a lot."

Michelle draped herself around Abby's arm, "Come on, sit. At least for a minute."

Abby sighed and reluctantly allowed her friend to drag her into the restaurant. Spying a table that had just cleared, Michelle hurried, grasping Abby's hand to ensure she followed close behind.

Abby's eyes widened as the table was just on the other side of a pillar separating them from Brett and the fans he was speaking to.

Ordering glasses of wine, Michelle excused herself to visit the ladies' room, leaving Abby to hunker awkwardly at the table alone. She tried not to listen to the conversation behind her, but to be heard over the rumble of the busy restaurant, voices had to be broadcast.

"I'm so glad you two could make it. Have you been to the con before?" Brett asked.

"Oh, yes. A couple of times. We have been to the open set experience for *Hope's River* as well," one of the ladies said.

"And the charity dance event in Nashville," the daughter said.

"Wow, you two are really big fans, aren't you?" Brett asked.

"The biggest!" the daughter said. "About all we watch are sweet romances."

"What's your favorite?"

"*Hope's River.* We like the movies, too," the daughter replied.

"I like the more heartfelt ones. Your movie *The Tree Farm* is right up there," the mother said.

"Thank you. I enjoyed that one myself. It was a bit of a different role for me," Brett replied.

"Watching you and your movie family tackle real-life issues and at Christmas time to boot, it hit home. Our household had certainly been there before," the mother said.

"This stuff really means a lot to you. Why… is it so important? Important enough to travel around to the meet and greets? Don't get me wrong, we all enjoy it too," Brett asked.

"I was real sick for a while," the mother said. "There are times when a bit of warmth is difficult to come by. Sure, the stories can be… familiar, and maybe real life doesn't turn out the way it does in the movies. But the movies provide a bit of hope that just maybe they can. For an afternoon, it feels like there is reason for hope. If pain flairs, if memories weigh heavy, if hearts are weary and broken, for just a little bit, they *feel* healed," the mother said.

Brett's voice cracked a bit, "That may be the single best answer to why we do what we do. Thank you for sharing that."

"You're so lucky to do what you love," the daughter said.

"Yeah, what I love…" Brett's voice sounded distant. "Thank you both for taking the time to visit with me. I really enjoyed our conversation. I hope we see each other throughout the weekend."

"Thank *you!*" the mother and daughter chorused.

Abby was startled as Michelle returned to the table, breaking Abby away from her unintentional eavesdropping, "Are you good?"

"Yeah," Abby said, her mind somewhere else. "You know, I think I'm going to get room service after all. I'm sorry. I really need to get my beauty sleep if I am going to be worth anything tomorrow."

"Don't be sorry, I get to drink two glasses of wine! Or better yet, there are plenty of people to share with. I'll make a new friend," Michelle said cheerily.

"Thank you for understanding. Put the tab on my room," Abby said.

Michelle smiled, clutching her two wine glasses and preparing to join the greater group of crew and attendees, "I already was going to."

Abby chuckled and hurried out of the restaurant. Seeing a pair of elevator doors begin to close, she stuck her foot between them, triggering them to reopen.

Brett looked up to see Abby stepping inside.

"Hey, boss!" he offered a thin smile.

Abby cocked her head, "Shouldn't you be off with your costars?"

"Manny tried to get me to go, I just thought, given the mixed crowd, I had better not," Brett said. "Besides, I got to spend time with the attendees. It was nice. I like to hear their stories and honestly, I find meeting with them inspiring."

"Inspiring," Abby nodded.

"Yeah," Brett nodded. "They are the ones watching the movies. Hearing what makes the stories resonate for them and make a connection, it... it gives me a bit of a lift."

"Are you sure you weren't just dodging your actor buddies?" Abby asked.

"Maybe a little," Brett shrugged.

"You seemed to be getting along well enough with them today at the snowball fight," Abby said.

Brett smiled, "Why tempt fate?"

Abby agreed, "I suppose. You're *really* good with the fans, by the way."

"Yeah, they are really good for *me*. A reminder of why we do what we do," Brett said.

"It's not the fame and fortune?" Abby grinned.

"If it were fame and fortune, we'd be working in Hollywood, not for Christmas movie studios. We, *I*, love knowing our stories are wholesome and touching. Sometimes it is good to be reminded that we are successful at that," Brett said.

As the doors opened and the two walked slowly out and down the hall, Brett added, "That was one of my hesitations on working with you. I have been questioning my career path since the, uh, paparazzi incident."

"Why? It was one mistake," Abby said.

"Yeah, but it put a blemish on my character. Our movies are all about character. Characters with solid morals. That's why I haven't been cast since," Brett admitted.

"I see," Abby said softly. "Well, I wish studios could see you with the fans at the convention. The way you helped our guest, Vanessa. The producers and casting directors would get a different perception of Brett Walker the paparazzi slayer."

Brett laughed, "Yeah. Maybe."

He paused awkwardly as Abby stopped by his side, "Uhm, this is my room."

Abby blushed, "Right, I'm sorry. I was just enjoying our conversation."

"Your room nearby?" Brett frowned as his eyes scanned the hallway.

"No. This isn't even my floor," Abby's cheeks grew redder as she turned and began walking back toward the elevators. A thumb pointing over her shoulder, she stammered, "I should, uh, good night, Brett!"

"Good night, Abby," Brett called, his face still sharing his confusion as Abby back pedaled her way down the hall.

When she had moved several doors away, she offered a sheepish grin and spun on her heel. Moving quickly toward the elevator, she refused to turn around, but she could feel Brett Walker's eyes on her as she walked.

Groaning to herself, she stabbed at the elevator button, willing the doors to open so that she could disappear inside.

As they finally opened, Abby shot a look down the hall. Forcing a smile, she watched Brett give a little wave from the doorway of his hotel room.

Snapping her head back in front of her, she took a long stride into the elevator to escape.

Fifteen

Abby's beleaguered body slogged her way through the convention center doors, making a beeline for the coffee cart. She was surprised to see a line already formed. She was not surprised to see a throng of crew members and vendors circling Brett Walker.

"Good morning!" he called over the small crowd.

"Good morning," Abby said.

"I've got yours and Michelle's coffees coming," Brett said.

"I'll carry hers," Abby smiled, receiving a chuckle from the actor.

"Wise choice," Brett said. Seeing the VIP line stream into the convention center, Brett waved his hand.

Abby turned to see the mother and daughter from the previous evening wave back.

Brett pointed at the coffee stand and waved them over. Letting a few people in front of him, he introduced them to Abby, "This is Rhonda Jude and her daughter Makayla. They are true fans of Christmas movies."

"I see, it is a pleasure to meet you both," Abby said.

"This is Abby Wells, Maggie's daughter. She has taken over the convention on behalf of her mother," Brett said.

"We met your mother. She was a sweetheart. I am so sorry for your loss," Rhonda said.

"Thank you," Abby said.

"Let me get you two a coffee or cocoa," Brett offered.

"That's okay, we are going to run and get in line for photos. You are on our list today," Makayla said.

"I can save you one line, right here," Brett offered.

Rhonda and Makayla looked at each other before shrugging.

Brett placed their order and they moved out of the way near the gingerbread house. "How about this as our backdrop? Abby, would you mind?"

Abby accepted. Taking Makayla's phone, she took several photos of the three. About to walk back to the coffee stand, Brett stopped her. "Would you mind taking one more? With my phone?"

"Of course," Abby nodded. Snapping the photo, she was once again paused as Rhonda and Makayla wanted a photo with her in it as well.

Abby was shocked. Aside from Michelle, no one had asked her to be in a photo at the convention. Nervously planting herself between the mother and daughter, she smiled as Brett took their photo. Just as they were relaxing, Brett called out. "What's a dinosaur's least favorite reindeer?"

All three scrunched their noses. "What?"

"Comet!" Brett said.

It took them a moment to realize Brett's horrible attempt at a joke, which they all found hilarious.

On the other side of the camera, Brett mashed the photo button.

"Bad dad jokes now?" Abby scoffed.

Brett smiled as he admired his handy work, "A lot of people are nervous in front of a camera. Getting them to laugh, no matter how bad the joke, can get a much better picture. See for yourself."

Abby reluctantly looked at the photo of herself, Rhonda and Makayla. Looking surprised, she said, "All right. Not bad."

"Let's get our coffees. Our order is up!" Brett said.

Michelle came running up, nearly colliding with Brett's outstretched hands clutching cups of coffee. Raising his arms and swiveling away prevented another disaster.

"Whoo! That was close," Brett said.

"Sorry," Michelle winced. "It's just, you are up for a podcast interview."

"Oh, okay. If you promise not to spill or run into anyone else with a cup of coffee, I will allow you to escort me," Brett said, receiving chuckles from the ladies. Over his shoulder, he called, "See you all later?"

Grabbing her coffee, Abby looked at Rhonda and Makayla, "Care to watch?"

They nodded eagerly.

Free seating in the room was scant. At the front of the room sat a table with a pair of microphones. A young woman greeted Brett and held a hand out for him to take a seat at the microphone opposite of her.

With a finger in the air, she got everyone's attention before hitting the record button.

"We are here with Brett Walker on the Night Before Christmas Podcast. I'm Jane Marshall, your host. Brett, thank you for joining me," the woman said.

"My pleasure, Jane," Brett said.

"Is this your first time at Christmas Con?" Jane asked.

"No, this is my third and so far, my favorite," Brett smiled into his mic.

"Oh, why is that?" Jane pressed.

"The people. The fans here are so great. They and the crew that put Christmas Con together are what make it so great," Brett said. "Check that. Not fans and crew… but friends."

"Friends, I like that," Jane replied.

Abby watched from the doorway. Brett was warm and thoughtful throughout the interview. The questions he received were softball, but he handled them with depth just the same. Some of the responses, especially giving tribute to her mother, made Abby smile.

"I never knew what to expect from Christmas Con. It was my first ever fan-meet. And it spoiled me. The atmosphere that Maggie Wells created was magical. Like being here today with all of you is," Brett smiled and extended his hands in a motion, encompassing the audience.

"It sounds like you enjoy your time here," Jane said.

"I do. I really do. It's good to connect with the folks who watch our movies. I take a lot away from the experience," Brett said.

"What is your favorite thing about acting?" Jane asked.

Brett looked thoughtful for a moment, "Learning from my characters and the situations they find themselves in. I mean, I never ran into my old high school girlfriend while touring an apple farm, but I get to put myself in situations that I as a person haven't faced. It is almost like a trial run."

"Well, if you ever do get to that apple farm, it sounds like you are well prepared for the journey," Jane smiled.

When it was over, Jane thanked Brett and they were both met with an ovation from the crowd. While he was overwhelmed with fans wanting a photo, Brett singled out an older lady who couldn't move as fast as the rest. A simple gesture from Brett and the audience parted so that he could close the gap to her.

"What's your name?" he asked.

"Rosie."

"Rosie, how are you doing? Thank you for coming to listen," Brett said.

"You remind me of my grandson," Rosie said.

Brett smiled, "I do? Well, I feel undeservedly special. Would you like a photo?"

Rosie blushed, "I would like a hug."

Brett's smile grew wide, "Of course."

Arms outstretched, he wrapped them around the woman as though she were his own grandmother. When they parted, he asked, "Now, how about a photo?"

"That would be nice," Rosie nodded.

An audience member took their photo. Brett stayed in the room until everyone had had an opportunity to visit with him. Before he could look up, the doorway where Abby had stood was now empty.

Abby had walked out of sight and hurried down the hallway. It was a pleasure to watch Brett with the audience, but she did not want to give the impression she was spying on him. Her plan was foiled by a frantic staff member who stopped her mid span of the hallway.

"There you are!" the woman flailed hysterically.

"What's up?" Abby raised a brow, distinctly aware the room behind her was emptying into the hallway.

"It is time for the Santa's Workshop for Kids," the staff member said.

"Okay…"

"There isn't a Santa," the staff member cried.

The podcast attendees streamed by, with Michelle and Brett trailing behind them.

Suddenly, Abby grinned, "Sure there is."

Having been within earshot of the conversation, Brett turned pale, "Oh, no. No, no, no!"

Abby looked directly at Brett, "It's for the *kids*."

"You have time in your schedule," Michelle said, scanning her tablet.

"Please don't make me do this," Brett pleaded.

"You will get such a good report from me. Imagine the headlines- 'Brett Walker Good Samaritan Saves the Day as Santa Claus.'"

"I would like to go on record that I am doing this in protest. I do not like this idea, at all," Brett said.

"But you *are* doing it," Abby ginned.

"How did I get roped into doing this?" Brett groaned.

"By punching a photographer," Michelle said.

"I was being rhetorical," Brett growled.

Brett slipped into the Santa suit, grumbling the entire time.

With each layer he donned, the wider Abby and Michelle's grins became.

"You look great, if I may say so, Mr. Claus," Michelle said.

"We need your glasses and a little more padding for your stomach. We don't want the kids to think you've been skipping their milk and cookies," Abby said. "And smile through those Santa eyes. Santa smiles… a lot."

"I am smiling!" Brett pouted.

"Hmm," Michelle squinted as she adjusted his beard, which had been covering his mouth. With a scowl, she said, "That's not a smile!"

Forcing a toothy, sarcastic grin between his Santa beard and moustache, Brett sighed, "Let's do this."

After an hour of 'Ho-ho-hos', Brett, Abby, and Michelle met backstage.

Brett couldn't wait to whip off the Santa hat.

"You were very convincing as Santa Claus," Abby said.

Brett glowered while slipping free of the belt around his coat so that he could slip out of the warm fuzzy suit and belly prosthetic.

"I agree. I think if you ever want to hang up your Christmas romance hat, you have a calling in Santa movies," Michelle added.

"I think I'll stick to starring across from the Queen of Christmas, thank you very much," Brett said, still working his way out of the rest of the Santa costume.

Looking out across the center, Michelle scrunched her nose, "Shouldn't the Holiday Hostess Workshop be starting?"

"It should," Abby said, glancing at her watch.

A frantic director pointed at her headset.

"Oh, hang on," Abby slipped her earpiece in and turned her radio on.

"Ms. Wells, we have a little problem on the Holiday Hostess set," the director said.

"What kind of little problem?" Abby asked.

"Well, you know how there wasn't a Santa? I found out why. Santa shared a cab with the Holiday Hostess. They both have the flu," the director said.

"Oh, no," Abby replied.

"Oh, no, what?" Michelle asked.

"Santa and the Holiday Hostess are sick," Abby replied. "We will have to cancel."

"Oh, no, we won't!" Brett declared.

"What do you mean?" Abby frowned.

"It's your turn to step up," Brett said, scratching his chin from where the beard had hung for the past hour.

Abby shook her head, "I, I can't do that."

Michelle grinned in Brett's direction, snatching the radio from Abby, "Don't worry, we'll be right over!"

"Seriously, I can't be the Holiday Hostess," Abby said.

"Yes, you can. I watched you orchestrate the transformation of a concrete warehouse into a winter wonderland fit for a Christmas movie set. You certainly have the eye and the touch," Brett said.

"Sure, I can decorate stuff. I can't speak in front of people," Abby protested.

"I'll help. Come on," Brett grabbed Abby's arm and started marching her along with Michelle close in tow.

Climbing up on stage, they looked out onto a boisterous crowd. Abby's cheeks paled, and her knees wobbled.

Brett touched her shoulder softly and stepped forward to the roar of the crowd. "Hello, everyone. I'm Brett Walker. While I have had the blessing to play on many beautifully decorated sets, I am the last guy you want showing you how to wow guests at your next holiday party. Ms. Abby Wells, however, the one we can all thank for this convention's beautiful decorations, is exactly the right person. Everyone, give Abby a big round of applause."

The crowd clapped and cheered as Abby collected herself. Staring at the table in front of her, she began to get the concepts that the real Holiday Hostess was to share with the audience.

Clearing her throat, Abby stuttered before saying, "Thank you all for joining us. I can't say any of what I'm about to show is magic, but if we pull it off, your guests just might think so. "

The crowd offered a light cheer, ready to see the presentation. As Abby demonstrated different themes and styles of Christmas décor for the home, how to upscale place settings for next to no budget and how to assemble a photo-worthy charcuterie board, she began to find her groove and the audience followed right along with her.

Brett stayed by her side, filling in color commentary when Abby paused to collect herself, was caught up in an "uhm moment" or mistakenly looked out at the crowd and was instantly overcome by stage fright.

Abby was so focused on creating her flowery meat display, she forgot to address the audience.

"Wow!" Brett exclaimed. "You make that look so simple. It's stunning!"

The camera zoomed in on Abby's latest creation. As she turned the glass she used to place the layers of meats in the form of a flower, she flipped the glass over revealing the final look.

"I never would have guessed that's how you do it. That looks easy enough that I could do it," Brett said. Scanning the audience, he grinned, "I hope someone is recording this so I can remember how to do it at home."

"Here, why don't you give it a try right now?" Abby asked.

Brett looked stunned for a moment. "All right, challenge accepted!"

Placing the glass that she used in front of Brett, Abby nodded toward the board.

"Right. So, I start by laying the slices here and then layer here…" Brett started.

Abby leaned in. Placing her fingers over his, she guided them over a bit. "You want them closer together, so that when you flip it over, it makes a nice, flowing petal."

"Clearly, this is done better as a team sport," Brett said, receiving laughter from the audience.

The pair shared smiles and laughs together as they cobbled an hour's worth of entertaining and useful presentation.

The biggest response from the audience was when Abby turned to grab a few additions for her charcuterie board and caught Brett trying to sneak a piece of capicola. Seeing him in the corner of her eye, Abby spun and smacked his hand. The timing was perfect, making the audience roar with laughter, especially as Brett pulled away and pouted.

When the charcuterie presentation was over, and the audience had plenty of time to ogle the final result in detail as the studio cameras zoomed in on the board and displayed it on two large screens in the back of the stage, Abby lifted the tray and offered a bite to Brett.

He grinned and accepted. As Abby looked at the audience, Brett quickly snatched several more pieces to layer on a cracker.

Hands on hip, Abby gave a scolding look before bursting in laughter herself.

Setting his snack aside, Brett looked out at the audience, "That is it for Holiday Hostess. Give it up for Abby. Didn't she do great?"

The audience cheered as Brett snuck a few more pieces from the tray and rushed off stage with Abby in pursuit.

Behind curtains and out of view, Abby stumbled back in relief.

"See, that wasn't so bad," Brett said.

"It was actually kind of fun. I wish to never do that again," Abby said. Looking Brett in the eyes, she said, "Thank you."

"For what?" Brett scoffed.

"For saving the day, yet again," Abby said.

"Like I said," Brett shrugged. "I'm one of the team."

Abby bowed her head slightly, "I'm glad you are."

Brett and Abby looked at each other, each seemingly interpreting the moment before Michelle's voice careened backstage, "You guys were great! I never knew you had it in you, Abbs!"

"I wouldn't say it was easy, but Brett certainly made it easier," Abby said.

"Off to grab a bite in the green room if Brett isn't too full from his charcuterie looting," Michelle said.

"You know, that sounds pretty good," Abby said.

Sixteen

Abby followed Brett and Michelle away from the stage area as they worked their way across the convention center. Always drawing a crowd, they allowed their progress to meander.

Taking time to stop and visit the vendors as they passed by, Brett stopped at a jewelry stand. Cocking his head as he looked at a photo, he asked, "Is that Juliette Magness?"

"Yes, Juliette wore that necklace in *An Island Prince*," a woman behind the counter said.

A second woman moved another photo for Brett to see, "Your buddy Manny Vega wore this bracelet in his last movie."

Brett pointed, "He told me about that. The proceeds go to a charity."

"Well, a portion of the proceeds. Ten percent of everything we net goes to charity," the woman said.

"Well, it's a pleasure to meet you," Brett extended his hand across the table. "I'm Brett Walker."

"We know!" the jewelers exclaimed in unison.

"I'm Stevie Lynn; this is my mother, Sandy," the young jeweler said.

"A mom and daughter team. I like that. Let's see what you've got," Brett buried himself in the earrings, bracelets and necklaces offered at the stand. Looking over his shoulder, Brett asked, "How about you?"

"Me? I'm no one," Abby blushed.

"You're the Holiday Hostess. Besides, it's for a good cause," Brett pressed.

Abby just smiled and shrunk away, feeling embarrassed.

Using the crowd billowing around Brett and the jewelers, Abby scooted down a few vendor stations. Finding a stack of books, she grabbed the first one she saw and buried her nose in it to collect herself.

"Ah, you grabbed one from the 'naughty collection'. That's a good one," the vendor smiled from behind the table.

"What?" Abby asked, lifting her eyes above the book.

The vendor opened her arms to showcase the entire display, "We have our 'naughty and nice collections.' These books are all sweet, very much like what you find in the movies represented here at Christmas Con. On the other hand, like the book you are holding, these stories tend to be filled with a bit more holiday spice."

"Oh!" Abby dropped the book before apologetically putting it back in its place. Taking an exaggerated step to the 'nice collection', Abby perused the books.

"You a big reader?" the vendor asked.

"When I have time," Abby said.

"If you like stories like in the movies, you will like these sweet holiday romances," the vendor said.

"Are you the author?" Abby asked.

"One of them. Our publisher set this space up for us. We are taking turns manning the booth. During peak hours, you'll usually find all of us here, unless pulled away for a panel. The publisher is wandering around here somewhere, and Nancy, she writes all the sweet stuff. You've probably watched movies made from her books," the author said.

"Oh. I would like to meet them. I'm Abby Wells. I like to personally thank all of the vendors," Abby said.

"I'll be sure to pass that along. I'm sure Jen, she's our publisher, will be back in a bit and Nancy is usually here with me. Maybe come back by?" the author suggested.

"I would like that," Abby nodded as a pair of hands clapped around her shoulders.

"To the green room we go, milady," Michelle called steering Abby back down the aisles.

Letting Abby go, Michelle cooed, "Ooh. Books…"

"Okay, I'm ready!" Brett joined them. Raising his wrist, he said, "Look it!"

A gunmetal bracelet gleamed from the edge of his sleeve.

"Look!" Michelle smiled, her fingers flicking a pair of blue earrings.

"Nice," Abby approved.

"And, I went out on a limb…" Brett held out a box for Abby.

Abby opened the box, not knowing what to expect. As the cover opened, it revealed a pendant necklace.

"It's the Christmas star for the star of Christmas Con," Brett beamed. "Here, let me help you put it on."

Abby's skin seemed to glow red hot as Brett gingerly scooted her hair to the side so that he could reach around her and clasp the necklace.

Abby reached up and clutched the pendant, "Thank you. It's beautiful. You didn't have to do that."

"It's for a good cause!" Brett raised his eyebrows. Glancing at his watch, he said, "I gotta get back to my station. Bring me something from the green room?"

Michelle nodded, "I'll be right behind you."

As Brett disappeared into the crowd, Abby looked up at Michelle who still playing with her new earrings.

"What?" Michelle asked.

"I can't figure him out," Abby said.

"Maybe there's nothing to figure out. Maybe, what you see is just that. He isn't putting on an act. All the stars here are so kind and genuine," Michelle said.

"Maybe. Even him?" Abby shrugged.

"Even him," Michelle said.

Abby looked toward the crowd Brett had slipped into.

"Second podcast is in an hour. Want to watch it? Like, from *inside* the room this time?" Michelle asked.

"You caught me lurking, huh?" Abby said with a wince.

"Yeah, you lurker," Michelle bumped Abby with her elbow.

"See you in an hour," Abby said.

Abby settled into a seat in the back of the room. Brett and the host chatted on the stage as the room filled in. Michelle winked at Abby from her spot in the front of the room where she monitored the audience.

When the room was filled to the brim, the podcast hostess counted down from three with her fingers.

"Good afternoon, live from Christmas Con. I am Kay Sullivan of the Romance After Dark Podcast. Here with me is Brett Walker, star of some of your holiday sweet tooth favorites like *The Christmas Café*," the host announced.

"Thank you, Kay, it's great to be here. It's great to be at Christmas Con," Brett smiled as he settled back into his chair, a leg crossed over his knee.

"You haven't been on my show for a while," Kay said.

"It's always good to catch up," Brett said.

"Any new works you can share with our listeners?" Kay asked.

Brett smiled his winning smile, "None that I can open the lid on yet. Let's just say there are some very exciting things in store."

"You don't have any Christmas movies coming out this year. Is that in response to your incident with the paparazzi photographer?" Kay asked.

"It has just been a year to focus on some other things, but I look forward to being on everyone's televisions in a new movie next year," Brett said, beginning to shift in his seat.

"So, what exactly happened?" Kay asked.

Brett chuckled uncomfortably, "That is all sealed up in the civil court case, part of which says I can't talk about it, just water under the bridge."

"How about being at the Christmas Con with Jessica Landon? For those living under a rock, Brett and Jessica were a longtime star power couple until earlier this year," Kay pressed.

"We… we've gotten along fine," Brett said, leaning forward in his seat, both feet pressed into the floor. "I even gave her a shot at winning the charity snowball fight."

"You two were the front-page couple, romance movie darlings. What happened?" Kay asked.

Brett was noticeably uneasy with the interview, "I'm not one to kiss and tell, Kay. Let's just say, sometimes people drift apart."

"My fans love the juicy gossip. Are there any other ladies in your life right now?" Kay asked.

Brett shook his head, his eyes pleading with Kay to change her line of interview, "I have been focusing on my career and my life. Learning what an adult Brett Walker is really supposed to be."

"What about you views on romance… Christmas romances in general?" Kay pressed. "Let's hear this clip."

Pressing a button, a recording of Brett's voice from an internet clip had him declaring that Christmas romances were unrealistic and silly.

Waving his hands in front of him, Brett said with gritted teeth, "That was part of a conversation and not the whole story."

"How about you share that story with us all now? Set the record straight. How does Brett Walker feel about Christmas romances?" Kay asked.

"I, uh," Brett's eyes moved from Kay's to the crowd. "I think romance… relationships in general can be as difficult and challenging as they are beautiful. When it comes to the holidays, we put so much pressure on ourselves to make them perfect… we sometimes miss the point that it is the love and the togetherness, not the sparkle and shine, that makes it all special."

"Well, I certainly hope you get back in the saddle soon, both in the movies as well as with your lady friends," Kay said.

"When we get back, we learn from Susan Mitchell what it is like to kiss Scott Conan," Kay said and stopped the broadcast.

Slipping off her headphones, she said, "Thanks for being on, Brett."

"Yeah, it was a great time," Brett snapped. Forcing a smile to the crowd, he nodded toward Michelle for them to slip out the back way.

Abby sat stunned in her seat. She had admittedly never listened to Kay's program, but she was a hit with the romance crowd. She watched as Michelle led Brett out of the room.

Seventeen

Abby slipped through the crowd and raced up to Brett and Michelle. The look Brett shot her gave Abby chills. Part hurt and part betrayed, he looked away.

"Brett!" Abby pleaded. "I had no idea Kay was going to ambush you."

"You booked her," Brett said.

"She was on Mom's list. That is the first time I ever listened to her podcast. It is likely my last," Abby admitted. "Mom wouldn't have someone at the convention that would do a hatchet job on one of the stars… or anyone. This convention is about peace, joy, and hope."

"Hmm," Brett grunted.

"I'm sorry," Abby said.

Brett slammed his hands in his pockets. Shaking his head, he said, "I don't know. Maybe it's time the truth all came out. Kay's questions aren't new. They just hit a little too hard."

Abby placed a gentle hand on Brett's shoulder.

His pocket buzzed. Pulling his hand out, he glanced at the screen, "I need to take this."

Brett's distant eyes swept over Abby like she wasn't there before he turned and walked away.

Abby watched the usually spirited actor slump away, looking wounded. Her booking had wounded him.

Brett stepped outside, ignoring the cold, wintry air.

"Liza…" he said into his phone.

"Hello, Brett," his agent's voice came clear though his phone's speaker.

"I suppose you saw the podcast," Brett said.

"I did. I have to say, I enjoyed this morning's better," Liza said.

Brett sighed through the phone, "You and me both."

"Kay Sullivan came in a little hard. Are you all right?" Liza asked.

"I think I am done," Brett said.

"At the Con? You need this," Liza said.

"No, I've been thinking about it. I may be done done," Brett said.

"Brett… take away your experience with Kay, what has it been like so far this weekend?" Liza asked.

Brett stared out at the parking lot. A light wisp of snow from a flurry scattered in the chilly breeze. "To be honest, I was starting to get it. Starting to understand why the movies we make are actually important. Seeing that we have the power to impact people in ways we never see from the other side of the camera. I was starting to get excited about acting again," Brett admitted.

"There you go. Forget about Kay Sullivan. She needed a ratings hit and she used you to get it. Don't let her get to you. Don't let her take away from your experience at Christmas Con," Liza said.

"Yeah," Brett nodded. "The thing is, Liza, I don't even know if her questions were unfair."

"They were a bit uncoated and out of place for the theme of the event, but honest questions," Liza said.

"I think that's the problem. I was feeling like I was getting over all of that, ready for a fresh start," Brett said.

"Great. Then let's move forward," Liza said.

"I just think that I need time. How do I go back in there, face the audience after that interview?" Brett said. "Face my costars?"

"Face Jessica?" Liza pressed.

"Yeah," Brett nodded.

"You just do. Find the good in the con. Embrace it, smile, and move on," Liza said. "You need an endorsement, a role, a request to read for a role. You are on thin ice, if you forgive the wintry pun."

"What do I do?" Brett asked.

"I want you to get onto social media anyway you can," Liza said.

"Like the selfie thing?"

"Exactly the selfie thing."

"I hate the selfie thing."

"Brett…"

"Fine. I'll do the selfie thing," Brett relented.

"The social media clips of you helping at the event and your first panel were very positive. The producers just can't get past if you are smiling in front of the camera only or not. They want the old Brett back or even better, a more mature, less fist-flying Brett 2.0," Liza said.

"I'm smiling," Brett grumbled through gritted teeth.

"Good, because I had Abby sign you up for the next event. I believe it starts soon," Liza said.

"What now?" Brett asked.

"Just go inside. Find Abby and don't forget…" Liza started.

"I know, smile," Brett hung up the phone.

Realizing he was starting to shiver, as much as he didn't want to face the fans and his costars, he very much wanted warmth.

In the corner of the event space, a large, clear snow dome had been erected. Inside, machines churned out snow that had piled up a foot deep on the floor and continued to billow down.

Abby nudged Michelle, who waved Brett down. He cast a quick glance at Abby who stood on Michelle's side. Abby returned an apologetic look.

"So… what do we have here," Brett said eyeing the dome, still rubbing his arms from being outside in the cold.

"We have our indoor snowman building contest. Four stars pair up with a randomly drawn participant from the audience. You have forty-minutes to build a snowman. Fan-favorite win," Abby said.

Brett nodded, his face still wearing a morose look.

"You should smile. It's going to be fun," Michelle said.

"Yeah, everyone keeps telling me to smile," Brett breathed.

"Good luck," Abby said meekly.

With a nod, Brett flashed a broad smile as he made his way through the crowd and to the entrance of the snow dome. There, he found himself standing alongside Marie Claire Downs clad in a winter hat, faux-fur lined white coat, and snow boots. On his other side were fellow actor Trevor Dalton and actress Margot Meads, each equally well-attired for the wintry event.

Seeing Brett was woefully prepared, his new friend Rosie stepped forward and handed him a crocheted hat she had purchased from one of the vendors. "It was for my grandson Robin, but I can get another one," Rosie said.

Brett smiled and gave Rosie a big hug, whispering in her ear, "Thank you, Rosie."

"All right, time for our fan pairings!" the convention DJ called out. Reaching his hand into a Santa hat, he produced four tickets. "Raquel Baez, Vanessa Senni, Jessica Reel and Nicole Clatterbuck."

Brett greeted Vanessa who beamed wildly for getting to work with him, "How are you doing? Ready for this?"

Vanessa beamed, "I am great!"

"Let's win this!" Brett smiled.

"And… go. There are forty-minutes on the clock!" DJ Frost called out.

In a rush, the contestants poured into the snowy dome. Each had their own station with a platform near the edge of the dome for easy viewing.

"So, what's the plan?" Brett asked, digging through the props and borrowing a scarf, which he quickly tossed around his neck.

Vanessa shrugged, "How about we recreate the final scene from The Tree Farm?"

"Right, where the kids are asleep and Aaron and Cara look out over the trees with the snow falling," Brett nodded. "Okay… how do we do that?"

"We need a backdrop," Vanessa said.

"Are props legal?" Brett asked.

Vanessa shrugged, "They didn't say they weren't."

"Fair enough, but let's save that as a secret weapon for the end. I'll work on Aaron, you work on Cara?" Brett suggested.

"You got it!" Vanessa took off excitedly.

Leaping and sliding on her knees, Vanessa began rolling the bottom half of the snow woman.

Brett glanced at the other star contestants before dropping to a knee to begin working on the snowman. He thought about the final scene in The Tree Farm. After everything they had been through, the couple had a moment to themselves. To be together. To breathe.

Hand in hand, they watched the snow slowly drift down onto the scene, which was their Christmas miracle.

Making their way with the large foundation layer of snowballs, they began working on the mid sections.

Marie Claire's second snowball got away from her and began rolling towards Brett's. Arms out to catch the runaway snowball, Brett looked up to see Marie Claire lose her footing. Swinging from the snowball to the actress, Marie Claire's full weight landed in his arms, knocking them both to the ground.

Wind knocked out of them, they paused for a moment. Brett lay flat on his back, his arms supporting Marie Claire. Marie Claire rested on her elbows, staring directly down at Brett. The shock dissipated; they broke into smiles.

"Thank you, Brett," Marie Claire said.

"Glad to be of service," Brett said.

As Marie Claire rolled off him, Brett jumped to his feet and helped the actress up. Even through the dome, they could hear the roar of the crowd over the churning of the snow machines.

Marie Claire embraced the moment, grasping Brett's hand and holding it up in the air triumphantly.

Following her lead, they swung into a bow before the crowd.

Marie Claire looked at Brett and pointed to her rogue snowball in the back of the dome. "I should…"

"Yeah," Brett nodded. Giving a quick wave to the crowd, Brett dove back into his snowman creation.

Abby and Michelle watched along with the crowd outside of the dome. The competition itself was good theater with occasional snowballs lobbed back and forth between the teams and the starts to very good snow people.

The Marie Claire and Brett affair, which was already the title of many social media posts was certainly a highlight for most.

"Well, he certainly seems to have bounced back quickly," Abby said.

Michelle's head snapped to her friend, an eyebrow raised, trying to discern the tone of her voice. "You okay?"

"Yeah," Abby nodded. "Just hard to tell what's real and what's acting anymore."

"Abbs, you've met them all. They are as genuine as they get," Michelle said.

"Yeah, they seem to be," Abby said, her voice void of tone.

Michelle slapped her hip.

Abby cocked her head.

Pulling out her phone, Michelle said, "It's Brett. He is requesting our help."

"Help with what?" Abby frowned.

"Looks like he and Vanessa would really like to win the contest," Michelle said. "Come on!"

Following Abby to the vendor aisle, Michelle asked, "Can we spare a few convention dollars?"

"Sure, why?" Abby asked.

Michelle pointed to a handmade wooden sign.

The vendor nodded, "Would you like it wrapped?"

"Oh, no. We'll take it just as it is," Michelle smiled. "Go on, pay the woman."

Abby pulled out the convention credit card and completed the purchase.

"Time's almost up, let's head back!" Michelle urged, quickening her pace.

Arriving at the dome, they walked up to the edge of the plastic where Brett and Vanessa were completing the finishing touches on their snow people.

Michelle held the sign up facing them. Brett held his thumb up.

Meeting at the entrance, Brett took the item and thanked them. Looking at Vanessa as the big red timer was counting down. "Care to do the honors?"

Vanessa smiled. Walking behind their snow people, she planted a sign behind them that read "Welcome to the Tree Farm."

Taking a step back, they surveyed their creation.

"I like it," Brett nodded.

"I do too," Vanessa agreed.

Sharing a high-five, they stood at the ready as the timer buzzed.

"All right, Christmas Con! Give it up for our snowman contestants! Wow, these look really great," DJ Frost said.

Walking in front of the dome, he gave all of the vignettes a quick look before reversing and stopping at each one. "Group 4 starring Margot Meade and Nicole

Clatterbuck. A parent snowman with a kid snowman building another snowman. I get it. Cute!"

Moving to the third group, DJ Frost eyed their work, "Yes! Two snow people decorating a little snow tree, I like it. I like it. Good work, Trevor Dalton and Jessica Reel."

"Brett Walker and Vanessa Senni…" DJ Frost took a step back. "Oh, well played, you two. A scene from Brett Walker's movie The Tree Farm. Oh, look at that, their snowy foreheads touched together, their little stick hands in one another's. Great visual storytelling, you two."

"Last but not least, Maire Claire Downs and Raquel Baez. You have created… oh, I get it. You made a snow tree, nicely decorated, by the way. You found rocks from out front and placed them around the tree," DJ Frost looked out at the crowd and raised his microphone in the air, "You all know what they made?"

The crowd chorused, "Rocking Around the Christmas Tree!"

"Very clever, very clever. But is it a winner?" DJ Frost asked to a mixed response from the crowd.

Moving from station to station, DJ Frost asked the crowd, "If you think team one won, let's hear your voice!"

"Team two?" the crowd erupted.

As DJ Frost moved to the other teams, it was clear who the winners were.

"There you have it! Team two with Brett Walker and Vanessa walking away with the gold!" DJ Frost called to the crowd.

The contestants stood next to their creations for a photo while Brett and Vanessa held their hands in the air triumphantly.

Brett looked out at the crowd. He wasn't happy being tossed into a competition right after getting fed to the lioness of Kay Sullivan and her podcast. He looked at Vanessa and the scene from one of his more poignant roles.

He was glad he'd done it.

Eighteen

Abby wandered the convention center space. Seeing how the vendors did for the day and wishing them a good evening. As she rounded Star Alley, she caught a glimpse from Brett's eyes. The close of the day's convention couldn't come soon enough.

Saying goodnight to the rest of the actors and the conventions staff that aided them, Abby went to the office to retrieve her own things.

"Hey, Abbs," Michelle called, following behind her to collect her things as well.

"How was the rest of the day?" Abby asked.

"If you mean, what mood was our hijacked actor Brett Walker in, I would say mixed. Not his usual self but moments where a glimmer of it were able to shine through," Michelle replied.

Abby said, "If I had known…"

"I know," Michelle nodded.

"We ready?" Abby asked.

"Are you going to try and sneak away tonight?" Michelle asked.

"Are you going to let me?" Abby pressed.

"No," Michelle shook her head. Grabbing her friend's hand, she tugged her along toward the convention entrance.

A weary Brett Walker was at the door finishing signatures for lingering fans.

"Walk with us?" Michelle offered.

"Sure," Brett nodded.

Abby couldn't tell if he was exhausted or just emotionally done for the day.

As they reached the main corridor of the hotel, he started toward the elevators.

"Aren't you coming?" Michelle asked.

Brett turned and frowned, "Coming where?"

"Christmas Carol Karaoke," Michelle said.

Abby offered an apologetic smile.

"Uhm, no. I don't think so," Brett said, pivoting to continue toward the guest rooms.

"But you're signed up," Michelle said.

Brett spun, a horrified expression washed across his face, "I'm what?"

"Yeah," Michelle said. "Look at the poster. That's your face."

Brett's eyes followed Michelle's extended finger and his head fell.

"You *are* on the poster," Abby affirmed.

"Oh, no. No, no, no, no," Brett stammered. "As if my career wasn't already in enough jeopardy, it is most certainly going to be over if I sing."

"It would probably go viral. All publicity is good publicity," Michelle sang.

Brett's head drooped as he eyed Michelle, "You say that to the guy that is on career probation for a video that went viral."

"Two videos. One punching the photographer, which honestly, probably didn't hurt you so bad. The video knocking romance movies, however…" Michelle said.

"Thanks. I didn't really need a scorecard," Brett said. Looking at Abby for help, she just shrugged.

"We can't wait to watch you sing!" the mother and daughter Brett met in the lobby called from down the hall.

"Hi Rhonda and Makayla," Brett waved and forced a smile.

"See, your fans are excited," Abby said.

"I really need a new agent," Brett muttered. "Let's go slay some songs."

Abby tilted her head, "Did you mean sleigh or slay?"

Brett just glowered.

Abby and Michelle grabbed Brett by his arms and propelled him down the hallway. They could already hear the carols playing through the ballroom doors.

Flashing their badges to the security guard, they walked in. Several Christmas trees, their lights pulsing to the music, were on display. The room's columns were wound in red string lights like candy canes. Four bars operated at full capacity while a large crowd found seats around round tables.

At the back of the room was a stage, flanked by two large screens that displayed images from a camera pointed at it. Two additional screens in the back of the room fed lyrics for carolers who got off track.

A pair of candy cane-wrapped microphone stands stood at the ready.

DJ Frost once more heralded the crowd.

"Welcome everyone! This is Christmas Carol Karaoke. We have designated spots filled in for your favorite Christmas movie stars, but fear not, there are plenty of spots in between for you and friends to rock around the Christmas tree tonight!" DJ Frost called.

"Let's kick this show off, we start with a woman who not only has starred in multiple movies, a long-running television series, but also has three albums to her credit, Ms. Jessica Landon!" DJ Frost announced.

Jessica Landon took the stage. A ruby-gemmed dress sparkled in the stage lights as she approached the microphone.

Abby's jaw dropped at the sight of the radiant actress, "Oh, my!"

Looking down at her well-worn attire from working the convention floor all day, she felt like she had stumbled into the wrong room.

"Good evening, everyone! Let's start things off by getting warmed up. Do you mind helping me?" Jessica said into the microphone.

Leading the crowd into a round of familiar Christmas tunes, she then launched into a riveting rendition of "O Holy Night".

When the echo of her voice finally faded from the massive speakers, the audience jumped to their feet in applause.

"Well, *that's* an opening act," Michelle gasped.

Brett looked uneasy.

"How about, I go get us some drinks?" Michelle offered.

Abby looked across the table at Brett, "I am so sorry about the day."

Brett took a deep breath and looked at Abby, "It wasn't all bad. I'm just afraid it is going to very quickly get a whole lot worse."

"Oh, it can't be that bad," Abby said.

Brett raised a brow.

"At least you don't have to follow Jessica," Abby said.

Brett winced.

"Too soon?" Abby scrunched her face.

Brett laughed, shaking his head.

Michelle arrived with drinks that were only all too well appreciated.

"Keep 'em coming," Brett gasped, rubbing his palms on his pants.

Abby stifled a laugh. She had never seen this confident, almost over-confident man nervous. Deflated after the Kay Sullivan interview, yes, but this was a new experience.

They watched the list get closer and closer to Brett's name. Using a cocktail napkin, Brett dabbed at beads of perspiration on his forehead.

DJ Frost bounced on the stage in front of the crowd, thanking a convention-goer for her robustly sung "All I Want for Christmas".

"And now, out of the red corner, give it up for Brett Walker!" DJ Frost announced.

With a final sigh, Brett stood up from the table and nodded at fans and costars as he meandered his jelly-like legs up to the stage.

Abby and Michelle cheered wildly as he took his time.

Climbing the steps, Brett thanked DJ Frost and grabbed the mic. Holding up a finger for DJ Frost to keep the low background music going for a bit longer, Brett addressed the audience.

"Thank you all for being here, I thank those who are not here to listen to me sing even more," Brett said.

The crowd roared with laughter.

"Look, the season isn't about individuals. It is about togetherness. Building community and *sharing*," Brett said.

Abby and Michelle looked at each other, not sure where he was going with his pre-song speech.

"So, I'd like to share this moment. Make it a duet," Brett grinned. His eyes moved through the crowd with plenty of hands streaking up in the air to be his partners. Landing directly on Abby, she shrank down in her seat, and her face turned white.

"Abby Wells, come on up. Enjoy this moment with me in front of all our friends. I mean, we're all like family, right?" Brett said.

The crowd cheered.

"Let's give her some encouragement, everyone!" Brett said, rallying the crowd to cheer as Abby reluctantly made her walk to the stage.

Stepping up, she took little steps to the second microphone.

Before she picked it up, she covered it with her hand and looked at Brett. Growling through a forced grin, she said, "I will hate you forever for this."

"Thought you already did," Brett shrugged.

With a nod to DJ Frost, the music started.

Clearing her throat, Abby brought the microphone to her lips and croaked, "I really can't stay…"

"But, baby, it's cold outside…" Brett chimed in. Taking his hand, he gently pulled Abby's microphone a couple of inches away and smiled at her.

Abby's eyes panned the crowd. They seemed to pick up every actor and actress that sang before. Jessica

Landon watched the duet with great interest, causing Abby to swallow hard.

"Beautiful, what's your hurry?" Brett sang as he locked his eyes with hers.

Their bodies slowly rotated to each other and away from the crowd.

"I wish I knew how," Abby's voice began to regulate as her nerves calmed.

"Your eyes are like starlight now," Brett sang.

A tiny crease of a smile was produced as Abby added, "To break this spell."

Their focus on each other in the flashing Christmas lights, they fell into a rhythm and their expressions suggested that they just might be having fun.

The rest of the room faded away in the bright lights, leaving the two of them on stage. With the moment coming to be about the song, their voices came out cheery and soulful.

"I ought to say, "No, no, no, sir…""

"Mind if I move in closer…"

Eyes locked on each other, their smiles became evident in their singing.

As they sang the last verse together, "Baby, it's cold…out…side!"

The music stopped and the audience erupted.

Abby's face glowed red, Brett's barely a shade lighter. Taking her hand, he forced a bow before escorting her to the nearest exit.

The room was an indiscernible roar in Abby's ears. The faces she walked by were odd images in the flickering candlelight. Reaching their table, her pulse roaring, the color in her cheeks an odd battle of pale white and red fiery crimson.

"Are you okay?" Michelle asked, her words sounding as though they were in a tunnel.

Grasping her beverage that she'd left on the table, Abby downed it in several desperate gulps.

Brett looked at Abby, her distant eyes trying to focus, "You want to get out of here?"

Abby nodded vociferously.

"I'll help her get some air. You stay and enjoy yourself," Brett suggested to Michelle.

Michelle looked at her friend who nodded.

"Okay. If you need anything, give me a call," Michelle said. "I'm just waiting for Manny's song."

"Ooh, record that for me, will you?" Brett asked.

Michelle laughed, "I will."

Smiling at attendees as he walked with a steadying arm around Abby, Brett made their way out of the ballroom. Locating the balcony doors on the other side of the corridor, he pushed them open.

Leading Abby to the balcony rail, he held her steady.

"You okay?" Brett asked.

Abby took in a deep breath of cool air. The crisp night cooled her cheeks.

"Yeah, that was a bit much, I guess," Abby said.

"You did great!" Brett said.

"I sounded like a frog," Abby said.

Brett shrugged, "Maybe in the beginning, but you found your stride. You sounded way better than me."

Abby grimaced, "I had to *sing* my lines. You got to speak most of yours."

"I had to sing a few, like at the end, for sure," Brett said.

Abby's eyes did not share an amenable tone. Her body shivered.

"Come on, let's get you inside," Brett said. "We haven't had dinner. How about we find a nice, *quiet* spot to lie low?"

"That sounds good to me," Abby nodded.

With most of the convention clustered in the ballroom, they were able to find a quiet and dark corner of the restaurant.

As the waiter brought them their drinks, Abby and Brett settled into their table.

"Let's agree to never do that again," Abby said.

Brett grinned. Holding his hand across the table, Abby slipped hers inside his. "Deal."

One of the bartenders from the ballroom walked by with an armful of wine bottles, "You two made a great duet. You had real stage chemistry."

Abby's cheek glowed beet red as Brett smiled behind his wineglass.

"Never… again," Abby asserted.

"I didn't sign myself up," Brett waved his hands in front of him.

"Fair enough," Abby said. Her face falling serious, she said, "I'm sorry again for this morning. I didn't know it was going to go that way."

Brett sighed, "It's not the first time. I'll probably continue to be hounded until the whole story gets out. Maybe it should. Make it old news."

"You can share it with me," Abby said, her voice soft. "What happened between you and Jessica?"

Brett played with his glass in the candlelight.

His eyes moved up to Abby's.

"We met on our first set together. We hit it off on camera… and off. I had a rule about dating costars, most of us do. We are all friends, family. But there was something special about Jessica," Brett shared.

"We started dating right after shooting ended and the film was in the can. By the time the movie came out, we were a couple. Well-broadcast, appearing on talk shows together couple," Brett said.

Brett looked off into a dark, nebulous corner of the restaurant, "I thought she was the one. She didn't feel the same. I… I just wasn't sharp enough to realize it. I wasn't prepared for those words. Well, I *was* prepared, but for an entirely different ending. One night, after attending a friend's premier, I had it all worked out. I should have known with it being a premier, paparazzi would be all over us."

His eyes swung back to Abby, "I chartered a little starlight boat ride. Just the two of us and the captain. She saw the blanket, the champagne, the flowers. I dropped to one knee, and… she said 'no'. She wasn't ready for marriage. She wanted to focus on her career and she was sorry for allowing us to get too close."

"Brett, I'm so sorry," Abby said.

Nodding, Brett said, "The captain turned the boat around. Paparazzi were waiting on the dock for us. One said something about 'my girlfriend' kissing other men for a living, and I hit him so hard he and his camera ended up in the water."

Abby placed a hand to her mouth, "Oh!"

"There was no shortage of other photographers to capture the moment," Brett said.

"I'm sorry," Abby repeated.

"Yeah," Brett sighed. "It has been a rough ride."

"That's why you went from sweet holiday romance actor to James Dean," Abby said.

"If James Dean was a moping actor without an acting gig, then, yeah," Brett nodded. "Doesn't help to be caught on a hot mic saying holiday romance was stupid."

"You were coping with your breakup with Jessica," Abby said.

"Tell the rest of the world that," Brett said. He raised his eyebrows and refilled their wine glasses. "How about you? What's your story?"

"Me?" Abby gasped.

"Yeah, you. You said you hadn't intended to follow in your mother's footsteps," Brett led her.

"I didn't. It was Mom's thing. While it's clearly amazing. I had other plans," Abby said.

"Oh yeah? What are Abby Wells' dreams?" Brett asked.

"I want to be a writer," Abby said, her voice demure.

"Hmm. Maybe I could read some of your writing," Brett suggested.

"Really?" Abby was incredulous at the suggestion.

"Yeah. What do you write?" Brett asked.

"Fiction, about life. Life where happy endings arrive by the last page," Abby said.

"That's funny, I act in those kinds of movies. Maybe I will star in one of your stories, someday," Brett said.

Abby blushed, "I wouldn't mind that."

They sat back in their chairs as the waiter brought their food.

When the plates were cleared and the last of the wine had been poured, they looked across the table from each other.

"It's been a long day. We should call it?" Brett suggested.

"Okay," Abby nodded. "Thank you for the duet."

"Sure. Anytime," Brett grinned.

Abby scowled, "One time was good, but thank you just the same."

Brett laughed, "Good night, Abby."

"Good night, Brett."

Nineteen

Abby woke before her alarm. It wasn't that the evening before wasn't busy and exhausting. There was a draw to the convention center. Something in the back of her head was pulling her out of bed. Getting ready, she was the first to arrive. She stood at the entrance as the night guard turned on the lights.

At first, the event space was bathed in light, illuminating the stages, the massive merchandise area and the vendor spaces.

Then the Christmas vignettes, photo op set pieces and the Christmas trees came to life.

Abby walked the convention center weary from the long weekend but motivated for the final day of the excitement-filled event. She was brimming with Christmas spirit. Yet, there was a hollow pit in her stomach.

As she wandered the space, it had truly become a winter wonderland. Trees with glimmering lights, patches of snow, a sea of red, green, silver, and gold baubles hung in all directions.

Abby took a deep breath. It was so much more than all of that. It was the people. They all arrived raw in expectations. For the actors, it was another stop on their public relations to-do list. For the fans, it was the hope of a photo or signature with a Christmas movie star that touched them in some way. For the crew, Abby observed, it was delivering a gift to thousands of people.

Scanning the ornate convention center, Abby sighed. "I'm sorry, Mom. I don't want to see the convention end. But I'm not the one to keep it going. I don't have what you have. Besides, preparing for this one nearly cost me my job."

"Ma'am?" the night guard called.

Abby blushed, embarrassed that she'd gotten caught talking to herself.

She frowned as the guard rushed over, holding up an envelope.

"I found this when I was checking the locks in the storeroom, I thought you might know who it belonged to," the guard said, handing the envelope over.

Abby inspected it. It had an ornate letter 'A' on it. Abby smiled and said softly, "Thank you. I believe it is intended for me."

"Well, I'm glad it found its owner," the guard said. As he turned around and started to walk away, he called, "Sorry to interrupt your conversation!"

Abby smirked as she tapped the envelope against her fingers.

Wandering over to the little park bench, Abby sat. Taking a deep breath, she slid the little card out from the envelope.

My dearest Abby,

I always yearned to walk through a Christmas village like the ones in my favorite holiday movies. I loved how it would draw the community together, where families could be made whole from life's struggles and how strangers might become friends.

Creating a space where dreams became reality, those glimmers of hope that seemed to only exist in fiction could find their way into actual lives -that is why I worked so hard to build what I have built.

It is a magical world I had always intended to share but never wished to force upon you. My greatest wish was always for my daughter to be the most wonderful form of whatever her dreams were made of, not of mine.

Love forever,

Mom

Abby slid the card back in its envelope and slipped it in her pocket. Deflecting deeper thoughts, she kicked her legs out playfully, "I do love a dress with pockets. A wonderful invention!"

"Ma'am?" a voice called, nearly making her jump. The morning janitor making rounds turned the corner of the little artificial park, dusting broom in hand.

Abby blushed, "Sorry. Just talking to myself… again."

"Carry on, ma'am. It's only a worry when things start talking back," the janitor said, shuffling past and around the next bend.

Abby laughed to herself as she patted the envelope in her pocket.

She sat in the park a few minutes longer until the whir of an espresso grinder broke through the silence. The murmur of voices began to slowly rise above the set pieces and the convention center officially sprang into life.

Not daring to get caught talking to herself a third time, she got up to join the human world.

The coffee cart was already busy. The line resembled more of a blob than a line. Abby wasn't surprised to see the reason why.

Brett Walker stood amidst the convention staff who swarmed around him. Abby smiled. He always took the time to visit whether he was still waking up, exhausted at the end of the day or humiliated by a podcaster.

Seeing Abby, Brett smiled above the crowd and waved her over.

"I was just about to get coffee for everyone," Brett said.

"Oh, no. This one is on me. Everyone has worked so hard this weekend. I can't thank you enough. I know Mom would have been proud," Abby said.

"Fair enough, but I think that warrants a trip to the front of the line," Brett suggested.

Abby said good morning to the event staff as she waded through the rough line.

"What'll you have?" Abby asked.

"Light eggnog, double caff latte," Brett smiled.

"Eggnog, wow," Abby said.

"'Tis the season," Brett replied.

"You know what? I'll have one, too. Thank you. And the rest of the line is on the event," Abby said, handing over the convention credit card.

Brett leaned over the barista stand and said, "Hey, does it ever slow down?"

The barista paused between tamping the grounds and inserting them into the espresso machine. Scrunching her nose, she said, "After the morning rush, just before lunch it starts to slow down."

"I would like to buy coffee... or cocoa for the vendors. Can I do that?" Brett asked.

The barista looked anxious, "I mean, yeah..."

Brett cocked his head, "It's a lot, huh? What if I came by and helped deliver them?"

The barista brightened, "That would work."

"All right, it's a deal," Brett said. Looking at Abby, he asked, "Think you can help me get everyone's orders?"

"I can do that," Abby nodded. "That is very nice of you. I think they'll enjoy the delivery more than the drink."

Grabbing their coffees, they wheeled away from the coffee stand.

As they walked by, a person stepped out of line in front of them.

Abby and Brett froze.

Brett bowed his head slightly, looking at the person through scrutinizing eyes, "Kay."

"I was hoping to run into you," Kay Sullivan said.

Abby bristled to speak, her anger forcing her words out in a rush, "I'm sure you were. Another hit job for your ratings?"

Kay took a deep breath. "That's fair."

Looking at Brett, Kay said, "Look, I'm sorry if I ambushed you. But, those are the questions everyone is asking. The tabloids are asking them, the networks are asking them, the fan boards are asking them. Yes, I was hoping to get the scoop, but it was also a chance for you to put some of them to rest."

"The soothing sounds of old wounds tearing open doesn't really make for good rest," Brett said.

Kay shook her head. "Scars and questions behind the scars are why the networks haven't placed you in a new role. Getting the fans behind you would help."

"The networks understand the scars," Brett defended.

"They do," Kay nodded. "They write stories about redemption. Stories about broken trusts re-earned. But they need to know you are on the path before they feel comfortable signing you."

"Thank you for your career advice less than twenty-four hours after torpedoing it," Brett snapped.

"If it's any consolation, watching you this weekend… you have opened my eyes to you, Brett. You are very generous and kind to your fans," Kay said.

"Yeah, well, too bad you didn't share that with your audience," Brett said and abruptly walked off.

Kay watched him walk away, "I hope I get the chance to!"

Brett disappeared toward the green room. Kay's head fell.

"You really did a number on him. He was on the way to change and healing this weekend," Abby said.

Kay looked at Abby and nodded, "I can see that."

"You really want to share the *real* story?" Abby asked.

"I'd love to," Kay said.

"Follow him for the rest of the event. See what everyone else here has been seeing. Share *that* version of Brett Walker with the rest of the world," Abby said.

"I have podcasts scheduled…" Kay started.

"Cancel them. You have a bigger story to tell," Abby said, her tone pointed.

Kay nodded slowly. "Maybe I will…"

"Abby!" a voice called out as Abby walked through the vendor aisles.

"Good morning, Nancy," Abby smiled.

"You have been asking a lot of questions about my writing and publishing journey this weekend. They kind of remind me of when I was just starting out. I was a young lady with ideas and some scribbles on a page. I didn't know how to get those scribbles turned into a story that others could enjoy. I mean, I had the story part, but not the how," Nancy said.

Abby looked curiously at the well-known author.

"I heard through a whisper that you were an inspiring author," Nancy said.

Cocking her head, Abby asked, "Michelle?"

Nancy grinned and shook her head.

Abby looked surprised.

"It's okay. Sometimes in this industry, who you know is nearly as important as the quality of your manuscript," Nancy said.

"I have written a story or two," Abby nodded. "I haven't had much time to do anything with them with my full-time job. Sent out a few queries, collected a charming set of rejection letters."

"I have an entire treasure chest full of those," Nancy said. "Fortunately, an agent saw promise in my words and submitted my first coastal cozy romance to a growing publisher. It isn't an easy road, but if you truly love your stories and your characters, every step along the journey is worth it."

Abby blushed, "Thank you, Nancy. You are very inspirational."

Nancy smiled, "Oh, I needed an encouraging word or two tossed my way over the years. I'd be happy to read one of your manuscripts. Maybe even pass it along to my agent, if it fits her portfolio."

"I… I'd like that. I don't know what to say," Abby gushed.

"Say, Merry Christmas. This event is all about growing and creating friendships, Abby. No matter where your book journey goes, you have a writer friend named Nancy Naigle."

"I'm thrilled to call you friend," Abby said and took Nancy's hands in hers.

Nancy brushed her hands aside and instead, enveloped Abby in a big hug.

"I knew your mother. She was a special lady. I see a lot of her in you, Abby," Nancy said.

Abby blinked. Surprised by tears that spilled out of her eyes, she swiped her cheek. "I'm sorry…"

"Nonsense. Tears aren't always a response to sadness," Nancy said.

"I suppose they aren't," Abby sniffed and swatted her cheek. "I'm… I'm going to get some air."

Nancy nodded, "And be sure to send me your manuscript."

"I will," Abby nodded and walked toward the exit near the loading docks.

Stepping outside, the cool air teased against her tear-stained cheeks. The weekend was a swirl of emotions. She felt like she was tossed in the middle of a blizzard. She was turned and twisted and battered by memories of her mother. The unexpected affection of the attendees of the convention. The support of the convention crew. The surprising kindness displayed by each and every one of the actors and actresses.

Swallowing hard, she knew she had tough decisions to make.

Twenty

Abby didn't move. She stared up at the night sky, watching the snowflakes softly fall. The silky flakes tickled her cheeks as they landed.

Her mind wandered to a memory that stabbed her in the heart. She stared out a window at a snowy landscape. Fresh snowfall drifted down over trees still lit for Christmas even though the holiday had passed and the new year had just been welcomed in.

Turning away from the window, she realized she was being watched. A pair of kind, though weary, eyes stared at her. With a feeble pat of an I.V. adorned hand on the white sheets of a bed, Abby was beckoned over.

With a thin smile and a nod, Abby complied.

Sitting carefully, she looked deeply into the eyes that held an unyielding gaze.

Despite the sounds of the hospital room machines, despite the tubes and cords draped over her, despite the sterile white environment, Maggie Wells wore her usual confident, elegant smile. To Abby, even lying in that hospital bed, she looked elegant. She looked like an actress playing a role.

Abby's heart sank, Maggie wasn't playing a role but was fighting for her life in a very real hospital bed.

"Child, don't look so sad. This day was going to come one way or another. I am so, so happy it is with you by my side," Maggie said.

The words admitted so much of what Abby's heart had already known. They tumbled through the air and hit her ears with a fury. Tears poured from Abby's eyes.

Maggie's taped and tube-constrained hand reached out, her fingers finding Abby's in a soft if muted touch.

"I'm so sorry, Mom. I should have been there. I should have come," Abby sobbed.

"Nonsense," Maggie said. "I wanted you to live the life you were supposed to live. Christmas Con was my world. You were always welcome in it. You were its inspiration. But it was my dream. The door to that dream was always open to you. But it was never intended to steer you from your own dreams, Abby."

"I was living the life I was supposed to live with you, Mom," Abby said.

Maggie smiled, "I had so much more I wanted to give you…"

"You've given me so much. So much more than I could ever ask," Abby said.

"Still…"

"I should have been at the Christmas Con," Abby snapped.

"It isn't about the convention, Abby. It is the spirit that comes from it. It is capturing it and finding a way to give it to others. *That* is the real gift, the gift I wanted to share with you," Maggie said.

Abby clasped her hand in Maggie's.

"I am so proud to have been able to call you daughter," Maggie said.

"You are and always will be my mother," Abby said.

"That day. I saw you through the nursery window. I didn't hesitate. I am certain it was God's hand guiding me. I knew what I had to do. What I wanted to do. I was supposed to be there to take care of you," Maggie said.

"And you did," Abby sniffed, swiping at her cheek with her spare hand. "You are an amazing mother."

"My real dream wasn't to create and operate a Christmas convention. It was to ensure that you and other children in similar situations can feel the spirit of Christmas, no matter the circumstance. I wanted you to feel loved, to *know* you were loved. And to feel the joy of what Christmas is really about," Maggie said.

"I never got to know my parents. But I feel like I did. Through you," Abby said.

"Those might be the kindest words I have ever heard. I see them in you every day," Maggie said.

Abby smiled, "There is a lot of you in me, too. Sometimes, I wish there was more."

"Why do you say that?" Maggie frowned.

"You are always so strong. So confident. Even here, even now. You amaze me," Abby said.

"I have the good Lord by my side and I got to see you grow into a wonderful woman. I got to help my dear friends' legacy blossom into a woman that I know they would be very proud of. I know I am," Maggie said.

Abby gave Maggie's hand a gentle squeeze.

"Things happen. Life is hard, even cruel at times. It is how we react. How we grow and carry on out of the hardship that defines us. It isn't about the pain. It is about the character that we develop from it and how our perseverance can serve others. That is the beauty of life. Love, community, sharing," Maggie said.

"That is why you love Christmas Con," Abby said.

"I love Christmas Con because of the looks on people's faces. People who have lost loved ones. People who have lost jobs. People who are estranged from their families. People enduring pain on the inside that no one can see, and yet, there are smiles. Christmas is all about hope. Christmas Con is reminding those who are struggling to recall hope and find it in the community. In the stories that the Christmas movies portray," Maggie said.

"To see the smiles on those faces when they meet a star, when they talk about their favorite movie with other fans, when they make new friends… only one smile makes me happier. Yours," Maggie said.

Abby nodded. The sting of pain of not being there for her wouldn't go away.

"I have never admitted this. There are years where I struggled. Especially when you were in college and couldn't come to the conventions. My own Christmas spirit was in peril," Maggie said.

"You? I can hardly imagine," Abby said.

"When those children come in from the charity program to see Santa and their eyes light up, it is a gift. Whatever trouble and strife and loss led them to that position, to see their smiles… oh, Abby. Christmas spirit is truly something magical. Whatever life throws you, even a brittle old woman in a hospital bed, always have faith in the Christmas spirit," Maggie said. Her eyes grew weary. The visit had sapped her strength.

Abby saw the energy drain from her mother. She nodded, her throat tight, she could barely eek out a reply.

"I love you, Abby."

"I love you… Mom."

Twenty One

The start to the convention's third day had a different feel to Abby than the prior two days. Aside from the new Sunday-only faces, the attendees lacked the nervous energy and wide eyes of taking everything in as they entered the space.

Instead, they had a direction to them and a familiarity with each other as though they were strolling down the main street of their hometown. Strangers from Friday greeted each other like friends and neighbors by Sunday. Abby felt it, too.

Passing the vendors, she smiled and waved. "Hi, Abby!" they called.

"Hi, Raquel!" she called back.

She realized, at least as far as being at the con went, *her* nervousness had subsided.

Turning an aisle, she saw Michelle escorting Brett. Michelle flagged her over, "Are you coming to watch?"

Abby cocked her head, "Watch…"

Michelle's eyes went wide, "Blind snowman building contest at the dome. It's going to be a riot!"

"It was one of Mom's creative ideas, I'd better see how it plays out," Abby said.

Brett looked confused, "I don't get it. Snowmen without eyes? Is it a charity event for a blind school?"

Abby laughed, "No. The *builders* are blind-folded."

"Oh. Yeah, I get it. That makes a whole lot more sense," Brett nodded.

"Are you in it?" Abby asked.

"No. I took home the trophy from the first snowman contest. I am just an observer this time," Brett said.

"Supporting his friends," Michelle said.

There was a large crowd outside of the dome. They watched and waited as the stars lined up. They would take turns with convention guests either wearing the blindfold or providing the other with instructions as they attempted to make their snowman.

"Look, my snowman is still there!" Brett beamed with a proud smile across his face.

The platforms the original snow people were on were moved to the back, replaced with new, empty platforms.

"No attempt at a repeat?" Manny Vega's voice cut through the crowd as he and his escort joined them.

Trailing in his wake were Jessica Landon and Marie Claire Downs.

A fan, excited by the celebrities gathered in front of them, asked for a photo. Agreeing, they moved off to the side to pose with the fan.

Michelle nudged Abby and whispered, "That duet last night, you two were pretty chummy."

"Just finding a focus point that was not a face in the crowd. I thought I was going to pass out," Abby said.

"Nice of Brett to take you to 'get some air'. I kind of thought you'd come back," Michelle pressed.

"Getting outside was helpful. But I realized I was done for the day. I needed a quiet little dark corner to hole up in," Abby said.

"With which he was happy to oblige," Michelle said.

"I think Christmas Con has a way of getting people to respond in ways that they ordinarily wouldn't. It is the Christmas spirit. We are all friends. Neighbors. Families when we are here," Abby said.

"Mm, hmm," Michelle chided.

"I don't know. It's just circumstances. I mean, look at them," Abby whispered.

They both cast their eyes on the group of actors, now lined up for photographs from several guests.

"What about it? They are people like you and me," Michelle shrugged.

"Beautiful, successful, famous people," Abby said.

"Two out of three isn't bad," Michelle grinned.

"I'm not any of the three," Abby refuted.

"First off, you are most certainly beautiful, my dear friend. You are successful. And fame is overrated," Michelle said.

"Well, thank you. But… I can't even claim successful anymore," Abby said.

Michelle gasped and turned to her friend, "What do you mean?"

"My job, the one I went to school for, that made me not available for Mom as much as I would have liked… it is over at the end of the year," Abby said.

"What happened?"

"My company is retracting. Everything is online and digital now. They don't need people like me to actually meet with customers," Abby shrugged.

"You were doing so good. I'm sorry, Abbs," Michelle draped an arm over her friend's shoulders. "What are you going to do?"

"I don't know. Work has consumed my life for the past five years. I guess, I'll have to start all over again with another company," Abby shrugged. With a nod, she indicated that they were about to be joined by Brett and his friends.

As they walked over, Marie Claire nudged Brett. "There is a very sweet romance that takes place on a Carolina beach that they are casting for. I head to my second callback after the holiday. I'll put in a good word for you," she said to him.

Abby couldn't help but watch the actress' enormous blue eyes smiling at Brett.

"Yeah, I would appreciate that," he said. "I'm ready to get back on set."

Jessica glanced at Brett, a slight smile crossing her lips, "I'm glad to hear that."

"Let's just hope the studio is glad to hear it," Brett said.

Manny clapped him on the back of the shoulder, "If not, I've gotta buddy producing a boxing movie next year."

"Manny!" Marie Claire and Jessica cried in unison.

"What? Too soon?" Manny asked.

"Hey, guys, the contest is about to start," Brett said. Giving a look to Abby and Michelle, he gave a flat smile.

DJ Frost arrived with his mic in hand, "Are you ready for the craziest contest this side of the Arctic Circle? I don't know where this one falls in the world of reindeer games, but it is going to be a blast. So, here is how it works. There will be four teams again, but this time, only one team member gets to build their snowman at any given time. Working in two fifteen minute shifts, they operate as a team. One will give instructions and be the eyes for their teammate who will be blindfolded and have to build without one of God's greatest blessings—sight!"

The crowd roared.

"Let's introduce your contestants!" DJ Frost called out the four teams.

The stars started with the blindfolds as the selected guests called out instructions. The chaos that followed had the audience laughing hysterically.

One snowball ended up on a competing team's platform. One snowball rolled away, leaving the actors to feel along the snow for most of their turn looking for it. The others made reasonable bases as they went to work on the second and third sections.

By the time the teams switched, there were two snowmen with proper tops, middles and bottoms. One had a bottom and middle, but the top had slid off. The last was three snowballs were nowhere near each other.

When the celebrities took their blindfolds off, the crowd roared again as the actors and actresses took stock of their handy work. The one with the reasonably complete snowman was rather proud. The one without a single ball stacked shrugged at the audience.

As the final fifteen minutes ticked by, three snowmen had their relative shapes. One had arms sticking out their front and back while their face was pointed and in an entirely different direction. One had eyes, nose and mouth scattered awkwardly within a relative diameter of where the face would be.

"And time!" DJ Frost called. Grasping his knees with his hands, he doubled over, laughing.

"All right, all right. Step away from the snowmen. Contestants, go ahead and take your masks off now," DJ Frost said. "What do you think? Good job?"

The contestants laughed together, collectively shaking their heads no.

"What do you think, audience? Ah, it was a good time anyway, am I right?" DJ Frost asked.

The crowd cheered loudly.

"Another hit from your mom," Michelle whispered to Abby.

"I, am so grateful, I could use my eyes," Manny said.

"And you still lost," Brett grinned.

Manny elbowed Brett in the ribs and pointed, "Rematch. Next year!"

"You're on!" Brett said, his eyes sweeping over Abby. Looking at Michelle, he asked, "What's next, boss?"

"You have an hour before your next photo session," Michelle said.

Manny checked his watch, "Mine starts… now! See you later, Brett. Ladies!"

Jogging off, Manny reunited with his escort and they disappeared.

"I need to go too," Jessica said, after seeing her escort waving from the walkway.

"I've got time. Want to get a bite in the green room?" Marie Claire asked.

"I, uh, I've got something I need to do. Catch up later?" Brett asked.

Marie Claire nodded.

Brett looked at Abby and Michelle, "You two want to help?"

Michelle scrunched her nose, "Help with what? Actually, it doesn't matter, I need to set up your next session. I will see you in an hour. You two behave."

Abby looked at Brett who smiled. "Well?" he asked.

"Sure. I'll help," Abby smiled back.

Twenty Two

Abby followed Brett over to the coffee stand.

The barista smiled at them as they walked up, "I already started on the order. Thank you, Abby, for running around and collecting their favorites."

"Happy to help," Abby said.

"You're sure about all this? It is going to be a hefty tab. I'll toss in a discount," the barista said.

"No, don't do that. If you really want to do something, give a bit to the toy drive," Brett said.

The barista nodded, "That's a good idea. While it's going well, I hear it is falling short of the goal."

"That would be my fault. I used the last several years as projections to create this year's goal. Mom must have come up with some magic donations I wasn't aware of," Abby said.

"If trying to help too many children is your biggest fault with the convention, I'd say you are doing pretty well," Brett said.

"It has been a wonderful Christmas Con, Abby," the barista said.

"Thank you, it wasn't easy trying to follow Mom's footsteps. She was incredible," Abby said.

Abby looked across the bar as the next set of drinks was being made.

"Don't sell yourself short. Everyone has been really happy with how things turned out," the barista said.

Abby's eyes caught Brett's, whose were staring at the espresso machine. "Are you okay?" she asked.

"Yeah…" Brett nodded, his brows furrowed.

Shaking a finger in the air, he said, "I might have an idea about how to boost the toy drive over the line."

"Here's your first eight drinks. Only sixty-two more to go," the barista set two containers full of lattes and cocoas and teas on the bar.

"We'd better get these delivered," Abby said, grabbing a load.

Brett followed suit.

Carefully, they worked their way through the vendor aisles, systematically delivering well-deserved hot beverages to the proprietors working their way through their third day of the con, their fourth day of convention center activities.

Reaching their first table, Brett set his drinks down so that he could personally grab the cups, read the names and hand the beverage to the vendor.

Jewels, an artist doing fan art, blushed when the movie star handed her a drink. "Thank you, Mr. Walker," she croaked.

"Brett. Thank you for being here," the actor said.

"Thank you," Abby echoed.

Jewels stared at Brett, holding her cup right where he had handed it to her.

Brett shuffled, "Would you like… a photo or anything?"

"Yes… a photo… please," Jewels stammered.

"Here, I'll take it. You two hold the coffee cup," Abby said.

Brett leaned across the table, cradling the coffee cup while Jewels slowly turned her eyes away from Brett and focused on the camera lens of her phone.

"Got it!" Abby sang.

Brett ensured Jewels had a solid grip on the cup before he let go. "It was nice to meet you, Jewels," he said.

"Yes. Meet you, too!" Jewels blurted, setting her cup down.

"We, uh, we better keep moving, Cindy probably has the next set ready," Abby said.

Working their way down the aisle, they delivered to the caricature artist and the chocolatier-—but not before scoring samples from the mom-and-daughter team from Jewels for Hope. Brett showed off his bracelet for them, and they took a photo.

Grabbing their second set of drinks, they stopped at the authors' table. Nancy greeted them, thanking Brett for her beverage. While she enjoyed a moment with the movie star, she leaned in toward Abby, "I read the first few chapters of your manuscript last night. I'm going to pass it on to my publisher."

Abby's eyes went wide, "Really?"

"It's good. I like your characters and I think the story is unique. There are a couple of style things the editors might want to play with, but I think they'll like it," Nancy said.

Abby leaned across the table to hug her, but Nancy waved her off.

"No, no. I'm coming out there, and doing this right," Nancy said, scooting around her table. She gave

Abby a big hug, and Brett snapped a photo with his camera.

"Thank you, Nancy!" Abby beamed.

"No problem. It was wonderful to meet you," Nancy said.

"It was great to meet you, too," Abby said as she picked up her drink tray to visit the next vendor.

Emptying their trays, Brett leaned in on their way back for another round from the coffee cart. "Nice job. I know it isn't easy to put yourself out there."

"Thank you," Abby blushed. "We'll see if her publisher even likes it."

"It's a quality shot on goal. Not much more you can ask of yourself than that," Brett said.

Abby nodded. She frowned as she saw a figure lurking around the corner of a Christmas tree, watching them gather drinks from the barista stand. As Brett reached for a new tray full of drinks, Abby spied Kay Sullivan, her camera in hand following them.

Biting her lip, Abby decided to keep her discovery to herself, for the moment.

"What was the idea that you had?" Abby asked.

Both with trays full of beverages, Brett said, "How about we find some time after lunch and we invite guests to the coffee stand? They pay a donation and have coffee with, oh, I don't know, a movie star or at least a guy who used to be a movie star."

"First, it is a great idea. Second, you'll be in a movie by February, you watch," Abby said.

Brett shook his head, "I don't know. The network is more than a little sour on me."

"This is the warmer, cuddlier Brett Walker. Handing out coffees and finding ways to make sure kids in need have toys for Christmas. Sounds like an actor who is a perfect fit for the network," Abby said.

"Thanks. I think I needed the pep talk. Especially after the Kay Sullivan podcast," Brett said.

In the corner of Abby's eye, she saw the podcaster duck between two booths to film their interactions with the vendors.

When they made their last trip and their last delivery, Brett ensured that he had had the opportunity to visit with each and every vendor.

Abby stood in the shadows, allowing them to have their moment with the actor.

Bringing their trays back to the barista, they shared Brett's idea.

"I don't know," the barista frowned. "If we want it to be really successful, we need a lot of people. I don't think I can handle it."

"Oh," Brett said, dejected.

"But, how about this?" the barista said. "We do a cocoa bar. I can make a big batch, have another making while we go through the first. That could manage a couple hundred people, at least!"

Brett looked at Abby, "Would that work?"

Abby nodded, "We'll call it Cocoa with a Star. Let people know it is for a good cause. I think they'll love it."

"Tell me when and I'll have everything set up," the barista said.

"We'll work out the details. Thank you," Abby said.

The barista beamed, "My pleasure."

As Brett and Abby walked away from the stand, Brett asked, "How do we get the word out?"

"I have an idea or two," Abby said.

"You know, so do I," Brett said. "We make a pretty good team, you and I."

Abby blushed, "I guess we do."

"Come on, we have work to do," Brett said, ready to bolt across the convention floor.

Abby eyed him with curiosity.

The actor grinned, "Trust me."

The words gave Abby pause, though the smile Brett Walker wore and the gleam in his eyes were in earnest.

Slowly, Abby nodded.

Twenty Three

Word around the convention center spread quickly. A line formed nearly a half-hour before the Cocoa with a Star Fundraiser was about to begin.

Cindy, the barista, set up a lavish bar with a variety of toppings from the quintessential marshmallow to peppermint to cinnamon and of course, whipped cream for the top.

Brett circulated the convention floor as his own barker, "Come on, everybody. Cocoa for a cause!"

Like the pied piper, fans followed along behind the actor. Vendors closed their shops to join in on the fun.

Leading a long line to join an already large group, Brett deposited them near the coffee stand.

Michelle and Abby created a roped-off area with dozens of tables scattered for guests. Each was adorned with a mini Christmas tree.

Guests would purchase a ticket for cocoa, which the barista sold at cost so most of the money could be directly donated to the toy drive. Attendees were also encouraged to donate directly if they felt called to do so.

Bouncing on her tiptoes, Abby watched as the crowd grew. Whispering to Michelle, she asked, "You think this will work?"

Michelle shrugged, "You posted a tough number to beat, but look at the crowd. I mean, I'd follow Brett Walker if he asked me to. I'd empty my purse in the donation bucket to have cocoa with him."

Abby looked at her friend, "We have sat at the table with him."

"I know. It's for a good cause, silly," Michelle said.

"True," Abby said.

"Come on. If we didn't have his agent asking him to volunteer and gotten to know him this weekend, you wouldn't follow him around a convention center?" Michelle asked.

Abby watched Brett work up the crowd. Shaking her head, she said softly, "I don't know. I like how down to earth the stars here are. I'm not the follow-an-actor around type."

Michelle studied her friend for a moment. Pursing her lips, she considered saying something, but instead just grunted a "Hmm."

"Hmm, what?" Abby asked.

"Nothing," Michelle's voice crescendoed, declaring nothing that wasn't a truthful reply.

Abby didn't have time to press as Brett looked at Cindy to see if the barista was ready for the guests a few minutes early. Receiving a nod, Brett led the guests in, not before purchasing a cocoa and making a donation himself first.

As the guests quickly poured their cocoas, they gathered at the table. Brett leaned casually, his elbow propping him on the tabletop as he stirred his own hot chocolate. Perking up, he greeted them. Raising his cocoa cup in a toast, he touched each one of theirs.

From Abby's perch in the corner of the roped in area, she could hear Brett ask each and every guest their name and ask them where they were from and if they had been to Christmas Con before.

When he completed the circuit, he eyed tables where guests looked anxiously over their cocoas at the first table. Excusing himself, he moved from table to table, ensuring each guest got to visit with him, take photos and spend a quality moment with a star over cocoa for a cause.

When he had made a complete circuit and other guests were filing in, he grabbed a can of whipped cream from the bar and hung an open bag of marshmallows from his belt. Playfully, he made his way around the tables he had already visited and tossed marshmallows into their cups or held the whipped cream can dangerously high above their cups to see if he could make it in. The tactic quickly devolved to a lineup of guests waiting for a shot of whipped cream directly from the can.

Shaking the can after a sputtering start, he asked Cindy for a new one, which she obliged, tossing it in the air across the event space.

Snatching it, Brett shook it, flipped it upside down and resumed his unorthodox duties of sharing dollops of whipped cream. As a new round of guests found their seats, Brett excused himself to say hello.

Michelle laughed at Abby as they watched the actor's antics, "I think you created a monster."

"Is the creation the monster or is the creator the monster?" Abby asked.

"Okay, Doctor FrankenChristmas. Whatever this is, it is pretty amazing," Michelle said.

"It is," Abby nodded, watching the line to enter the cocoa space inexplicably grow.

Guests graciously made space for more to join.

When Brett's circuit brought him near Abby and Michelle's table, he leaned in and whispered, "How are we doing?"

"We shattered our goal, Brett. We are way over," Abby said.

Unwrapping a candy cane and jamming it in his mouth as though he were chewing a cigar, he smiled, "All right! Let's keep this thing going!"

"Wait. Look!" Michelle pointed.

"Looks like we definitely aren't done yet," Brett grinned, the candy cane clenched in his teeth as he ran off to greet new guests.

Manny Vega and Marie Claire Downs led a whole new slew of recruits to the cocoa area, motivating Cindy to make a third batch of cocoa.

Abby and Michelle scrambled to find help expanding the space with more chairs and tables and forfeited the ropes enclosing the area.

Manny grinned at his friend, "Couldn't have you stealing all the fun… or the good karma."

"Even Jessica is impressed with you this weekend. She said she has seen a whole new side of you, Brett Walker. So have I," Marie Claire said.

"Just doing my civic duty. Besides, it's for the kids!" Brett shrugged.

"Don't be so modest Brett," Marie Claire said. Her eyes swept the audience. Slipping out of her seat, she said, "This is pretty incredible, Brett Walker!"

"Than…" Brett started.

Eyes wide, he pulled back as he was overwhelmed by Marie Claire's arms wrapped around him and her lips pressed against his.

"You and I need to catch up after the convention. We need to have a discussion with the casting director for my next movie," Marie Claire whispered inches from his lips.

Offering a smile to those watching, Marie Claire made her way out of the cocoa area. Before she left, she turned and winked at Brett.

Brett's head swiveled around the room, looking shell-shocked.

From across the cocoa area, Abby froze. Chair in hand, she stood and watched.

Manny ribbed his friend, "What was that?"

"I… don't… know…" Brett said. Briefly looking off in the direction Marie Claire had gone.

Ignoring the escalated clamor from the cocoa guests, Brett scanned the area for Abby.

Finding her looking horror-struck, Brett moved in her direction.

A throng of guests at the fundraiser pulled him back to his duties. Despite his eyes searching for Abby, there was nothing he could do. Collecting himself, he focused as best as he could on the guests. Manny helped as he chimed in.

In the corner of his eye, Brett watched Abby look back briefly in his direction, a sickened look on her face as she turned and walked away.

His eyes followed Abby until she disappeared. Collecting himself, he forced a smile and focused on the crowd who remained at the fundraiser.

Holding his hands high in the air, he gathered the audience's attention. "Everyone, thank you so much for coming to the Cocoa with a Star Fundraiser," Brett said, his eyes sweeping across the attendees.

"I have enjoyed getting to meet and visit with each and every one of you. The convention website has my *real* social media pages. Please, follow them. Say hello. Put in a note that we met at Christmas Con. *You* are who makes Christmas Con special. The roles that we play, we are driven by the hope that we can in some way reach you at some point in your lives. That we can bring a hint of Christmas spirit into your homes," Brett said.

"The power of Christmas Con allows us to do something else very special. That is to give back and bring a little Christmas spirit to those who really need it. With your help and with this event, we met and shattered the goal for children the charities Christmas Con has chosen to give to. That means even more children in need who may receive a gift this year. Thank you," Brett said, as the cocoa audience cheered.

When he was done speaking, his eyes drifted back to where he had last seen Abby.

Abby's heart was in her stomach. She squeezed her eyes shut for a moment, just so she could collect herself long enough to disappear. As she tried to slip away, she passed Kay Sullivan.

The podcaster's eyes glanced at Abby and then back at her camera screen.

Even the podcaster known for pushing the limits, didn't know what to do with the footage she had just captured.

Finding the nearest corridor she could use to avoid people, Abby meandered the back hallways and ducked into her office. Slipping through the doorway, she rolled out of sight. Clutching her hands to her chest, she pressed her back into the wall.

"How could you be so stupid, Abbigail Wells?" she scolded herself.

Twenty Four

Head in her hands, Abby fumed. The roller coaster weekend that seemed to be on a perpetual cycle of exhilarating highs and stomach-churning lows felt like it had finally gone off the rails. What really made Abby mad is she felt like she was in control of the roller coaster car when it hit its apex of destruction.

She was mad at herself. Her knuckles slowly knocked into her head as her mind was still dizzy from the ride.

Abby's thoughts brought her to the convention center half a decade prior. Maggie had been excited as they had the cast from a big Hollywood film as special guests that year.

The lead actor, Trace Gannon, had won several awards for his action movies and was a box office splash with a handful of lighter films. He came into town like a tempest. Despite the lengthy list of personal needs to be provided, he seemed rather cordial.

Maggie admitted that they had a connection from before she became a mother. She fancied that was one reason they were able to land the Hollywood crew.

Arriving early, the debonair actor met with Maggie for coffee and then for dinner. At breakfast the next morning, Maggie was a giggling schoolgirl in a manner Abby had never witnessed.

Gannon had wooed Abby, as well. He looked like the shining star from the past that was a missing puzzle piece for Maggie. She had been so wrapped up in being a mother, supporting foster programs and developing the Christmas Con, romantic relationships had taken a bus-length backseat in her life.

Trace Gannon looked to change that.

Maggie was giddy as she leaned across the breakfast table from Abby, "It was an amazing night.

Like out of a movie. Candlelight. Dancing. Even a carriage ride!"

"Mom, it sounds wonderful. You deserve it," Abby said. Reaching across the table, Abby placed her hand over Maggie's, "I love seeing you so happy."

Maggie swooned.

Abby sipped her coffee, "You said you knew him from before?"

Maggie nodded, "We were college sweethearts. I thought he was the one."

"What happened?" Abby asked.

"Hollywood happened. He got his first big break at a wild whim audition during a trip we had taken together. He got the part. It wasn't the lead, but Abbs. He did so well. After that first movie, a studio gave him his first lead role and he was hooked," Maggie said.

"What about you two?" Abby asked.

Maggie looked distant as she remembered, "It was like he walked through a portal. He left for the acting job and… never came back."

"Mom," Abby's grip on Maggie's hand tightened.

"It's all for the better. His career took off and I found my purpose. No regrets," Maggie said.

Abby studied her mother's face for a moment. She looked like a love-struck teenager. "And now?"

"I don't know. In a way, it feels like we're right back where we left off. Only he has Oscar awards and I have you," Maggie said. "He told me last night, I never left his heart. After all these years."

"Well, how could you? You're amazing," Abby said.

"There's more. He wants to become a part of the foster care foundation. He said it is one of the reasons he got the crew to come to Christmas Con," Maggie said.

"The foster care foundation? Why?" Abby asked.

Maggie shrugged, "Children are a part of his life he never got to enjoy."

"Well, it all sounds great. Just be careful," Abby said.

Maggie smiled.

Abby lifted her head from hands. Her memories made her chest heave and her mood sour even more.

She remembered a very excited Maggie asking Abby to escort Trace Gannon from the Green Room to Santa's village.

Walking into the room, she heard Gannon's voice. Not wanting to interrupt, she slipped in quietly.

"I know, I know," he said into his phone as he paced in a corner of the Green Room. "I'll be back in L.A. on Monday. I've got to do this thing. I mean I do one Christmas movie and every year after that, I have to pretend to be that guy. It's nuts but I like the royalties, you know what I mean? Anyway, it's not all that bad. The lady that runs the convention is an old college flame. I've got her running circles."

Abby cocked her head as she slowly entered the room.

"Remember that part I played… I was the secret agent who had to woo a soccer mom to get close to her and her organization? It's basically the same script. I mean, sometimes the writers get it right," Gannon laughed. "She's no super model, which, by the way, that's another story I have for you, but she's all right. Anyway, I've got to get back to it. I'm gonna pose for this charity thing. The P.R. guys are gonna love it."

Gannon hung up the phone. Spinning he, saw Abby Wells staring at him.

"Hi ya. Maggie's kid, right?" Gannon stammered. Pointing at his phone, he said, "That was just a bit."

"I think *you* are just a bit. Your whole shtick is an act. You don't deserve to be in the same room as Mom," Abby said, her eyes twitching as she tried to rein in her temper.

"You don't know what you're talking about. Do you know who I am? People came from all over to see me at Maggie's little convention," Gannon said, uprighting himself and snapping the lapels on his jacket.

"People who care about Christmas, and oddly enough, others than themselves, came from all over to attend Christmas Con. You, you're just a sideshow. A sad, once and done farce," Abby spat.

"What's going on?" a voice called from the Green Room doorway.

Abby turned to see her mother with a confused expression.

Trace Gannon began to speak, but Abby cut him off. With an angry finger raised in front of him, Abby confessed to her mother, "I overheard Mr. Gannon here, tell one of his L.A. buddies that he is playing you. And everyone else here, me included. He is after a little goodwill with your charity. I'm afraid his plans for you might be even more devious."

Maggie looked past Abby's shoulder, "Is this true?"

"Well, not all of it," Gannon scrunched his face and took a step toward Maggie.

Abby instinctively moved in between the two, "What part isn't true?"

"Rekindling old feelings, that was kind of fun," Gannon said.

Maggie slapped herself on the forehead, "Oh… my… word… You were playing Secret Agent Jack Stone.

How did I miss that? I'm the unwitting soccer mom who falls for the agent in a whirlwind weekend. I am so…"

"No, you're not," Abby snapped. "Give Mr. Gannon here credit for being an alarmingly talented actor with a snake charmer smile."

"What do we do with you, now?" Maggie asked, approaching the actor.

"We, uh, we continue the weekend, without anymore pretense. I'm sorry, Maggs. I didn't mean to…" Gannon started.

"Save it!" Maggie snapped. "You can finish out your celebrity photo sessions and then I don't need to see you again."

"What about the charity?" Gannon asked.

Maggie produced a terrifyingly angry look that Abby had never seen before, "You will be nowhere near those kids, Trace. They deserve better than you. So do I."

Maggie spun, grabbing a box of candy canes from the counter, "This is what I came for."

Abby walked alongside her, "I'll take them, Mom."

Grabbing the box, the pair stormed out of the Green Room. When the door closed behind them and they were in an empty hallway, Abby slung a free arm around her mother.

"Are you okay?" Abby asked.

Though her eyes were teary, Maggie nodded, "I'm fine. It brings back memories from years ago. Broken hearts heal, but they become more fragile each time."

"Aw. You were right, he doesn't deserve you," Abby said.

"I've never had a deep relationship since," Maggie said.

"It is a shame. You have so much love to give. You are so beautiful, Mom," Abby leaned her head on her mother's shoulders.

"Thank you, baby. You are the light of my life," Maggie said.

"You're the light of *mine*," Abby said. "And so, so many others. Speaking of which, you have about fifty children who you are about to shower with love and light. You good?"

Maggie sniffed. Straightening herself, she smiled, "I am better than good. Let's go spread some Christmas cheer!"

Twenty Five

Abby sat in her office, her head buried in her hands. Wanting to shrink away from the world, she knew she had to make it through the final day of the convention. Sucking in tear-choked breaths of air, she tried to collect herself.

A knock at the door made her raise her head up, swiping at her cheeks with her sleeves.

"Can… can I come in?" Michelle asked.

Abby scowled, "When have you ever asked?"

"Things were a bit… weird. I figured I'd try something new," Michelle said, her face making a meek gesture.

"Well, that's that," Abby said, trying to shake herself out of her malaise.

"What's what?" Michelle asked.

"How stupid am I, Michelle?" Abby groaned.

"Not stupid at all!" Michelle snapped.

Abby stared at her friend. "No? For even a second thinking… pretending that there could be something with… a guy like Brett Walker. Who am I? What a joke!"

"It's not a joke," Michelle scowled at her friend. "You would have to be blind to not see that something was going on this weekend."

"Sure. Pity, humility, caught up in a moment…" Abby said. "Until the real world came into view. His real counterparts arrived. Seriously, he used to date Jessica Landon. He almost married her. And now… Marie Claire… she is ridiculously beautiful with those ridiculous blue eyes…"

"She is pretty, but so are you," Michelle said.

"I'm a librarian-on-a-blind-date pretty. They are movie-star pretty!" Abby spat.

Michelle couldn't help but to laugh at her friend's self-indignation. "Abbs, stop it. I'm not saying things are supposed to work out or even that spark was going to ignite. Maybe it will, maybe it won't. But you listen to me, if you think for even a second that you aren't worthy of Brett Walker's attention, we're gonna have to resort to fisticuffs."

"Fisticuffs?" Abby frowned.

Michelle shrugged, "I don't know. It's a thing."

"You're impossible. But I'm glad you're my friend," Abby said, a slight smile making its way across her lips.

"What are you going to do?" Michelle asked.

"I'm going to get myself together and I'm going to close out this convention," Abby said.

"I meant about Brett?" Michelle asked.

"There is nothing to do, Michelle. There is no thing. I'm just his warden as he pays some strange career work release sentence. That's all. He's quite possibly a nice guy and I quite possibly read too much into it, especially after I thought he was a self-centered, narcissistic egomaniac. Turning out to be such a nice guy, act or real, was a bit of a surprise. Surprise!" Abby said.

"Hmm," Michelle studied her friend. "Okay, you pull yourself together, but once you do, I want you to come find me. Don't make me have to find you."

"I promise. As soon as I clean up this mascara and tidy up a bit, I'll be on the convention floor doing what I came here to do," Abby said.

Michelle paused by the door, shooting her friend a dubious look, "Okay."

As soon as Michelle disappeared down the hall, Abby slumped her head back into her hands.

"Get a grip, Abby. It was never real. You are here for Mom and that is all that matters," Abby mumbled to herself.

Slapping her hands on the desk, she said, "Okay, let's make yourself ballpark presentable."

Opening the desk drawers looking for something that resembled a mirror so that she didn't have to walk down the hall to the ladies' room looking like she did, she was surprised to find herself yanking a sticky drawer.

Freeing it, she found it empty other than an envelope that seemed to drop as the drawer emptied. To her surprise, it had an ornate letter 'A' on the front.

With a raised brow, she retrieved the envelope. Gingerly opening it, she pulled out the card that was enclosed.

Dearest Abby,

This world I forged can be a strange one. Beautiful, but strange.

Melding fantasy with reality can create blurry lines between what is realistic and what is nothing more than fanciful fiction. Living in a world of hardships, heartbreak and loss while entertaining a world of happy endings, stolen kisses under the stars and lost loves that are always found in the end can be confusing at best.

Here is what I have learned- hope is real. Love is real. Family can be more than who you are related to.

The people that I have been blessed to associate with over the years are real. They are genuine. They are people of faith. They are people of character. Their gift to the world is a gift of hope. When life seems hopeless, their message in what may appear, at times, seemingly unrealistic stories, is that there is hope.

Yes, life is hard. Yes, life is scary. Is there a guaranteed happy ending? No. But there is undeniable hope. There is love if you are willing to accept it. Is it from a prince or a pauper? It doesn't matter. It doesn't matter if you are a princess or a house maid. Love transcends place, it transcends pain. If you are willing to accept it. Accept your losses. Accept love. Life will give you both. Sometimes without warning.

Forever my love,

Mom

Abby looked around the room, searching for a hidden camera, a ghost anything to explain these messages left by her mother.

The office was empty. The hallway was empty. No one was in the hall when she entered. No one could have foreseen that is where she would go when she left the fundraiser early.

Clutching the letter to her chest, she tried to understand the message. Wincing, she couldn't imagine how those words would in any way alter her current situation.

Shrugging, she said to herself, "He's not a bad guy. He was just being nice and I mistook his kindness for something more. That's all. It happens."

Shaking herself, she straightened up and headed out of the office, prepared to complete her role in bringing the convention to a successful close.

As she entered the convention floor, she smiled at guests and staff as she walked by, not realizing how plasticine her feigned smile really was.

The whispers seemed to echo and cascade from all around her.

"Did you hear about Marie Claire and Brett Walker?"

"She kissed him. Right there in the middle of the fundraiser!"

"What a beautiful couple! How do you think Jessica feels?"

"Do you think this means they are going to be in her next movie together?"

"Are they dating?"

Abby felt like ghosts were swirling around her, taunting her.

Shaking her head, she tried to block out the chatter and focus on her next task, preparing for the closing panel.

Brett Walker smiled and waved as he exited the fundraiser. His phone had been going ballistic in his pocket. Pulling it out, he saw his agent, Liza Accorsi, splashed on the screen.

"Liza!" Brett called, as he ducked into an empty hallway.

"Brett, I trust day three has been exciting," Liza said.

"Well, yeah," Brett frowned into his phone. "I mean it started off good. *Really* good. I bought the vendors coffees. Abby and I delivered them. It was very rewarding. And then, I heard the fundraiser was struggling, so I set up a special event- Cocoa with a Star. It went gangbusters… until…"

"Until what, Brett?" Liza pressed.

"Until Marie Claire came up and kissed me," Brett winced.

"I know. Wasn't that brilliant?" Liza asked.

"Brilliant? What?" Brett stammered.

"I got together with Marie Claire's agent. We thought it would be a jumpstart for both of you. I mean, she was convincing, right? I've seen enough angles on social media to think so," Liza said.

"Social media…" Brett scratched his head. "What are you saying, Liza?"

"It was a bit. A stunt. By all accounts, it worked brilliantly!" Liza said. "The studios are buzzing. A different studio called. They want both of you to come for a reading. Their movies are a bit edgier, but maybe that's where you need to be now. Embrace the bad boy status. It could work for you."

"Liza, I am who I am. I don't need to change for anyone," Brett said.

"What's wrong? I thought you'd be thrilled. Put the Jessica baggage to bed once and for all. Marie Claire is gorgeous. She's an up and comer," Liza said.

"Liza, these are real lives. Real people are involved here. This isn't a movie set," Brett said, his voice heated.

"Brett, what is really going on? Is it the convention girl? I've seen the photos, she is quite pretty. Does she act? Just asking…" Liza started before Brett cut her off.

"Liza, I have to go. I need to fix things," Brett said.

"Brett…"

Brett hung up the call. When Liza immediately called back, he hit the cancel button.

Wheeling out of the corridor, his head swiveled as his eyes searched for Abby.

Twenty Six

Christmas Con on afternoon of day three felt different than the other two days. It was like Christmas morning and the presents had all been opened. The mystery and excitement of wrapped presents was gone, but it was still a wondrous feeling.

Instead of secret packages, it was new discoveries. In place of enjoying new toys at the Con, it was enjoying new friendships and memories.

Abby felt like she had opened a gift where she had misread the tag. The pretty package wasn't meant for her. She drew a deep breath. It was all right, because it meant the gift could find its way to the rightful owner. And she was okay with that.

Stiffening, she held herself upright and re-entered the world of Christmas Con. Updated to-do list in hand, she was content to focus on her final day tasks. Christmas Con had been a success, and she was going to carry it through, just as she had planned, for her mother.

In the corner of her eye, she spied Brett. Knowing he was scheduled to be at his booth, she thought she would slip through unscathed and unnoticed. With the remainder of the day's agenda in hand, she was confident she could work around him.

"Abby!" Brett called.

Abby studied her list harder than she needed to and kept walking.

"Abby!" Brett's voice called, sounding closer. The sound of dress shoes clapping against the hard concrete floor chased after.

"*Abby!*" Brett pleaded, his hand reaching out for her shoulder.

With a sigh, Abby stopped. She remained frozen, staring ahead for a moment while she forced a neutral expression.

Turning, she ducked her shoulder away from his hand.

"Abby, it was not what it looked like," Brett said.

"Is anything what it looks like with you? I feel like I'm on one big movie set," Abby said.

Brett frowned and looked around as they stood just outside of the little snowy park trail vignette.

"You know what I mean!" Abby snapped. "It looked like a beautiful, up-and-coming costar kissed you."

"Yeah, okay, it *was* what it looked like, but it wasn't real!" Brett exclaimed.

"It looked real to me. Acting. Real. The lines just sort of blur with you, Brett. You meet me as the brooding, troubled actor. You come here as the misunderstood, kind, giving philanthropist. You make me feel, if just for a moment, like I might actually matter. But, at the close of the curtain, nothing really matters. Take a bow, walk away and seek out your next audience. I get left with an empty bowl of popcorn and rolling credits," Abby said.

Brett, suddenly aware they had drawn a crowd, shuffled, "Abby, let me explain. Let's go somewhere and…"

"I have work to do," Abby looked at her watch. "And you probably have a line of fans that would really like to get a picture with you."

Brett dropped his head to the side, fighting for the words to reach her.

"Go to your station, Brett. Thank you for your help with the fundraiser. Your acting skills were top notch," Abby spun and walked away.

Brett tried to follow but a photographer got in his way trying to film Abby's retreat. "Hey! Let her be!" he growled.

With a handful of the photographer's shirt, he spun him around. The photographer winced. Brett realized his fingers were pulsing in and out of making a fist. Letting the man go, Brett slumped, "Let her be."

The photographer nodded and hustled off in the opposite direction of Abby, but not before taking a picture of a forlorn Brett Walker looking toward where Abby had disappeared.

Sighing, Brett started making his way back to his booth. He knew Michelle probably had her hands full with his absence.

Passing the gingerbread house, he spied Kay Sullivan tracking him with her camera.

"You!" Brett snarled.

Kay stood up, "I can kind of see why you might occasionally want to take a swipe at the paparazzi."

"Kay…" Brett glowered.

"I'm sorry. It might seem like I was lurking. Well, I *was*, but not in the way you think. I think there is an untold Brett Walker story unfolding here," Kay said.

"I'm not so sure there is much of one," Brett mumbled.

"What you did for the charity, that was something special," Kay said.

Brett shrugged, "I tossed around a little star power, that's all."

"That wasn't why people came. Well, it's not why all of them came. It certainly isn't why they filled up the donation buckets," Kay said.

"Look, I don't know what you think of me. I kind of don't care anymore. But I *do* care about other people who are caught up in the misinformation, the partial information, the one side of the story. It hurts people. *People.* All of us. We are people. Even us who put a character out there on a screen. When the camera goes off, we are real people. We have real lives. Real feelings. Real families. They all matter. We aren't toys for people to play with. People think they know us. Behind the smiles and fancy clothes, we're just people," Brett said.

"I know," Kay said. "I know. And I'm sorry if I had a hand in anything to the contrary."

Brett looked at Kay with a skeptical eye.

"I watched you at the fundraiser connect with people in a genuine way fans don't always get. Visiting with them, you weren't Brett Walker the actor, you were Brett Walker," Kay said.

"Yep. The out-of-work actor who has a problem with photographers," Brett said.

"That is the tabloid story, sure," Kay said.

"Isn't that what you were driving at on your podcast?" Brett asked.

Kay's head fell, "It was. I was wrong."

Brett scowled, "Why are you telling me all of this?"

"Because, I think you got a raw deal. And I am sorry if I was perpetuating it," Kay said.

"And?" Brett asked.

"I might be able to help," Kay smiled.

Cocking his head to the side, Brett studied the podcaster, "Help how?"

"Help the world see what I have seen this weekend," Kay said.

Brett shook his head, "An unemployed actor who can win on screen but fail miserably in real life?"

"That's not what I've seen. I just think you need the right real-life leading lady," Kay said.

"You do what you think you need to do. Just be mindful of those who didn't sign up to be in the public eye. I need to get back to my booth," Brett said.

Kay watched him walk away. The gregarious, leaning toward over-confident bounce in his step was vacant from his walk.

Abby successfully melted into her comfort zone of existing in the background. Navigating her way through the convention center floor, she ensured the vendors had what they needed. She maintained that the day's final events were ready. She checked on the convention staff to ensure their spirits continued to soar as they neared the finish line.

Tasking Michelle with all things celebrity, Abby was able to avoid star alley and the green room. She was content to work her way through the detailed notes her mother had placed for the final day of the convention.

According to her mother, carrying on the momentum of the previous two days was key, but sprinkling memorable surprises was important to seal a lasting impression for the guests. She had a big one planned. She assigned the tasks so that they could operate without her. She could play her role from behind the curtain, where she belonged.

Clutching her clipboard, she leaned against the wall, using a giant stack of decorative gift boxes as a hideaway. Attendees who had only met two days ago walked together and laughed together. They exchanged hugs and phone numbers and mailing addresses.

Abby smiled at the interactions. Letting her body relax, she dropped her clipboard.

Squatting to pick it up, she gathered the papers that had spilled, which comprised a collection of day three notes Abby had taken out of the binder. She noticed the back page was handwritten.

Pulling it out of the stack, she read,

My dearest Abby,

By the time you are reading this, lives have been changed. Friendships have been forged. Hearts have been warmed.

There is magic in the gathering of people at Christmastime. Not in a swirling hocus-pocus sort of way, but in a follow-the-Christmas-star sort of way. Those moments where you can get lost in the reflection of an ornament, twinkling lights, or imagining a Nativity scene coming to life.

It is a feeling of hope. Of community. Of friendship. Of family.

Look around you. You will see all of that forged from the raw beginnings of strangers entering a weekend of nostalgia to forming new and very real memories.

Look around you. You have had a hand in helping those friendships and memories come to life.

That is the magic in the gathering of people at Christmastime.

That is the magic of Christmas Con.

Love forever,

Mom

Abby slipped the note back behind the paper on the clipboard. She followed her mother's instructions and looked out onto the convention center floor.

Silly notions of false romance aside, it had been a wonderful weekend. She had made countless new friends and she had made a collection of memories that she would hold forever. She felt closer to her mother since she had in a long time.

Her mother was right. Christmas Con was magical. She was happy to have been a part of one last journey into the spirit of Christmas.

Twenty Seven

Abby played with a Christmas toy on her desk. Spinning it in her hands, the friendly little stuffed reindeer reminded her of a memory she didn't know she had tucked away.

She took in a deep breath, and her heart quickened.

A muddle of images flashed through her mind, like a jumble of puzzle pieces that were lined up but missing adjacent bits. Slowly, the images came into view. Flashing lights of competing reds and blues lit up an otherwise dark night. Snowflakes fell heavily all around.

Abby couldn't move, trapped by heavy straps pulled painfully taut. Faces of strangers swirled all around her, studying her. They moved both calmly and frantically at the same time. Looks of concern oscillated with consoling smiles.

Impossibly large hands reached out to free her. A knife cut through the straps. Abby could feel the pressure release as another pair of hands pulled her away and wrapped her in a powerful hug.

She could feel the cold of the night air and the wind swirling around them. The flashing lights grew brighter. More strange faces appeared and then disappeared. As she was placed in a car seat, her eyes caught a glimpse of metal. Twisted and crumpled atop a sea of shattered glass on an icy roadway.

The flashing lights gave way to darkness. The car windows were fogged over as dim streetlights fought their way through in measured intervals until the car stopped.

Hands once more reached in to grab her. More faces she didn't recognize carried her to a cold and empty room. Voices chattered indecipherably in another room.

The faces returned. Like a package through the mail, toddler Abby was transported through a system of disjointed stops and stays.

One of the hands and one of the stops found them at a door. A wreath hung on it. It wasn't like the cold and sterile doors she had been ferried through to this point of her chaotic journey.

A hand let go of supporting her to knock on the door.

The arms bounced her gently as they waited.

The door opened, revealing a room bathed in warm light. Bright and cheery decorations filled the room. A smiling, nervous woman came into view. Her eyes landed on Abby's.

Maggie Wells accepted the child into her arms, giving Abby the warmest hug of her life. As Maggie closed the door and cooed at the child in her arms, she placed a fuzzy little reindeer in the child's tiny little hands.

Maggie brought the child, bounced from official site to official site into her home. Her forever home.

Abby's mind reeled.

She was back outside the door, but it wasn't winter.

Maggie kneeled down and gave Abby a hug.

"Are you ready?" Maggie asked. "It's your first day of school, are you excited?"

Abby looked at her mother with large, saucer shaped eyes and nodded unconvincingly.

Maggie smiled. Producing something from her pocket, she handed it to Abby. "Here, so a part of me can travel with you."

Abby accepted the item Maggie held out for her. Abby smiled, "It's a reindeer!"

Maggie nodded. "You are my little Christmas miracle."

"But it's not Christmas," little Abby frowned.

"No, but Christmas spirit lasts all year long," Maggie said. "Here."

Maggie took the reindeer from Abby and clipped it to her little pink backpack.

"I'm always with you here," Maggie said, patting Abby's chest with her fingers. "This little guy is just to remind you."

"I like him. Okay. I'm ready," Abby said, her voice resolute.

"Thatta girl," Maggie said with a smile.

Walking hand in hand, they waited for the bus. As Maggie watched for the yellow vehicle to rumble down the street, Abby looked up at Maggie. The heavy engine of the bus chugged, and Abby squeezed Maggie's hand.

Maggie knelt down and enveloped Abby in an enormous hug.

As they pulled away, Abby caught the look in Maggie's eyes. She looked as frightened as Abby was.

"I'll be right here when you get off the bus," Maggie assured, trying to blink away her tears.

Abby nodded.

"I love you, Abby."

"I love you, Mom."

As little Abby stepped through the bus doors, her mind flashed again.

A flicker of a candle lit up the darkened room. The candle dipped down to an unlit one Abby held in her hand. As the two wicks joined together, Abby's candle bloomed to life in a brilliant dance of light.

Abby and Maggie sat in front of the Christmas tree. The candlelight illuminated the ornaments. Maggie cupped one in her fingers and brought it closer to the light. A heart-shaped ornament held a cropped photo of a couple, a couple Abby had only known in the tiniest fragments of her infant memory.

Abby looked at Maggie.

Maggie's voice was soft, "Abby, you are the greatest gift the Lord has ever given me on this earth. But, that gift came with a heavy heart. I lost two very dear friends in a snowstorm. They were actors heading home from auditions. Their car hit a patch of ice. They never made it home."

Abby's eyes blinked with a twinge of sadness.

Maggie set her candle on the floor. Abby sat hers next to it.

"They had a little girl. Barely welcomed to the world, right before Christmas. The moment I learned of it, even through the heartbreak, I knew what I had to do," Maggie continued.

"My friends did not have a lot of family. Neither did I. We had become family. Just like you and I, Maggie said.

"You and I?"

"Abby, your mother and father died in a car crash when you were just a baby. It would have been your second Christmas together. I was not going to allow you, their daughter, to spend Christmas alone in a county facility. A judge rushed the case with the holidays coming and you… you came home. To me," Maggie said.

Maggie waited for what must have felt like an eternity for Abby to respond. At first, the child's expression was blank. Her lips didn't move. Her expressive eyes were steel.

Tears began to well and Abby fell forward into Maggie's arms.

"I don't remember my parents. I only remember you. You're my mom!" Abby sobbed, swiping away at her tears. "You're still my mom, right?"

"Of course, Abby. Forever my love! Forever my love," Maggie said, pulling Abby in tight.

When Abby released her grip, she studied Maggie in a way that a child's eyes studied their mother.

"I have something for you," Maggie said.

Reaching under the tree, she pulled out a neatly wrapped box and handed it to Abby.

Abby slid the lid open. In the Christmas tree and candlelight, she pulled out a little stuffed reindeer.

"That reindeer has a secret," Maggie said.

Abby looked at her mother with a curious glance.

"Look at the tag on his collar," Maggie said.

Abby found the metal tag and held it close to a bulb on the Christmas tree.

"To Abby, forever my love. Mom," Abby read.

Tears welled in her eyes. Clutching the reindeer tight in her arms, she in turn fell into Maggie's.

They watched the lights dance through the night, holding each other close.

Abby's vision returned to the little reindeer on her desk in the convention center event office.

The reindeer had a tag, but the only inscription was "Comet".

"Well, little guy. Maybe you'll have a deeper message scrawled on you before long," Abby said.

Taking the reindeer, she placed it in a box she had lined with tissue paper. Easing on the wrapped box lid, she tied the entire package together with a bright red bow.

Carrying the present to Santa's village, Abby placed the package amidst dozens more, equally wrapped with festive trappings.

She remembered standing in that very spot with her mother. Abby smiled at the memory. Maggie was more excited and more nervous in welcoming the foster children to the event than she was the movie stars and fans.

Abby wasn't nervous. She was grateful.

Twenty Eight

Abby thanked the crew as they put the finishing touches on the prep work. Candy cane stanchions led from a special entrance into the convention center right up to Santa's village.

Walking what her mother had dubbed "Candy Cane Lane", she reached the doors where the special guests waited inside the lobby. Pushing the doors open, she surveyed the excited crowd.

A woman standing in front smiled, "Abby Wells. I haven't seen you in years. Your mother… she was an angel. Thank you for having us again."

"Thank you for coming and being the most magical part of Christmas Con," Abby said. Addressing the crowd of eager children, each bunched in squiggly lines with their foster family, "Welcome everyone! Christmas Con is a fun event where fans get to meet their favorite movie stars. It is a spectacular event. But this… this is what it is all about. Thank you all for coming! Come on, let's go have some fun!"

Leading the charge, Abby was joined by four brave crew members dressed in elf costumes who helped funnel the children into Santa's village.

Two crew members in festive attire, one wearing reindeer antlers on her head. The other wore a sweater ringed with white fur, a string of large Christmas lights serving as a necklace for a giant gingerbread. Welcoming guests as they arrived, they handed out cocoa and cookies.

Abby wrangled the children onto a giant red, circular rug. In front, sat Santa's throne.

"I know you are all ready to meet Santa!" Abby called out to a loud cheer. "I am pretty excited, too. But, we all know how busy he is this time of year, so I thought we'd have a little fun while we wait for Santa. What do you think?"

The children cheered.

"We have some special guests that I think some of you might recognize," Abby said.

With a nod, two actors dressed in reindeer character costumes from a popular children's cartoon came out and waved at the crowd.

Abby beamed and clapped as the characters danced in front of the group. Each entered the crowd and pulled the kids up to dance with them. As they made their rounds with their holiday theme song playing, both characters converged on Abby and pulled her into the fray of dancing children.

When the song was over, the characters led the children back to their spots. Flanking either side of the big chair, they gave their attention to Abby.

Abby slid her hair off her forehead and smiled at the foster families, "Wow. That was a good way to get things started, wasn't it? It's good to get the energy out, which is perfect, because our next special guest needs your attention."

Encouraging the kids to retake their seats, Abby said, "Who likes stories?"

The crowd cheered.

"I like them, too. My mother, my adoptive mother- I was a foster child too -used to read books to me all the time. My favorite ones, ones I still have on my bookshelf today, were Christmas stories. Would you like to hear a story? Better yet, would you like to hear the story? The original story that those funny reindeer came from?" Abby stood in front of the crowd.

As the children cheered, an audience had formed outside of Santa's village and ran down the stretch of Candy Cane Lane. Brett Walker stood beside Michelle and whispered, "She is amazing out there."

Michelle looked at Brett and nodded, "She's in her element. She enjoys working with the kids."

"It shows," Brett said, admiring how Abby commanded the crowd. "You could barely get her near the stage before. Now look at her."

"She and I wore those elf costumes more times than I could count. It is way more fun than it sounds," Michelle laughed. "The kids are great."

"What a nice part of the convention. I've never seen anything like it," Brett said.

"It was Maggie's creation. She wanted people to get a first-hand perspective of who the charity drives that the con supports really help. The foster children, the families who bring them into their homes and the adoptive parents who make them part of their forever family," Michelle said.

"Wow," Brett said. "It's fun to see her like this."

Michelle smiled at the actor.

"Kids are pure. They don't judge. They just want to love and know that they are loved," Michelle said.

"That sounds like something Abby would say," Brett chuckled.

"I may have quoted her," Michelle grinned.

Brett watched the reindeer clap as Abby introduced their next guest as the writer of the children's book. The author sat and as Abby quieted the crowd, the author opened a book with a pair of familiar reindeer on the cover.

"I know that story. It's about a reindeer and his dad. You know, I had a shot at doing the voiceover for Hayden the reindeer," Brett said, looking very proud of himself.

"You did?" Michelle cocked her head at the actor. "It was cute and surprisingly… touching. You didn't get the part?"

"No, I did. I turned it down. I was too proud to do the voice for a children's cartoon. One of many, many bad decisions I have made over the course of my career," Brett said.

Michelle looked at Brett. She had come to appreciate the frankness the actor had developed as the weekend wore on.

"Well, I hear another book is coming out by the same author about a mischievous little elf. Maybe you'll get your shot at redemption," Michelle said.

"Talk about being typecast," Brett grinned.

They turned and watched the children in the audience breathless as the author turned the page and continued the story.

When the author reached the last page and closed the book, Abby led the audience in a cheer.

"What did you guys think? Who read that book before or had someone read it to them? Aren't the illustrations beautiful?" Abby said. "We have another surprise- you all get a signed copy!"

The reindeer pulled books out of boxes behind the big chair and handed them to the author who personalized books for each guest in Santa's land.

When the last book was handed out, Abby readdressed the crowd. "That was a good story, wasn't it? I like it too. You know, the first story of Christmas happened a long, long time ago. It was a story about a baby. A baby who came into the world in the most unusual way. Most of us are born in a hospital with doctors and nurses. This baby was born in a stable. His bed was a food trough animals ate out of. His parents used straw for his bedding.

"This was not an auspicious start. That means, it wasn't elegant or pretty or even what most people would consider normal. But there he was, this little baby. From lying in a food trough in a stable, he became the King of kings."

"Do you know who we are talking about?" Abby panned the crowd.

"Jesus!" many of the children shouted.

"That's right! And we celebrate his birthday at Christmas," Abby said. "People knew he was special right away. Wise men and kings and even simple shepherds came to visit this baby and give him gifts. As time wore on, many years afterward, the spirit of gift giving at Christmas continued. One man, a saint might have become the most well-known gift giver, at least of traditional presents. Any idea who that might be?"

"Santa Claus!"

"That's right. And Santa, who was a good friend of my mom's, loved Christmas Con. Because he loved visiting children, just like you, here in Santa's village. Are you ready to meet Santa?"

The kids erupted into a loud cheer.

Abby turned and clapped as a jolly man in a red, fur-lined suit walked out in front of the crowd.

"Ho-ho-ho!" Santa called out. "Merry Christmas!"

Abby giggled, "It's like being at a rock concert. Who would like to visit with Santa?"

Arms from every child flew up like a rocket.

"Santa, take it away!" Abby said.

Santa, joined by the crew members in the elf costumes, sat on the large throne. Each child took a photo with Santa, a few with encouragement from their foster parents, before receiving a wrapped present.

When each child had gone through the process and each sat back at their spot with a present, Santa twirled his fingers, "You may open your presents. Merry Christmas! Ho-ho-ho!"

Tearing through the wrapping paper, children squealed as they revealed classic toys from dolls to trains to wooden games.

The presents unwrapped, children played with one another on the red circular rug, and Abby thanked Santa and got the children to chorus along before Santa made his exit.

Addressing the audience, Abby's eyes extended beyond Santa's village to the larger crowd that had formed around it, "This, this is what is at the heart of Christmas Con. Children and families and community and love. These presents make up a few dozen of the nearly thirty-thousand we strive to give out to children who need a little extra love during the holidays. From the bottom of my heart to all of you who came to visit today, to all of you who attend Christmas Con and are a part of making all this happen… thank you. And Merry Christmas!"

Abby attempted to retreat from the focal point of the audience, but instead was swarmed with children and foster families who wanted to thank her personally and give her hugs. Her cheeks rosy, she accepted the attention and hugs, especially from the littlest guests.

Michelle slipped through the crowd, and holding her hands up, she got the attention of the crowd, "We are here for the kids, no doubt about it. Thank you, Abby Wells, for hosting this amazing event. We also support foster moms and dads and brothers and sisters, too! You might have noticed an audience has gathered around Santa's Village. There are a few friends who would like to meet you."

Brett Walker made his way through the crowd, followed by fellow actors Manny Vega and Trevor Dalton, along with crowd-favorites Jen Lilley and Erin Cahill. The children gave way to their parents' excitement, especially the foster mothers who gushed at the Christmas movie stars.

"You guys are the real stars, here," Brett said. His eye caught Abby's. He chuckled when he saw that she had managed to once more slip into the background.

Abby leaned against the convention center doors at the far end of Candy Cane Lane. She enjoyed watching the families enjoy their time. The event was well beyond the scheduled time slot, but she didn't mind. Seeing the children with smiles painted across their faces and families that opened their homes to children enjoy a bit of Christmas joy filled her heart.

At that moment, she somehow felt close to her mother.

Twenty Nine

Michelle found Abby as the attendees in Santa's Village and along Candy Cane Lane trickled out of the convention center.

She cast a caring glance at her friend, "Are you okay?"

Abby shook herself as she was caught staring at the foster families streaming out of the building. With a nod, she said, "Yeah. I'm probably as good as I've been all weekend."

Michelle placed a hand on Abby's shoulder, "You did good work. Inviting the foster children and their families in to participate was a nice touch."

"It was always Mom's favorite part. Amidst the nostalgia of heart-tugging movies, the glamor and fun of the actors and actresses the Christmas movie-like sets, this was Mom's favorite part. She would find a quiet corner and watch. She loved watching the kids interact with whoever she brought in for the event. Of course, no matter who she got, Santa was the big star of the afternoon," Abby said.

"I saw a news crew covering it," Michelle said.

"Hopefully, the charity and the foster program get some good press out of it," Abby said. Her eyes trailed off.

"What is it?" Michelle asked.

"I… I, uh, didn't think about what would happen with the foster program," Abby said.

Michelle studied Abby for a moment, letting her friend process.

"I was hung up, still am, on the vastness of the convention. Of managing such a big event. Working with the movie stars. Trying to ensure so many people are happy who come. I hadn't taken the time to think about the foster program," Abby said.

"There are a lot of ways you can serve foster children and their families outside of the convention," Michelle offered.

Abby nodded, "Sure. There are. Mom had built something pretty special."

"She did. Like you said, you aren't her. You need to carve your own path. I have faith that whatever that path is, it will be pretty special too," Michelle said.

Looking up, they watched as Brett Walker and his fellow stars began making their way back toward Star Alley for the final stretch before the closing panel.

Abby abruptly left Michelle's side and jogged over to the actors. Her voice was soft at first, "Hey! Hey!"

Brett was the first to hear Abby's voice and stop. His small entourage of friends stopped with him and turned.

Abby blushed, "Thank you for coming over. I could tell it meant a lot to the foster parents. Well, the mom's at least."

"You'd be surprised," Manny Vega said. "The dads seemed pretty happy to meet Jessica and Donna."

Brett laughed, "I had several admit they have a secret love for sweet Christmas movies. Guys have hearts too."

"They all like movies they can have on that they know are wholesome and safe for the family," Donna McCall said.

"Well, you were a hit, whatever the attraction," Abby said.

"I love the cause of serving foster families. You know, I work with a foundation that serves children all year long. I'd love to link your efforts and theirs. I might even have a few friends who might pitch in for appearances or auction items," Donna McCall said.

"Wow, that would be incredible," Abby said. "Thank you."

Donna said, "We should get ready for the closing panel. Let's get in touch after the convention."

Turning, she and the actors began walking off.

Brett stayed behind.

Abby looked into his eyes. In her peripheral vision, she could see Michelle slinking away.

"Thank you, Brett. It means a lot," Abby said.

"It's a good cause. Those are special people, I wanted the chance to say hello. Besides, there was Santa. I'm not sure what list I'm falling on this year, if I'm honest," Brett said.

"A mystery that has us all a little puzzled," Abby teased.

"It's good to see the reach our movies have beyond two hours of escape," Brett said.

"That was Mom's perspective. She found depth and warmth and heart beyond the sometimes tropey storylines. She wanted to share that. Build on it. Make a community with it. Do some real good," Abby said.

"And she did. And you did this year," Brett said.

Abby squirmed, "I held a few pieces together that Mom had already strung."

"You did a lot more than that," Brett insisted.

"This whole world, it's overwhelming," Abby said. Subconsciously, they slowly walked together toward the Green Room.

"It's a big undertaking. I have certainly learned that this weekend," Brett said.

"It's more than that. Yes, it's a big event. There are big expectations. Big personalities. Big spotlights. I feel like a vampire trying to avoid daylight. I'm not like you and your friends. The spotlight is the last place I want to be," Abby said.

Brett studied her for a moment. With consideration, he said, "Maggie thrived in the spotlight. Sure, she had a vibrant persona. She certainly looked the part in the way she carried herself and her elegance. But it was her heart that owned the moment. When she spoke, whether to the actors in the Green Room, to the event staff or to the guests, she spoke from the heart," Brett said.

The actor trailed off, his eyes suddenly distant. Abby tried to decipher what he was thinking.

"I could… I *have* learned a lot from her," Brett said.

In the background, guests were filling into the main stage seating area for the closing panel.

"I should go," Brett said.

Abby nodded.

Watching Brett walk away, the expression on his face seemed highly contemplative. Abby shook her head. The man. The weekend. Her life. They all seemed so complicated.

Thirty

Nearly the entire convention had gathered, overflowing the seating area by the main stage, for the closing panel. The last official celebrity event for the convention was a huge draw for the fans.

Every star who was featured at the convention was seated on the stage.

Three days of togetherness brought out the silly in them as they joked and goofed around while they waited for the panel to begin.

Manny played catch with the fans, tossing a stuffed Christmas reindeer, the mascot of the con, back and forth.

Donna McCall stood at the stage's edge, chatting with fans.

Actor and producer Cam Cooper signed Christmas Con buttons and tossed them into the crowd.

Brett Walker stood by the decorated tree. The usually boisterous actor started the final panel of the convention the way he started on day one, by himself.

DJ Frost stepped out onto the stage as the music volume dialed down.

"Wow! What a weekend, huh, everybody?" he called into his microphone, receiving a thunderous applause from the crowd.

Abby, intent on focusing on her afternoon duties, turned and watch from the edge of the vendor booths.

"All right, this panel is all about the love. We are going to hear from the celebrity guests one last time. This is their chance to share a message with you," DJ Frost said.

Starting with Donna McCall, the actors came up one by one to share a message with the fans. They thanked them for their interactions over the course of the weekend. They plugged their upcoming movies one last time. They shared moments with the guests who had come to their booth. They shared a few behind-the-scenes antics that occurred between themselves in the Green Room.

Brett Walker fidgeted from his seat at the end of the lengthy procession.

When he was the last actor to speak, he hesitated just a moment before taking the microphone. Standing up, he walked toward the edge of the stage as he addressed the audience.

"When I first came to Christmas Con, I saw it as a fan experience. A couple of days where you take some photos and sign some stuff, which is great. It really is.

What I've learned over this weekend, is that it is so much more. It isn't a fan experience, it is a *human* experience. I have been touched so much in meeting people and making genuine friendships over the past few days. And I mean that, truly. And, I have watched you all do the same.

For some of you, Christmas Con is a way to ignite your Christmas spirit. How can you not feel it as you walk this event space? How could you not feel it when eventually make your way home? Sure, you have the décor and fun nods to Christmas movies, but it is the people. It is all of you out there. I have never felt the spirit of the holidays absolutely radiate off people like I have here.

"To be honest, I didn't have it when I arrived. I showed up to meet you all. To visit with my friends here on the stage. But I've gotta tell you, I feel it. I feel it like I may never have felt it before.

"I was lucky enough to have met the visionary who created Christmas Con, Maggie Wells. I wish I could have gotten to know her better. I really do. She touched people. She was honest in her actions and intentions. She lived the spirit of Christmas. I have learned this weekend, that spirit is very much alive here still today.

"Maggie's love for Christmas and delivering Christmas cheer to people who need a promise of hope in their lives, is alive in her daughter, Abby. Abby likes to stick to the shadows and there are days I don't blame her.

Being in the spotlight is… exhausting. And at times exasperating."

Brett looked out at the audience and swallowed hard.

"But Abby, whatever shadow you have tried to sneak into, it is hard to disappear into the dark when you are a brilliant, bright, shining star!" Brett said. "You have a part of Maggie's light in you that makes your own, dazzling light shine like the Christmas star. A beacon of hope and giving and love. You don't have to live in the spotlight to touch so many people. Speaking on behalf of everyone who stepped foot in this convention center this weekend, thank you. Thank you for being *you*."

Brett's eyes swept the crowd as he took a breath.

Relaxing, he smiled, "Merry Christmas, everyone."

The crowd cheered. Those fortunate enough to have found a seat, rose from their chairs.

One by one, the actors on the stage rose to their feet. Marie Claire and Jessica shot glances at each other and exchanged smiles as they stood and clapped for their friend and fellow actor.

Brett waved and thanked the crowd as he retook his seat. He glanced and saw Kay Sullivan on the side of the stage, capturing his message.

"Well, with that mic drop," DJ Frost called into the microphone, "that does it for this panel. But don't fret, the party is not yet over. We have a couple more absolutely amazing events scheduled, and don't forget to visit the vendors. You can finish all your Christmas shopping before you leave Christmas Con. List completed, yes, please!"

As the panel rose from their seats, Marie Claire ran up to Brett. "I am so sorry. It was stupid. My agent thought it would generate some exciting buzz. What we thought would be a harmless stunt… it is a slap in the face to our craft and I'm sorry," she said.

Brett nodded, "My agent was in on it, too. It might be her last official act as my agent."

"Don't be too hard on her. It was silly. It was wrong. She didn't know… I didn't know…" Marie Claire started.

Brett's eyes instinctively swept the crowd before landing back on the actress, "I'm not sure I knew. Now, it might be too late."

Marie Claire smiled, "It's never too late. It is the season for miracles, Brett Walker."

Brett nodded.

Marie Claire reached out and touched Brett's arm, "I hope we can still be friends?"

"Of course," Brett said.

"No more silly stunts, I promise," Marie Claire said.

As she disappeared backstage, Brett saw a figure standing there. Her camera capturing the conversation.

Kay Sullivan shrugged.

The moment Brett's soliloquy was done, Michelle's head popped above the crowd as she sought out her friend. Figuring she would be in the back, she saw Abby's head disappear down the long hall that split the vendor area.

Slipping ahead of the audience dispersing to last minute shop the vendors or rush to be first in line for the final event, Michelle jogged to catch up to Abby.

"Abbs!" she called.

Abby slowed before she fully stopped and looked back at her friend.

"Abby!" Michelle jogged up to her. "Did you watch the panel?"

"Yes," Abby said, her voice flat.

"Well…?"

"Well, what?" Abby snapped.

"Did you hear Brett's message?" Michelle asked.

"Yes. It was an eloquent, well-delivered line," Abby said. "So, what?"

Michelle heaved, "I don't think it was a line, Abbs. I think, he was speaking to you."

"He was speaking to an audience of his fans and a bunch of cameras, hoping that his pretty speech reaches producers and studio executives," Abby said.

"Abby! When did you become so cynical?" Michelle gasped.

Abby smiled a thin smile, "It is a learned trait."

"Come on, Abby. Don't be like that," Michelle said.

"I am happy for him that Christmas Con turned out to be a great public relations move. I just don't want to be a pawn in it," Abby said.

"You are his shining star. The 'Queen of Christmas Con'," Michelle pressed.

"I am the queen of the con, all right," Abby retorted. "Who am I kidding that I could pull this off? That I could be anything like Mom. That Brett could be… anything other than who I thought he was before this weekend started."

"Abby, the convention is fantastic. All you have to do is walk the floor and you hear people gushing about it. Maggie was an amazing woman. So are you. Are you both exactly the same? No. And I don't think she wanted you to be her. She wanted you to put your Abby Wells spin on Christmas Con, and you have," Michelle said.

"Yeah," Abby snorted. "If by spin, you mean making a fool of myself and getting my hopes, my incredibly *false* hopes up. I fit in with Brett and the other actors like a fish on a cat farm."

Michelle scrunched her face, "What does that even mean?"

"I don't know," Abby snapped, determined to not let her face break into a smile. "I just mean I don't fit in. Look at me!"

Michelle took a step back, pursed her lips as she gave Abby a thorough once over, "You look beautiful. And it matches your kind, kind heart."

Abby rolled her eyes.

"I'm serious. You are gorgeous, if a bit uptight. But, Abbs, even if you weren't my stunning friend, you would fit in. Because everyone in that green room, everyone manning a booth along star alley is a kind human being. They are as real as someone you'd meet in a supermarket. They are down to earth and they are caring. They cared about your mom and they care about you. That is who they are. That is what Christmas Con is all about," Michelle said.

Abby huffed and looked away. "I don't know what to think anymore. I miss Mom. She was my ground. With her gone…"

"I know," Michelle said softly.

"I'm doing this for her. I am no Queen of the Christmas Con," Abby said.

Michelle sighed, trying to figure out how to appeal to her friend. Placing a hand on her friend's shoulder, she started to speak.

Abby spoke first, "Look, this is all almost over. By most reasonable assessments, it has been a wonderful success. Truth is, once the lights go out, I need to concentrate on my career, not whether a hunky actor is acting or being real with me. To be honest, I have more important things to worry about."

"Oh, Abbs," Michelle looked at her friend. Whether she wanted to admit it or not, there was heartbreak in Abby's eyes.

"I'll see you at closing time, Michelle. Cocktails tonight? On me. I'm going to need one," Abby said. "Or two."

"I'll be where you need me," Michelle said.

"See you in a bit," Abby said.

Nodding, Michelle watched her friend walk away, clipboard held tight to her hip.

Thirty One

Abby successfully found one of her beloved shadows. Finding an excuse to plunder through the nearly empty storeroom, she enjoyed the back hallway concrete tomb.

The room was silent. It was still. There were no expectations. There were no pressures for her to do anything for a moment, but be still herself.

Taking a breath, she closed her eyes.

Her heart tightened as her mind played back a conversation that took place fifty weeks prior.

"Mom, I've thought about it. A lot. You know I love Christmas Con, but mostly, I love spending time with you. You'll be busy anyway," Abby said into her phone.

"It's not the same without you," Maggie Wells replied.

"Oh, you don't need me to run a successful Christmas Con. Like you said, it has been a couple of years, and it only gets better and better without me there," Abby said.

"The convention is successful. I just like knowing you are there with me. You're my little angel. You are my confidence in the corner of the room," Maggie said.

"If there is one thing you don't lack, Mom, it's confidence," Abby laughed.

"Are you sure you can't at least come for one of the days?" Maggie pressed.

"You are going to have me fly halfway across the country for a day?" Abby asked.

"It would be well worth it to me," Maggie said, her voice resolute.

Abby sighed away from the phone, "I would, Mom. I have this project to get done. I want to make sure it is out of the way before Christmas so that we can have our holiday together without it hanging over my head."

Maggie's silence on the other end of the call told Abby she was pouting.

"Look, I'll put next year's Christmas Con on the work calendar as soon as it is posted. I will be there next year," Abby said.

"Yeah," Maggie's voice was soft and distant.

"Is everything all right? I'm used to your… persistence, but…" Abby asked.

"Everything is fine. If you change your mind, at anytime, I'll have the plane ticket booked," Maggie said.

"Mom," Abby drawled. "I will see you for Christmas. I'll be home in less than two weeks. I'm looking forward to it."

"Okay," Maggie said, clearly dejected.

"I love you, Mom."

"I love you, too, Abby. Forever my love," Maggie said. She seemed to linger on the call.

Abby noticed the delay just as she hit the 'end call' button. Looking at her phone, she breathed a heavy breath. Her thumb circled around the 'call' button to call her back. Before she could, her phone buzzed with a message from her boss.

The taste of salt on her lips brought Abby out of her memory. Tears streamed down her face. Her heart in her chest hurt so bad it reeled her backward, and she leaned against one of the storeroom shelves.

"Mom!" Abby cried. "I should have come. I should have been there. I am so sorry."

Abby clutched her heart. The tears stung.

Slowly, Abby slid down the shelf until she was squatting. Her head fell into her hands. For the first time in nearly a year, she prayed.

"Dear God, please let Mom hear these words. Please let her know how much I love her. How much I miss her. The world misses her. There is such a blank space without her," Abby prayed. "Let her know I am sorry that I didn't fight for every second that I could have spent with her. She deserved that. She deserved so much more. I'm sorry, God. I am grateful for everything in my life that you have given me. I am sorry if I haven't shown that. Lived that. I'm sorry."

Sobbing a tearful "Amen!", Abby let her head hang heavy, her chin on her chest.

She could feel her lungs working as she sat as still as she could. The world seemed to swirl around her. She was hot and she was cold. She felt a chill but not from the cold. It was a tingling.

Abby picked her head up. Taking several steadying breaths, she rose to her feet and wiped her cheeks, ignoring the smears of makeup she surely caused.

She hadn't wanted to take over Christmas Con. She was afraid of the memories and closed fist of nostalgia she knew being in her mother's realm would cause. She had no idea of the dizzying earth-spinning mind tempest it would erupt in her head.

She had no idea of the wild oscillations of her heart the weekend would produce.

Abby chuckled as she sniffed away the last tear, becoming more aware of the mess she had become.

Christmas Con made her feel alive. It made her happy and sad all at the same time. Mostly, as she held her hands once more to her heart softly beating heart. It made her feel enveloped by her mother.

Thirty Two

Abby snuck from the refuge of the storeroom and found a tucked-away restroom to tidy up. Glancing in the mirror, she groaned. Taking a breath, she pulled herself together and did her best to tuck away the signs of tears and replace them with a face of gratitude.

As she entered the convention floor, she was grateful to have had a moment to put herself back together. A few steps into the convention space, she was waved over.

"Abby!" Nancy's voice called out.

The romance author slipped into her booth followed by a woman Abby hadn't met yet.

"Hi Nancy," Abby said, producing a soft smile.

"That was quite the closing ceremony, huh?" Nancy asked.

Abby blushed and nodded, "I love how much Mom's event has touched people's lives."

"Your mother was Maggie Wells. A lovely woman. I thought of her as one of a kind, but now I find myself mistaken," the woman Abby hadn't met said.

"Abby, this is Jen, my publisher," Nancy introduced.

"Nancy has talked you up quite a bit. Nancy held lunch hostage until I read at least thirty pages of your manuscript," Jen said.

"Oh," Abby said, struggling to stifle a wince.

Jen smiled, "It has real promise. Well-developed characters, a unique though relatable story line. I would like for you to come to Charlotte and work with one of our editors."

Abby gushed, "That, that would be amazing…"

"We'll put you up in a charming bed and breakfast for a few weeks. All you have to do is show up and bring that creative mind of yours," Jen said.

Abby remembered the reality of having to find a job and get to work before her next rent check was due, and her face faltered a bit, "Can I work out a few things on the calendar? Maybe get with you after the holidays?"

Jen laughed, "Of course. After Christmas Con, most of our office is on hiatus until the new year, with exception of sales and marketing, and our writers, of course."

"Thank you. Thank you both. I don't even know what to say," Abby said.

Jen smiled, "Say 'Merry Christmas'. But know, this is an earned opportunity, not gifted. Your talent is genuine, Abby."

"Merry Christmas," Abby said.

"We'll talk after the new year," Jen said.

Abby's head spun as she tried to muster a response.

The ladies' eyes moved in concert over Abby's shoulders.

"I thought I might find you here."

Abby froze before slowly turning on her heel. "Mr. Walker."

"Abby." To the ladies behind the table, "Could I… steal Abby for a moment?"

The ladies' heads nodded vociferously.

Reluctantly, Abby thanked the ladies and agreed to walk with Brett.

"I was hoping we could talk," Brett said.

"About what?" Abby asked, a distinctive edge to her voice.

Brett walked a few steps as he drew a deep breath, "Did you hear the closing panel?"

"I did," Abby admitted. "They were… very nice words."

"Not just words, Abby," Brett said, his voice soft.

Abby stopped. Squaring up with Brett, she looked him in the eyes, "Brett, I don't know how your world works. But I *do* know that I don't belong in it. This weekend has proven to me that you are a good guy. A *really* good guy. But we are from two separate worlds. When the excitement of the weekend passes and you are called off to a movie set who knows where, your life will be there. Where it is supposed to be. Mine, mine will be looking for a job in an occupation that seems to be going extinct. That's my life. "

"I'm not so sure it is," Brett said.

"What?" Abby spat, preparing to be incensed.

"I think there is a light inside of you that is ready to come out. That *needs* to come out," Brett said.

Abby shook her head, "I don't know what you are talking about."

"You have stories to tell the world," Brett said.

"I have bills to pay," Abby said.

"What if you could have both?" Brett asked.

"And what if snowmen could come to life…"

"You have a gift and you have gifts," Brett said.

"Are these some sage words from a script that I am supposed to understand or suddenly swoon to?" Abby asked.

Brett cast his hands around the convention floor, "Your mother gave you a gift. Her vision, her legacy to live on in you."

"I barely have enough time in my job as it is," Abby groaned.

"How did your mother make a living?" Brett asked.

Abby stared at Brett, incredulous.

"You could have time to pursue writing and make ends meet by continuing what your mother started. A gift of hope to a world that needs truly needs it," Brett said.

"You know nothing of my mother or what my life is supposed to be or not be!" Abby snapped.

Brett nodded solemnly. "You're right. I'm sorry if I overstepped. I see… such a light in you. I just hope it gets a chance to really glow."

Abby looked at Brett. She huffed, "You know, being with you is like being with a magician. You never know what is an illusion or what is real. Oh, he's brushing my hair with his fingers. Oh, look, a shiny quarter being pulled from my ear."

Brett shook his head. "How I feel about you is no illusion. Look, I thought I was in love. I thought I was ready to get married. When Jessica wasn't, it threw me for a loop. It broke me. I didn't handle it very well and unfortunately, some of that was caught on camera on display for the world. In the end, it was probably a blessing. But, being here at Christmas Con, being here with you, I feel like myself for the first time in a long time."

Abby looked at him with a scrutinizing eye, waiting for the other shoe to drop. When it didn't come and Brett looked at her, waiting, she didn't know how to reply. Her fears overcame her, wanting to believe Brett's words.

Her lips fluttered and almost in surprise herself, Abby blurted, "And cut. End scene."

Brett looked deep into Abby's eyes. Her return stare was blank. With a sigh, he shook his head and walked away.

Abby stared after him. Her head was a swirling tempest of feelings. She was mad. She was angry. She was sad. She was confused. Mostly, she was overwhelmed.

With her own sigh, Abby held her hand to her forehead as if to conjure up a solution of some sort to her wild mix of feelings.

As Brett disappeared into the crowd, Abby held her breath. She wanted him to turn back and look at her. She was horrified that he might. She was hopeful that he might.

Taking a few steps in the direction he departed, she stopped abruptly.

"Abby, what are you doing?" she muttered to herself, looking up to see a couple walking by and look at her with questioning faces. Wincing, she shrugged, "To do lists… what is next? Always something, right?"

The couple remained tightlipped but offered hesitant nods in return.

Making a beeline for the relative safety of the hallway her office was in, she asked, "Serious, Abby. What are you doing? You're going crazy, that is what you are doing. Talking to yourself and going crazy."

The hallway felt like it was way longer than it should be. Abby felt like eyes from the convention floor were staring down the hall at her. She pictured them puzzling over the crazy lady who was talking to herself.

With quick little steps, she walked as fast as she could and have it still be called walking. Finally reaching the doorway, she rolled around the corner into the dark room. For several long moments, she kept it that way. Collecting herself and hiding in the dark.

Thirty Three

Abby had successfully snuck into her office and away from the bustle of the busy convention.

Leaning back in her chair, she tried to sort out which intrusive thought would have right of way in her brain.

Eyeing her bag, she leafed through it and pulled her heavily scribbled-on manuscript from its spot buried among convention notes and to do lists.

Letting it plop onto the desk, Abby looked at it. Her mind drifted to its setting. She could see her characters strolling hand in hand along snow-covered sidewalks of a town lavishly decorated for Christmas.

The emotions of her heroine swelled in her chest, and she contemplated taking a chance and choosing love versus returning to her life and the safety of what is already known over a terrifying new adventure.

Picking the manuscript up, a piece of paper stuck to the last page fell to the desk.

An ad for a job similar to the one she was struggling to keep. It was entry level, though the bullet points assured there was room for growth. Taking the job would mean moving to a larger city as well. She felt there was no twinge of excitement or even interest as she held the job ad.

With a sigh, she crammed it and the manuscript back in her bag- a problem for another day. The concept left a pit in her stomach.

Opening the Christmas Convention binder, she flipped through the pages in the back to ensure she hadn't missed anything as they prepared to close the event out.

Her eyes landed on pages she hadn't paid attention to before as they weren't relevant to the actual preparation or operation of the convention.

A series of spreadsheets spilled out a sample budget for the how the convention center operated. Her fingers slid down the lines as she tried to interpret the financial guidelines of the show.

"Abbs!" a voice at the door made her jump.

Michelle leaned into the office, her hands wrapped around the doorjamb.

Abby looked up at her friend.

"Ready for the last event?" Michelle asked.

"I'm, I'm not going," Abby said. Nodding toward the pages she had found in the book, her voice was deliberate. "I have work to do."

"You have a hole to hide in which I am going to drag you out of," Michelle corrected.

"No, I think I'm fine, right here. In my hole," Abby said.

"Abby, you *have* to go. This was your big idea. Your addition to this year's Christmas Con!" Michelle urged.

"Will it not function without me?" Abby asked.

"Abby!" Michelle's tone made Abby jump in a manner she hadn't since her mother had scolded her. Her eyes were equally convincing.

"Fine!" Abby huffed. "I will watch from the crowd. Way in the back of the crowd."

"You're the facilitator," Michelle said.

Abby slumped.

"You are almost done. If you want to quit, do it three hours from now. After the people leave and the sets are packed up, *then* you can be done. If that is what you want, you can walk away from Christmas Con forever. But for the next few hours, you are your mother's voice. You go out there and you speak for her," Michelle said.

Abby's eyes were wide almost in shock from her friend's harsh tone.

"Let's go!" Michelle demanded.

Reluctantly, Abby rose from the desk, letting the binder slam closed.

"All right, all right. I'm going," Abby trudged like a toddler sent to clean their room.

"And you put a smile on that face!" Michelle said.

"I'll try," Abby pouted.

As they reached the center of the convention space, the convention crew cleared out the stations and the sets that had been there. In their place, was a giant ring of chairs placed around a pile of wrapped boxes.

Guests stood in line, each with their own wrapped box in their arms, waiting for the event to begin.

News crews set up sentry with their cameras overseeing the giant ring of chairs.

Abby gulped, "Remind me, whose big idea was this?"

"Yours," Michelle said.

"Is DJ Frost still around? I think he would be a great facilitator," Abby said.

"He is, but he is working on the final set," Michelle said.

Abby drew a large breath.

"Come on. I'll at least stand with you," Michelle said.

"Thanks," Abby breathed. "Well, might as well get this over with."

Michelle waved to the crew manning the entrance to the event.

With a nod, they unlatched the velvet rope and let the crowd stream into the circle. They added their gifts to the pile that was initially placed in the center of the ring and selected their seats.

Abby strode toward the center of the convention center where space had been made for the world's largest white elephant exchange. News crews were on hand to capture the event and catalogue if indeed it reached the echelon status.

Michelle thrust an entirely stagestruck Abby into the center of the white elephant exchange. She faced a larger-than-expected crowd. News cameras with red lights noting they were recording gave Abby another surprised fluster.

Abby's lips fluttered, completely overwhelmed. Her eyes swept the audience, increasing the volume of her terror to ten. She spun in a small circle, fighting to get a word out.

Microphone in hand, Abby trembled.

For a moment, the audience lulled into a quiet hush to hear her before clamoring about her trepidation.

Suddenly, the crowd cheered.

Abby followed their eyes.

Brett Walker slipped through the crowd, "Excuse me, pardon me. Sorry I'm late!".

Walking up, he stood by Abby's side.

Abby looked at him, surprised, horrified, perturbed, and grateful all at the same time.

"May I?" Brett nodded toward the mic.

Abby nodded eagerly.

Taking the microphone from Abby's trembling hands.

Brett waved at the audience and whispered to Abby, "Sorry I'm late."

"What are you doing here? I thought you left?" Abby hissed.

"And miss the world's largest white elephant exchange? No way. Unless that is you don't want my help…"

"Oh, no. Please help. Please help," Abby stammered.

Brett raised a wrapped package in the air. Giving it a little shake, he added it to the mound of presents in the center of the circle.

"Welcome everyone! Sorry, I was running behind. I wanted to find the perfect White Elephant present," Brett said. "Now, since we're all here, why don't we get started?"

Brett panned the crowd, letting everyone settle in. Giving Abby a childlike smirk, he began, "If you have been to a white elephant before, then you know how this works. In the middle are mystery presents. The exact number of presents matches the participants. Instead of drawing numbers, we are going to start at a random point in the circle and go from there. Since this is the world's largest white elephant exchange, we have to keep things moving."

The crowd cheered and the news crews held their cameras high to command sweeping views of the giant circle.

"Before we begin, how about a warm round of applause to the mastermind behind the world's largest white elephant exchange as well as this amazing experience we have all enjoyed this weekend?" Brett held his hand out toward Abby who blushed as she gave a humble curtsy.

Brett smiled at Abby, "Take it away, Abby."

Moving the microphone away, he whispered, "I'll be here every step of the way."

Abby nodded a thank you and addressed the crowd, "All right. Thank you, Brett, for kicking us off and thank you all for being here. Now, let's have some Christmas fun. DJ Frost, if you can give us a little music…"

DJ Frost played a snippet of "Holly Jolly Christmas" while Abby walked the circle of participants. When the music abruptly stopped, Abby stopped.

Abby looked at the starting player. "Makayla and Rhonda. It has been a pleasure to meet you two this weekend. You get to start us off. Good luck and Merry Christmas."

Abby watched as Makayla selected a present from the pile and brought it to her mother. Returning to the mound of presents, she seemed to be seeking out a particular package.

Content that she had found the one she was eyeing, she scurried back to her seat.

"Open them up. Whoever is selecting next has a chance to steal a previously selected present or choose one from the pile of unopened presents. Once a present has been stolen twice, it is yours forever," Abby said.

Stepping back to watch the game play on, she shrank to the safety bubble of her surprise co-host.

"You're doing great!" Brett nudged.

"I'll give you an extra present if you just want to take over," Abby hissed.

"Nah. You've got this," Brett said. Studying the circle, he asked, "Do you have room for a few more seats?"

Abby shrugged, "I suppose, why?"

Brett looked over at the entrance of the game where a group of celebrities had walked up, each holding a gift.

Abby looked stunned. "What are they doing here? I mean, it's amazing…"

"I invited them. They said it sounded fun," Brett grinned.

"Yes, absolutely!" Abby nodded.

Michelle had already requested the convention center crew provide several more chairs.

In-between white elephant exchanges, Abby took to the microphone, "Every one, as you may have noticed, we have a few more players. Let's sprinkle them in among the circle and let them join the fun."

The crowd quickly stood. Stepping a few feet back, they created enough space to place the chairs every few seats. Led by Donna McCall gracefully entering the circle, the actors waved at the group, placed their presents in the middle and took their seats.

Manny Vega shook his present and danced his eyebrows at the crowd.

Cam Cooper walked all the way around the circle until he found his fan friend Rosie who lit up when he sat by her.

Marie Claire and Jessica Landon walked in together before splitting and walking opposite directions to complete the circle in the final two seats.

The crowd and the news crews lit up with the late entries.

"I can't believe you got them to come," Abby said.

"It wasn't that hard," Brett said.

"I just figured you'd all want to be on your way," Abby said.

Brett shook his head and smiled, "We love Christmas Con, too."

Abby's eyes smiled her gratitude.

As the gift exchange worked its way around the circle, Brett and Abby took turns announcing the presents and the exchanges that were made.

"Ah, a fine set of glass Santa hats. Perfect for your favorite holiday toast, I'm not sure those are going to be kept," Brett smiled. "Especially since I am pretty sure the box was signed by Manny Vega!"

The announcement caused a scurry for the next few selections as the shot glasses were in hot demand.

"Ooh, and we have one of our vendors to thank for this, Christmas tree ornaments with photos of none other than Brett Walker, Cam Cooper, Donna McCall and Jessica Landon. I mean, who doesn't want Brett Walker staring you down all season long to see if you are naughty or nice?" Abby said.

"I hope they are still there when I get to pick," Brett said, craning his neck to see where the gift landed.

Signed Christmas Con programs, lanyards and badges made their way around the circle as did a scribbled-in screenplay from Cam Cooper.

A video of blooper reels compiled from Christmas movies found its way into the game. Brett picked up the microphone and teased, "How come they are all of Manny Vega…?"

The crowd laughed.

When it was Brett's turn, he set out like a man on a mission. Stopping in front of a shrinking Makayla who clearly had hoped to have gotten away with her obscure selection, he held his hand out. Makayla pouted and slapped a USB drive in his hand.

Holding it up in victory, Brett grinned, "I have saved my career! In case you missed it, someone slipped in a video of karaoke the other night. This one is going home with me."

"Not so fast, Walker!" Manny Vega rose out of his seat. An evil grin spread across his lips. "You skipped me, and now that little gem is in mine. Second steal, by the way."

Brett scowled as Manny walked up to him. Slapping a pair of gingerbread man oven mitts in his friend's hand, Manny snatched the USB drive. Holding it high in the air, Manny panned the crowd, "Next time I am up against Walker for an acting gig, I'm tossing this baby to the casting director."

The crowd laughed as Brett looked horrified.

Cam Cooper slid a gift out from under his chair and with his foot, slid it to the center of the circle.

"Oh, look. There is one more gift," Brett announced.

Abby looked confused, scanning the circle.

"Ms. Wells," Brett held his hand out toward the present.

"I, uh, I wasn't participating," Abby frowned.

"There's a gift. You're the last one here," Brett shrugged.

Confused, Abby slowly made her way to the center of the circle. Picking up the present, she held it.

Brett walked up and said softly, "You might want to open it up later."

Abby nodded.

Spinning away, Brett smiled into the microphone, "Thank you all for playing the world's largest white elephant exchange with us. What a great way to cap off an already exceptional weekend. Speaking on behalf of my amazing costars, we look forward to sharing our movies with you and, of course, seeing you at next year's Christmas Con. Merry Christmas, everyone!"

The crowd cheered, and gathering in the center of the circle, they wished each other greetings and said goodbye to the stars.

As the crowd began to disperse, Michelle directed Abby to the back hall where the actors were waiting to say goodbye to her.

Donna McCall walked up to Abby and took her hands in hers, "You have been a wonderful hostess. You delivered an amazing experience for the fans… and for us. Your mother would be very proud of you."

"Thank you," Abby said through watery eyes.

Donna released her hands and wrapped her arms around Abby. After a few heavy breaths and choked tears, she stepped back. "Merry Christmas, Abby," Donna said.

"Merry Christmas," Abby sniffed.

Cam Cooper smiled, "I was thinking, would it be all right if we filmed clips for a new movie I am working on at Christmas Con next year?"

Abby's eyes widened. Her stomach had a lump as she knew there wouldn't be a Christmas Con, but she nodded in the moment, anyway.

"Merry Christmas, Abby!" Cam walked away, leaving Abby in the hallway with Brett and Michelle.

Michelle handed Abby the present from the white elephant exchange. Taking a few steps backward, she disappeared down the next corridor.

"There's only one thing left to do," Brett said.

Abby looked up with curious eyes.

"Well, are you going to open it?" Brett's voice was soft.

Abby pried the lid off the box. Sliding a piece of tissue out of the way, she uncovered a book. Grabbing the edges of the book, she allowed the box to drop.

"What is this?" Abby asked.

"A little something my friends and I put together for you," Brett said.

Clutching the book between one hand and her stomach, she used her free hand to pry the pages open.

The first photo was a snapshot nearly twenty years old. In the center of the photo was Abby's mother. Flanked behind her and on either side, were the actors that joined her mother for the very first Christmas Con. The subsequent pages were snapshots of her mother with various stars through the years.

Many of the photos were selfies the stars had taken themselves. Abby turned the pages with trembling hands.

"What? How?" Abby shook.

"I asked if anyone had any memories they could share. They started combing through their phones, their websites, old social media posts…" Brett shrugged. "It's a little rough."

"Brett…" Abby started. Tears began to well up in her eyes.

Her gaze fell to the book in her hands. A photo of a younger Abby with her mother's arm wrapped around her. They smiled together in front of the Christmas Con sign.

Covering her mouth, Abby turned away. Tears streamed down her face, her body shaking with powerful sobs.

Brett took a step back, fearing that he had made a mistake.

"Abby, I'm sorry. I thought…" Brett started.

Abby shook her head. Wiping her cheek with the sleeve of her shirt, she turned and said, "No. This is one of the most amazing gifts anyone has ever given me."

Brett looked through Abby's water eyes. He moved to hug her, but Abby slipped away, "I'm sorry, Brett."

Shuffling down the hallway, clutching the book tight to her chest, Abby disappeared.

Brett was left to watch her leave. The discarded gift box at his feet.

Thirty Four

Abby sat in her office. Propped up on her elbows, she leaned over the desk. Her eyes hovered over the photo album.

Opening the album up, she studied the first photo. It was taken at the first Christmas Con just over a decade ago. Abby traced her mother in the photo with her finger. Standing with a half dozen Christmas movie stars, she never appeared out of place.

Abby sighed, "I miss you, Mom."

Flipping through the pages, she leafed through photos of her mother with Donna McCall at the second

Christmas Con and every year since. Cam Cooper was a stalwart since the third convention.

Abby couldn't resist a chuckle at a photo of Brett and Jessica bookending her mother from last year's con. She had to admit, they made a cute couple.

Even in that photo, her mother was beautiful. She wasn't feeling well, but her smile was bright as ever. She loved the convention. As soon as one ended, she was planning for the next.

Abby ran her fingers through her hair. She was exhausted after her three days running the convention. She didn't know how her mother always looked fresh and energetic.

Finding the last page, her eyes draped over the photo of her and her mother. They looked so happy. Happy there. Happy to be together.

"Aw, Mom. What am I supposed to do?" Abby asked as if the photo could provide an answer.

"Knock, knock," Michelle stood in the doorway. "You okay?"

Abby nodded.

"That's pretty amazing, huh?" Michelle smiled, stepping closer.

"Were you in on this?" Abby asked.

Michelle shrugged, "I helped put the book together. The idea, collecting the photos, that was all Brett."

"Thank you," Abby said.

"I'm not sure I'm the one you should be thanking," Michelle said.

"You and a whole bunch of others," Abby said.

"We love you, Abbs. Everyone here loves you. You should know that," Michelle said.

Abby nodded, wiping her cheeks. Trading out the photo album for the convention binder, she flipped to a tab near the back of the book. Finding the closing checklist, she said, "I need to… I should…"

"We're fine out there. The last of the guests are mingling, saying their goodbyes. The crew is on standby, ready for take down. The vendors are making their last sales to attendees who didn't want to haul their purchases through the convention all day long. We're good," Michelle said.

Abby tugged the photo album closer. "How did she do it? I mean, you know how tiring this weekend is. She never showed it. Ever."

Michelle smiled, "You know that feeling when you give someone a really special gift? That feeling of warmth that lifts your spirit? That is what your mom felt with Christmas Con. The gift of Christmas spirit to those who needed a lift. A sense of community for those who were struggling at home. The bit of hope that Christmas movies bring but in real life."

Stepping up to the desk, Michelle flipped the photo album open, "Your mother wasn't tired running Christmas Con because it filled her with joy to give the experience to others."

Abby looked up and nodded.

"I'm going to see off the last group of celebrities… if you'd like to join me," Michelle sang, a mischievous smile creasing her lips.

Shaking her head, Abby's eyes returned to the book.

"Okay," Michelle nodded in understanding and disappeared down the hall.

Studying the photos, Abby didn't look up at the rapping on the door, "I'm fine, Michelle."

"Sorry to disturb you, Abby," Jessica Landon's voice said, coming from the doorway.

Abby spun, "Jessica! I'm sorry, I thought it was… anyway. What can I do for you?"

"May I?" Jessica nodded in toward the office.

"Of course," Abby said.

"I just wanted to catch you before I took off. Abby Wells, it has been a pleasure to get to know you. You are a wonderful person. You remind me a lot of your mother, but with your own amazing qualities. Christmas Con was… inspiring. I am excited to see what next year brings," Jessica said.

Abby blushed, "Thank you."

Jessica smiled and nodded. Starting to turn, she paused, "Oh. And be patient with Brett. He is a great guy. He just needed the right person to be his incentive to grow up. I think he has found that in you. Merry Christmas."

Abby reeled back stunned. "Merry… Christmas, Jessica."

Left again to herself, Abby's phone chimed. A special video on the convention's media page posted. Abby frowned and hit the link to play the video.

Kay Sullivan's podcast logo displayed on the screen before fading away to clips of the convention. Kay's voice played over the images.

Christmas Con, the annual event where fans of Christmas movies get to meet their favorite Christmas movie stars and feel just a bit like they are strolling through the winter land of one of the fabled Christmas towns.

Like most conventions, there is the standing in lines for photo ops, rows of merchandise vendors and some design features to give attendees the sense of setting. But, Christmas Con delivers something else. It is almost inexplicable in how milling about a giant warehouse-like space can manage to deliver the warmth of a small town at Christmas. From event staff, to fans, to vendors to the movie stars themselves, Christmas Con felt like walking down Main Street amongst neighbors, friends, and family.

As a celebrity vlogger, it is my job to dig up the dirt. Get the stories behind the actors. Sometimes, it is easy to forget that the people we watch on the screen are just that, people. People with lives, families and feelings.

Visiting with Brett Walker, I tried to dig into his tumultuous year. I tried to draw out the fist-flying playboy that the tabloids would have us believe. Not because it was true, but because it sold well. It was unfair. Having spent the weekend with Brett and his fellow Christmas movie costars, opened my eyes to this community. They are as genuine as the characters they play on your television sets. The way they interact with the fans, each other, and even the convention center janitors shows a glimpse into people who care about other people.

The feel-good stories they are a part of is who they are. They want to bring joy into households. Brett Walker is no exception. With no press around, other than me stalking him from behind Christmas trees and vendor booths, Brett took his time to visit with every fan. He supported the vendors. He initiated a last-minute charity drive to boost the convention to reach and surpass its goals.

There is a Brett Walker story, but it is not one of brawls and break-ups. It is a story about caring, about a living, breathing example of Christmas spirit itself.

If you weren't able to join us for this year's Christmas Con, mark your calendar. This is an event you won't want to miss. And you never know, you might even encounter a Christmas miracle.

This is Kay Sullivan, wishing you all, a very Merry Christmas!

Abby watched as the final scenes showed her and Brett laughing in the center of the white elephant exchange.

"Nice job, Kay," Abby said as she closed out of her phone.

Glancing at the time display on the screen, she got up from her desk. Walking out of the office and down the corridor, she stepped out onto the convention floor for the closing minutes.

The room felt like the end of a Christmas party. Attendees hugged one another. Vendors exchanged gifts and contact information.

Brett Walker walked among them. Stopping to say goodbye to fans he met over the weekend, hugging each as they headed out of the convention center. Making his way, he stopped at each vendor.

Abby didn't interrupt. Watching from the distance, she saw as the actor patiently work his way around the room.

Spying Kay Sullivan, he shoved his hands in his pockets as she made her way over to him.

"Hello, Brett," Kay said.

"Kay," Brett acknowledged.

"I'm sorry I ambushed you the other day. I was wrong and I'm sorry," Kay said.

Brett bobbed his head, "We all do things we'd like to reel back."

"I hope I was able to make some amends," Kay said. "I was glad I could get the convention to broadcast it on the main stage."

"It was a nice piece, thank you," Brett said.

"Well, I wanted to do something. But, there is someone *else* you need to thank for the idea," Kay said.

Brett frowned, "Why didn't you two just tell me?"

"It was her idea to stay in the background. Maybe, she just wanted me... and the world to see you for who you really are when you didn't know the cameras are rolling," Kay said.

Brett looked in the direction he had last seen Abby.

"Merry Christmas, Brett," Kay smiled.

"Merry Christmas, Kay," Brett said, walking toward where Abby disappeared.

Thirty Five

Abby walked to the exit of the convention center, saying Merry Christmas to the straggling guests, stopping to give hugs and swap contact information with a few of her new friends.

Rosie ambled up, wearing her ever-present smile, "Merry Christmas, Abby. Your mother would be so proud. You should be, too. Christmas Con was wonderful this year. So full of energy and love. That is why I come. That and cute actors, of course."

Abby laughed as she gave Rosie a hug, "It looks like you made plenty of friends with them, too."

"Oh, they are all so kind," Rosie smiled.

"Merry Christmas, Rosie. Please, keep in touch," Abby said, holding the door open for her. Abby couldn't help but think of her own grandmother. Rosie, a stranger on Friday, felt like family by Sunday.

Laden with bags from the vendors and celebrity memorabilia, Abby held the doors for Rhonda and Makayla. Like Rosie, Abby felt the mother-daughter duo could fit right in for Christmas dinner at her house.

"It was so good to get to know you two," Abby said, giving each a hug.

"Christmas Con gets better and better," Rhonda said.

"Thank you. I am glad. I had big shoes to fill," Abby said.

Makayla grinned, "The white elephant and the other games were so much fun. I hope we do them next year."

Abby swallowed, her eyes diverting from Makayla's for just a moment, "Yeah. Me too."

"Well, Merry Christmas, Abby," Rhonda said.

"Merry Christmas. And if you get invited to a movie set again, call me!" Abby grinned, holding her hand to her ear.

Abby watched them leave. As the door closed, she spun around and faced the convention space. The last guest of Christmas Con had left.

Her heart felt heavy. Her head was so full of conflicting thoughts, she felt dizzy.

Watching the crew quickly shift from caring for guests to convention breakdown, she sighed. Glancing at the little faux winter park, she snuck away for one last time.

Following the well-traveled little trail, the snow-covered trees shielding her from the packing vendors and the convention crews preparing to stow decorations, Abby felt peaceful.

Smiling, she took her seat on the little bench and sat back, taking a moment to just breathe.

"I thought I would find you here," a voice said, rounding the bend.

Abby looked up at Brett, "I must be too predictable."

"You are dependable," Brett countered.

"That's a nice way to put it," Abby said. With a frown, she asked, "Not to sound ungrateful for the company, but what are you doing here? I believe you have served your time. You are free to go."

Brett nodded, "You were a tough, but fair warden."

Abby studied Brett for a moment, "I hope the project was successful for you."

"This weekend was way more than I could have ever hoped for," Brett said.

"It looks like you and Kay made up. You friends now?" Abby asked.

Brett shrugged, "It's Christmas."

Abby nodded.

"Her last bit was shown on the main stage screen. A nice tribute to the Christmas Con," Brett said.

"An accurate insight into the heart and mind of Brett Walker," Kay said.

"I don't know if a weekend is enough to reveal much," Brett said.

Abby cocked her head and looked at Brett, "I believe it can."

Brett looked down at his feet as he shuffled, "Look…"

Abby smiled, "Brett, two different worlds."

"I make movies about the subject all the time," Brett pressed.

"Because we watch what we can't have in real life. The idea of the city girl on the farm is cute. The high school crushes meeting back up in their small town is quaint. The prince, the singer, the movie star sharing a moment under the stars with the commoner… It's all fairy tales, Brett," Abby said.

"I think they are stories about hope and love. Love doesn't follow a script. You can't find the plan for it in a big binder that you carry around, hoping to satisfy each box on a checklist. You have to have an open heart. Then, all those things in life don't matter anymore. How you met. Where you met. Rich, poor. Famous or beautiful behind the scenes," Brett said.

Brett stared at unwavering eyes. With a solemn nod, he turned to leave.

Abby stood up, "Brett."

The actor turned to face Abby.

"The photo album… it was beautiful. Thank you," Abby said.

"Memories should be cherished," Brett said.

Pointing toward the convention space, he added, "Michelle said something about a closing speech?"

Abby slumped, "I am really not cut out for all of this center of attention stuff."

Brett shrugged, "Don't look at me. I can't save you on this one. It is all you."

With a nod, Abby followed him to where Michelle had gathered the crew by the giant Christmas tree. Greeting them as she walked up, she reluctantly took the microphone Michelle was holding.

Abby scanned the faces looking back at her. They were familiar. They were friendly.

Taking a deep breath, Abby spoke, "Mom had a vision eleven years ago to pull the warm fuzzy feeling we get when watching Christmas movies in our living rooms and create an event where that feeling can come to life. Christmas movie fans can walk into a town overflowing with Christmas spirit. They can meet and get to know the actors and actresses that make the movies that remind us what joy the season can bring. Love, family, neighbors.

You all helped bring that feeling to life for over a thousand Christmas movie fans."

"And some actors!" Brett's voice called over the crowd to a murmur of laughter.

"And a woman dealing with such loss that Christmas didn't have a lot of meaning to her this year. We don't know what our guests' lives are like. We don't know what heartbreak and loss they are dealing with. Christmas Con allows them to put their lives on hold, if for a weekend. Surround themselves with people who share a love for Christmas. A joy for community. A fondness for stories that some may find tropey while others, well, they find hope. Thank you all for all of your hard work. You made Mom's vision a reality again this weekend. You brought hope, community and Christmas spirit into people's lives," Abby concluded.

The crowd cheered. Michelle took the microphone from Abby who was all too happy to be free of it.

"Let's hear it for Abby. She managed a wonderful con this weekend with her own really smart additions," Michelle said to another round of cheering. "There is still a lot of work to be done, but not tonight. Tonight, we have our crew Christmas party. But don't run off yet, we have our annual group photo. Gather around the stage."

In a massive huddle, the convention crew lined up in three rough rows.

Michelle looked out over the crowd to see Brett Walker walking away. "Oh, no, Mr. Walker. You are part of the team. Get in there."

Brett paused. Seeing the insistent look on Michelle's face, he jogged in to join the group.

When the photographer was ready, Michelle descended the stage steps and took her position.

"Merry Christmas!" the group chorused as the photographer snapped the photos.

As the group disbanded, the convention crew scurried off in multiple directions.

Brett started toward the exit, but he paused.

The sound of tables screeching across the floor and the clatter of chairs rattling against racks caught his attention.

Turning, he watched as the crew began moving tables and chairs from what was the vendor area to the center of the convention center.

Crew members carried several Christmas trees from around the convention hall and repositioned them near where the tables were being lined up and chairs placed evenly along either side.

Red tablecloths were fanned out and parachuted in place while various pieces of smaller décor from the convention were repurposed as tabletop centerpieces.

Brett saw he was being observed and watched Abby and Michelle walk over to him.

"What's this? I thought the idea was to break down the event," Brett asked.

"It's our Christmas party for the crew," Michelle said.

"Mom called it the 'the family dinner'. You should stay," Abby said

Brett shuffled, "I've been distraction enough."

Michelle crossed her arms, "You're one of us, now. I think you have proven that."

Abby nodded, "Stay."

"What's the play? Do I need to contribute anything?" Brett asked.

"No. We have it all covered. It is a tribute to all the hard work the crew puts in before, during and after the con," Abby said.

"It is also a refueling of energy before our last final push to break everything down," Michelle said.

"It was Mom's tradition. She looked at everyone who worked with her as family. She wanted to celebrate that fact and enjoy an evening with the crew just being together," Abby said.

Brett nodded as he watched the final pieces of the long dinner table put into place. Caterers whisked in and began setting out place settings and bottles of wine in the center of the tables. Large cloche-covered dishes were set out along the table.

With a shrug, Brett looked at Abby and Michelle, "I'd love to stay. I haven't had a family meal in a really long time."

Thirty Six

Abby waited as the convention crew got settled before she approached the table.

She remembered walking to the dinner with her mother.

Young Abby looked up at Maggie Wells and asked, "Why is it called family dinner, Mommy?"

"Well, when you work with people for a long time and you share a lot together, you kind of become more than friends. You become like family," Maggie said.

"Like us? Because I had a different mom?" Abby said.

Maggie stopped and knelt to be close to her daughter, "No, not exactly, baby. You and I are special.

Mother and daughter, birth or adopted is a special bond. But it doesn't mean your family circle can't grow."

"Like the Christmas Con team," Abby said.

"Yes, like the Christmas Con team," Maggie said. "There is always something special with biological moms and dads and brothers and sisters. There is also something special in foster and adoptive families."

"Like from the charity. And you and me," Abby said.

Maggie nodded. "The truth is, family is what you make it. People who will be there for you and you know you can rely on, people who experience important events in life with you, they can be like family, too."

"Like friends? I have some *really* good friends," Abby said.

Stifling a chuckle into a smile, Maggie said, "Really good friends can definitely become part of your family circle."

"What's a family… circle?" Aby asked.

"It is all the people around you. Your mom and your dad. Me. Uncles and aunts. Cousins. That is your inner circle. On the outer circle but very much still a part of your life is the rest of your family circle. Those are the friends we've been speaking of," Maggie said.

Abby looked past her mother and at the convention crew assembling around the table.

"That's a big family," Abby said.

Maggie smiled, "It is. I am very fortunate to have met some truly wonderful people."

Abby wrapped her arms around her mother, "Me too."

"You are the biggest blessing and the most special of all of my circle," Maggie said, looking into Abby's eyes. Maggie drew a circle on her chest and pinned her finger on the very center. "This is where you are in my circle."

Abby smiled back.

"You know, this is one of my favorite parts of Christmas Con," Maggie said.

Young Abby looked at her mother with questioning eyes, "Why's that?"

"Because all of our hard work has paid off. We get to take a moment to come together and celebrate our success, but also each other," Maggie said.

"It has been a lot of work," Abby said. "I think it's nice you have a family dinner."

"I do too. I think it is important we all take a moment and set work aside for just a while and enjoy being together. I like to let the crew know how much I appreciate them," Maggie said.

Abby nodded. Slipping her hand in her mother's, young Abby and Maggie Wells made their way to the family dinner table.

To Abby's amazement, the table fell to a hush as her mother approached. All eyes fell on Maggie Wells. Abby could see the love and appreciation for her mother from every crew member seated around the table. Even a young Abby swelled with pride for her mother.

Abby smiled at the memory as she watched the team find their seats. Their weariness over the long weekend certainly showed on their faces, but so did the joy and Christmas spirit that flowed through them.

Maneuvering around the table, they gave each other hugs and laughed together. Abby was amazed at the buzz of energy that resonated from the group. When they had all gathered, they ensured everyone had found their seats together.

When most of the crew had claimed a seat, Michelle led Brett Walker to the table, seating him right next to the head of the table. Abby sighed, knowing what that meant as Michelle reserved Abby's seat, taking the spot just across from Brett herself.

Craning her neck, Michelle found Abby observing the table. Waving her hand and making eyes at the seat at the head of the table, she beckoned her friend to join them.

With a nod, Abby made her way to the table. As she walked, her eyes scanned the faces seated around the Christmas convention family dinner. Lighting on Michelle and Julie, her head elf, and even Brett. In her heart, she felt a familial tug.

When the crew saw her approach, they looked at her with the same respect and love that they had with her mother. Abby's cheeks flushed. Her eyes stung as they glossed.

Taking her seat, she smiled and waved at the people seated around the long table. Brett stood up and helped Abby slide her chair in before retaking his seat.

Michelle smiled at her friend and as if she was reading Abby's mind, she said, "You may not feel worthy to wear the crown, my Christmas Con Queen, but yet there it sits atop your head just the same."

Abby blushed. Mouthing "Thank you" to the table, she sat up and addressed the team. "Let's have some well-deserved fun and food. I'm starving!"

Thirty Seven

The energy of the convention crew after such a long weekend tickled Abby. Seeing them filled with energy and spirit just by being together was a gift in itself.

"You should say something," Michelle hissed.

Abby squirmed in her seat.

Brett gave an encouraging nod.

Michelle tapped her wineglass with a butter knife until all eyes were on Abby.

Abby stood, smiling at each one of the members of the crew.

"I always wondered how Mom did all of this," Abby said, her arms held wide moving in a small arch.

"There were moments I wondered why would anyone *want* to go through all this work for a weekend?"

The crew laughed.

"But then, I got here. And I got to watch all of you. I got to work with all of you. We got to experience the fans and their love for the movies, the stars, and for Christmas. We got to work with the celebrities," Abby's eyes fell with everyone else onto Brett.

"It all became really clear why anyone would go through all of this work. This very hard work that couldn't be done without you. Tonight, we celebrate you," Abby said, her glass raised.

"Us! We celebrate *us*," Michelle stood and corrected. Placing an arm around her friend, they raised their glasses to a warm cheer.

Brett joined the Christmas Convention team in toasting.

"With that, no more messing around. Let's eat. It's a party!" Abby said.

Christmas music began playing over the convention center speakers and the cloches were removed.

"Family dinner means family-style eating. Mom always thought it brought everyone together better than individual meals," Abby said.

Every other table had cuts of roast beef, turkey and ham. Bowls of potatoes and sweet potatoes made their way around the tables. Green beans and balsamic Brussels sprouts rounded out the feast.

"I was expecting pizzas or something," Brett said, his eyes wide at the offerings.

"The first year it was. The second year was Italian dishes. Mom felt something was missing. It wasn't an authentic family Christmas dinner. So, she found a caterer that could do just that and she has been using them since," Abby said.

"Nice touch. Your mom seems to have had this with everything she has done," Brett said, his eyes lighting on Abby's.

Abby said, "Mom was… so much. She was Mrs. Claus. She was a party planner. She was elegant."

"She was amazing. You are too," Brett said.

"I am clumsy. Disheveled. Distractible," Abby said.

Brett laughed, "I think Kay Sullivan should have followed you around. But in reverse, show you what the world sees in you."

Abby blushed.

"I mean, I'm the one who spilled coffee, took out a guest, and nearly lost a Christmas tree in the process," Michelle said.

"You didn't punch anyone out or exclaim in a viral social media clip that Christmas romances are silly and a waste of time," Brett said.

They laughed.

"Okay, we all have our strengths and challenges," Abby laughed.

Her eyes wandered to the rest of the table. After several long days of working together, they genuinely seemed to enjoy spending yet another evening together.

As plates were cleared, Abby and Michelle excused themselves.

Brett shot Abby a curious look.

"It's Santa time," she smiled. "Don't worry. Word has it you managed to make it on the nice list."

Brett laughed and swiped at his forehead, "Another close one this year."

As Abby and Michelle left the table, the actor was quickly pulled into competing conversations with the festive crew members.

Michelle looked at Abby, "So… the con."

Abby raised an eyebrow at Michelle, "What about it?"

"It was pretty amazing this year," Michelle said. "Built on your mother's foundation, but Abbs, it was better than ever. Minus an incident with a tree."

Abby laughed, "It was a wild ride that somehow managed to turn out okay."

"Okay? Come on, Abbs. It's me. Stop with the I'm just a girl who enjoys working behind a desk for a boss that barely knows me. Wait, that's right. I am looking for another one of those jobs," Michelle teased.

"What do you suggest? I need to make a living," Abby said.

"How did your mom do it?" Michelle asked.

Abby shuffled with her hands in her pockets, "Well, I sort of found a sample ledger in the back of the binder. It was just a sample, though."

"And?" Michelle pressed.

"And Mom, on paper, did pretty good. She did better than the top scale of my industry," Abby admitted.

"Well?" Michelle looked astonished that Abby hadn't jumped on the idea.

"I don't know. It's scary. Not have a regular job…" Abby winced.

Michelle squared up with her friend, "Abbs, you can totally do this. And, you'd have time to write."

Abby's heart fluttered, an excited smile leaked out, "You really think so? I thought about it. I dreamed about it last night. It just seems so…"

"I know, scary. Abby, good things in life are scary. Bringing Christmas cheer to thousands of people and working with high profile actors is scary. Finally getting your novel out there is scary. Finding *love* is scary," Michelle said.

Abby blinked at Michelle.

"You can spend January chasing down jobs in a fading industry or you can spend January with editors from Carolina Pines getting your book that you have carried around for years ready to share with the world. You can work on your next novel. And, you get to put to rest that sinking feeling that I know you get every time you think about your mother's legacy being memories in a photo album or a living, breathing event that carries on," Michelle said.

"Is this life really for me?" Abby asked. "Mom, she was bold. She was the elegant life of the party, the queen of Christmas Con."

"You wear that crown now, your majesty," Michelle bowed. "Are you going to defend your kingdom and help it thrive, or are you going to let it go to rest and be consumed with the vines of old memories?"

Abby frowned, "I think *you* should be a writer. That was good."

"Think about it, Abbs. And if you need an assistant…" Michelle nudged her friend.

"Okay. Okay. I'll think about it. I have been thinking about it. But, now, we have gifts to deliver," Abby said.

Abby and Michelle pushed two carts down the hall toward the convention space where the crew was gathered.

"Ho, ho, ho!" Michelle called.

Abby just grinned as they wheeled the carts laden with presents to the long dinner table.

"Merry Christmas, everyone!" Abby sang as she handed out presents.

Returning to their seats, Abby handed the last gift to Brett.

"You didn't have to do that, I'm not really…" he started.

Abby shot him a defiant frown, "You're sitting at the family dinner table, aren't you?"

"Yes, ma'am," Brett dipped his head slightly.

"And one for you, madame," Abby pulled a gift out for Michelle.

Michelle's eyes went wide, "I love your mom's gifts!"

"That one is from me," Abby said.

The sound of wrapping paper tearing was followed by oohs and aahs as the crew inspected their gifts. Abby's mother would always coordinate with one of the vendors for the following year's crew presents. This year's legacy gift was a snow globe with the Christmas Con mascot, a smiling, prancing reindeer wearing a Christmas wreath inside.

Michelle looked on, "Aw, it's so cute!"

"Don't worry, you get one of those, too. I got you something special. I couldn't have done this without you," Abby said.

Michelle tore into her present. With the wrapper off, she gently opened the lid of a box to reveal the contents. "Abby, it's beautiful!"

"It's the same necklace that Donna McCall wore in *My Christmas True Love*," Abby said.

"I love that movie!" Michelle clutched the necklace close to her heart.

"You always commented on that necklace. I found out it was made by one of our vendors, Jewels for Hope. Their handmade jewelry is worn by a number of actors and actresses. They even give a portion of proceeds to charity," Abby said.

"I love it, thank you, Abby," Michelle said.

Brett shook his snow globe and stared at it.

Abby watched with him as the little flakes glistened in the Christmas lights. It was the perfect symbol for Christmas Con. The thought made Abby shudder.

"Are you okay?" Brett asked, turning away from the snow globe that he appeared to prize.

"Yeah," Abby nodded. "Just a lot on my mind."

Michelle looked at her watch and said, "We should wrap this thing up. One more long day tomorrow."

Abby nodded and stood as Michelle brought the ever-boisterous crowd to order with her wineglass and butter knife.

"Thank you all for celebrating a very successful Christmas Con. I know Mom is watching us, smiling among us as we enjoy each other's company. Let's get some rest and we will tackle all of this and the rest of takedown in the morning. Good night, everybody!" Abby said.

The crew thanked her as they gathered their things to head back to the hotel.

Michelle glanced at Brett and then disappeared in with the crowd, leaving the convention center.

"Mind if I walk you back to the hotel?" Brett asked.

"I don't mind," Abby said, her voice flat.

Abby subconsciously kept a step apart from the actor as they walked. Nodding a thank you to the night guard who locked up behind them, they adjusted the collars on their coats to fend off the icy night breeze.

"Boy, it's chilly out," Abby shivered. "It can be cold, but hopefully dry for everyone's travel home."

Brett unraveled his scarf and without allowing Abby a moment to refute him, tossed it around her neck.

Abby offered a weak smile and said, "Thank you."

They were quiet for a moment as they walked, mirroring the other's pace.

"So, a lot on your mind…?" Brett asked.

"The convention, life, you name it," Abby sighed.

Brett stopped short of the hotel. Braving the cold for another moment and looked at Abby, "I want to thank you. This week has been one of the best weekends of my life. I know you weren't thrilled to work with me and frankly, I wouldn't have been either. Especially how I started out. But I am so grateful for the experience. To really see things from the crew's side, the fan's side. It reminded me why I love what I do. It isn't to put my face on the screen, but it is to bring a moment of joy into people's lives if even for a couple of hours."

Abby squared up at Brett.

"Sometimes, I think about the characters I play, and I think, 'why can't I be a just bit more like them'? I am envious of their lives sometimes," Brett said.

"Which lives? The city ones that end up in the country or the country ones that end up in the city?" Abby grinned.

"Funny!" Brett lifted his brows. "I guess, either. The ones with the happy endings."

"My mom would say, be the best version of yourself. That's all anyone can ask of themselves," Abby said with a shiver.

Brett cocked his head, "Have you fully followed that advice?"

Abby's voice was soft as her eyes darted away from his, "No."

"Come on, it's freezing out here," Brett held the door open for Abby.

As they shook the cold off, they paused in the hotel lobby. Shuffling for a moment, Brett nodded toward the hotel bar, "Night cap?"

Abby looked into Brett's eyes with glimmers of wanting to say yes, "No. We… I shouldn't."

Brett nodded, "Good night, Abby."

"Good night, Brett."

The actor started toward the elevator.

"Brett!" Abby called.

Brett paused and spun on his heel with a look of hope in his eyes.

"Your scarf," Abby held it out for him.

"Right," Brett nodded. With a dejected half smile, he retrieved his scarf and turned back for the elevator.

Abby watched him from the lobby. Waiting for him to hail his ride before she hailed hers, she glanced at the bar and whispered to herself, "Maybe I should have…"

Thirty Eight

Abby paused outside the doors of the convention center. She closed her eyes briefly before taking a breath and moving forward. The familiar face of the morning security guard met her at the door.

"Good morning, Paul," Abby said.

"Good morning, Ms. Wells," the guard said.

"Oh, come on. For five days, I have asked you to call me Abby," Abby said.

"Well..." the man started.

"Paul..." Abby stood with her hands on her hips.

He let out an exasperated laugh, "All right, all right. Abby it is."

"Thank you, Paul. Thank you for greeting me every morning," Abby said.

"It has been my pleasure. I remember your mom. You remind me a lot of her. She always treated everyone so nice," Paul said.

"Well, Mom was a special lady. I am glad a few things rubbed off on me," Abby said.

"More things than you might imagine," Paul said. Turning to walk away, he said, "Merry Christmas, Ms., I mean, Abby."

"Merry Christmas, Paul," Abby said.

Abby stepped further into the convention center as the light sequentially came to life. Whether it was the morning of move-in day, the morning before an event day or even takedown day, there was something special about the convention center. It was a peaceful calm before festive chaos and hard work. It was the excitement of what was to come or the filmstrip of memories of what the weekend had brought.

Her heart ached for the love and friendship and community she had enjoyed through Christmas Con.

"It would be a shame for all of this to go away," a voice called from behind Abby.

She turned to find Donna McCall standing in the doorway. Illuminated by pink and orange zested morning skies.

"Ms. McCall…" Abby said.

The actress smiled, "Please. Call me Donna. All my friends do."

Abby smiled back at Donna. "How did you… uhm, can I help you with something?"

"I am on my way to the airport but I realized I had forgotten something. A gift of sorts," Donna McCall said.

"A gift? In the green room? I can help you find it," Abby said.

Donna shook her head, "It's for you."

Digging in her pocket, the actress pulled out an envelope, very similar to the ones she had been finding from her mother. This one had her full name on it.

Abby took the envelope, confused.

"It's an invitation. To my New Year's Eve party in Nashville. Didn't you ever wonder where your mother went on New Year's?" Donna asked.

"Now I wonder why she never invited me as a plus one," Abby said.

Donna laughed, "I asked her the same. She said as you got older, the movie crowd wasn't your scene. I had always wanted to know what that meant."

Abby's eyes drifted momentarily as Brett Walker entered the convention followed by a stream of convention crew.

Donna's eyes followed, a grin splitting her lips.

"I, uh. I guess I got busy after college, focusing on my career," Abby said. "If I'm honest, I think the glamor and the beauty and the bigger than life vibrant personalities scared me."

Donna laughed again, "I can understand that. It scares me sometimes. Fortunately, the people I get to work with are even more beautiful on the inside than they are on the outside."

"I'm beginning to understand that myself," Abby said.

"It's true," Donna nodded. "Even a certain troublemaker. Raw deal that one got. But I put in a good word with the studio after seeing him here this weekend. Well, I should run to catch my flight."

"Oh…" Abby reached out. "What did you mean when you walked in? It would be a shame for all of this to go away."

Donna smiled, "Honey, I am very well-connected. There aren't too many rumors in this community that I don't hear about. I imagine this is all a giant undertaking. Uprooting your life to continue your mother's legacy, while a beautiful notion, might not be your path. I understand that this might be the last Christmas Con."

"Oh," Abby said. She was taken aback, her head spinning.

Donna grabbed her hands in hers, "Either way, please, I hope to see you for New Year's."

Abby nodded, "Thank you. For everything."

"Thank *you*, Abby. You're part of the family now, whatever path you choose," the actress said and turned to her waiting executive car.

Abby's head spun.

Michelle's smiling face burst through the doors, "Did you see Donna McCall? What was she doing back here? Even on a travel day, she is gorgeous!"

"Good morning, Michelle," Abby said.

Michelle's face fell as she was not getting the scoop from her friend that she had hoped.

"What are you doing for New Year's?" Abby asked.

"What?" Michelle scrunched her face.

"Never mind, we can talk about it later. We have a convention to pack up," Abby said.

As they joined the work crew, they gathered at the tables from the previous evening's family dinner. Abby was surprised to see Brett in his fancy clothes as he was the day he arrived.

With a grin, he pulled off his overcoat and his jacket, laying them on a chair. Removing his button-down dress shirt, he said, "Just kidding. I'm ready to work.

Michelle gulped audibly as she looked at Brett in his t-shirt, only partially tucked after being yanked by the removal of his dress shirt.

Breaking the spell, Abby clapped her hands together, "Let's do this! As much as I have loved spending time with you all, it is time to go home! It's Christmas!"

The crew snapped into a frenzy, making quick work of the tables and chairs before descending on the winter wonderland sets, booths and dozens of Christmas trees.

Brett launched right in. As they worked in reverse of the setup, he found himself undoing trees with Abby and Michelle.

"I wasn't sure we'd see you today. This is above and beyond the agreement with your agent," Abby said.

"I am freelancer," Brett said. "Reminds me, though. I need to get a new agent in the new year."

Abby cocked her head, "What do you mean?"

"After the Marie Claire ruse, I fired her," Brett said.

"Hmm," Abby thought about it for a moment. "According to Donna McCall, you might need one sooner than you think."

"Really? I'll have to tackle that as soon as I am home, I guess," Brett said.

Abby put her string of lights down and addressed Brett directly, "Maybe."

"Maybe?" Brett frowned.

"She's not all bad. Having you help with Christmas Con was a good thing, right?" Abby asked.

"It was a very good thing. The kind of thing that might have straightened out my thoughts on my career and maybe, maybe even myself," Brett said.

"Give her a second chance?" Abby asked. "It's Christmas."

Brett paused midway through removing a string of lights. He nodded, "I know a thing or two about second chances. I'll call her up. See if we can come to an understanding."

"That's the spirit!" Abby cheered.

Brett smiled, shaking his head.

"So, what's next for you?" Brett asked.

"I don't know. I mean, I really don't know. I've learned a lot about myself this weekend, too. I've also learned how much Christmas Con means to people. I don't want to be Scrooge and take it away," Abby said.

"More like Mr. Potter. Scrooge had stuff and didn't like to share. Mr. Potter was the take stuff away type," Brett said.

"You know a lot about Christmas," Abby said.

"It's part of the job," Brett shrugged.

Abby laughed, "I suppose it is."

"So…" Brett pressed.

"So, what?" Abby squirmed.

"How do you complete your dream and not send Christmas Con to Pottersville?" Brett asked.

Abby sighed, "I… I have an idea. But I'm afraid it won't work."

"It won't work because it isn't a great plan or it won't work because you are afraid it won't work?" Brett asked.

"I think the plan is okay," Abby said, her voice soft.

"It's okay to be afraid. I was afraid to try out for my first acting gig. I was afraid to come here," Brett said. "It isn't the things that we are afraid of that define us. It is what we decide to do with the fear."

Abby looked at Brett. "That might be the most profound thing I have ever heard you say on or off screen," she said.

"I'm struggling how to take that," Brett said.

"Thank you, Brett," Abby said.

"Okay, I'll take it in a good way," Brett smiled, returning to his work.

After a few minutes of working in silence, Brett asked, "Say, if you were to live your dream, writing, right?"

"I would love to be a writer," Abby nodded.

"Well, you have written. You have a publisher taking interest," Brett said. "Are you working on anything else?"

"I have been toying with a story idea," Abby said, a coy note in her voice.

"Oh?" Brett asked, removing another string of lights.

"It's about this really obnoxious man," Abby said.

"Really? Do you have a character profile in mind?" Brett asked.

"I have an idea," Abby admitted. "It turns out, he's really not so bad after all."

"Hmm. Not very realistic. I mean, do you think people really change?" Brett asked.

"Maybe," Abby shrugged. "I think, sometimes, when you strip away all the clutter, their true selves can come out."

"True selves," Brett repeated. "I think maybe your leading lady should be finding herself in this story."

Abby walked around the tree Brett was working on. Squaring up to him, she looked into his eyes, "I think she has."

Pressing up on her toes, Abby led her lips to Brett's. Together, they met. Among the trees in the little park vignette, they kissed.

A crew member disassembling the snow machine, spied the two. In a moment's inspiration, he turned on the machine to use up the remaining flakes.

Abby and Brett laughed as snowflakes cascaded softly over them. Looking up, the crew member shrugged with a wry smile.

"So, this is how they do it in the movies," Abby said, her lips close to Brett's.

"No. This is how *we* do it in real life." Brett gently cupped her chin with his fingers, and Abby wrapped her hands around his neck as they embraced in a deep kiss.

Separating, they laughed, dusting fake snow off each other's shoulders as the snow machine was wheeled away.

"What do we do now?" Brett asked.

"We..." Abby started.

A voice called from the far end of the nearly empty convention center. "Ms. Wells!"

The night guard came running up to Abby as the last of the trees were hauled off by crew members. The guard's footsteps echoed through the cavernous building.

"Yes?" Abby replied.

"I have something for you. A note said to give it to you right before you left," the night guard said, handing Abby an envelope.

Abby took it, tracing her fingers around the ornate letter "A" scrawled on the red sachet. "Thank you," she said, her voice low.

The night guard nodded, "We're locked up, so make sure when you push through those doors, you have everything you need."

"Thank you," Abby said again, staring at the envelope.

"What's that?" Brett asked, eyeing Abby's reaction to the delivery.

"It's from my mom," she said.

"Oh. Uh, I'll be… I'll be right outside," Brett said, grabbing his clothes from the solitary chair standing in the middle of the convention center. Slipping them on, he pushed through the doors and into the frosty night air.

Abby squeezed her eyes shut tight. She gripped the envelope with her fingers. Taking a deep breath, she opened her eyes and slid the notecard out of the envelope. Flipping it open, she read-

My dearest Abby,

By now, the hard work has paid off. There have been hugs. There have been tears. There have been friendships made that will endure years, if not lifetimes. Christmas Con is a gift.

I wanted you to carry on where I left off. I know it wasn't part of your plan. If it still isn't, I understand. If you are like me, the first con is every bit as terrifying and daunting as it is uplifting and beautiful.

It came to me out of inspiration. It comes to you out of obligation. I hope you don't feel that way anymore. I hope you found overwhelming joy in your time with the con.

The big question is, what is next?

Now that your heart is warmed and you are overflowing with Christmas spirit, this is the time to reserve the space for next year's Christmas Con. You won't regret it. I promise you.

I wish I was there with you. Know, in some way, I am right by your side.

Merry Christmas, Abby!

Love forever,

Mom

Abby put the note away in her pocket. Her head surveyed the empty convention center.

Bouncing on her toes, she took one last look back before pushing through the heavy convention center doors and into the cold evening.

Brett stood, blowing on his hands for warmth as he waited.

Abby looked up at him and offered a smile.

"You good?" he asked.

Abby nodded. "I think…" she started.

Glancing over her shoulder at the convention center, she said, "I told the night guard to have the manager call me tomorrow to reserve the center for next year. What do you think? Keep the white elephant exchange?"

"Keep the snowball fight and I'm in!" Brett grinned.

Abby collapsed into his arms, grateful for the steady company as her heart and mind swirled from the new world she was leaping into.

"You are going to do so great. By this time next year, you'll have your first book on the market. I can only imagine how cool Christmas Con will be next year. Just double-check your podcasters," Brett said.

Abby looked up at Brett, studying his eyes.

The actor smiled back.

Leaning in for a kiss, Brett whispered, "Merry Christmas, Abby."

"Merry Christmas, Brett."

About the Author

Seth Sjostrom is a serial entrepreneur, adventurer and author. His novels include the thrillers *Blood in the Snow, Blood in the Water, Blood in the Sand, Penance, Penance: Unredeemable, Penance: Absolution, Patriot X, Patriot X: Insurrection, Dark Chase* and *Dark Chase: Dead Run* as well as the romances *Back to Carolina, Finding Christmas, The Tree Farm, Letters from Santa, The Nativity* and *The Toy Store*. He recently released the first of his Beach House Mysteries series *Trouble on Treasure Island*. Seth partners with Hire Heroes USA and Special Operations Warrior Foundation with proceeds and volunteer hours dedicated with sales of his Patriot X series. Sales of *The Christmas Café* help to support Jen Lilley and Ale Boggiano's "Christmas is Not Cancelled" charity fundraising for foster children. Seth has also shares a portion of author proceeds of his Penance Series with the Mel Greene Institute to Stop Human Trafficking.

www.SethSjostrom.com
Twitter: @SethSjostrom
Facebook: @authorSethSjostrom
Instagram: @SethSjostrom

More Books by Seth

Christmas Titles
Finding Christmas
The Tree Farm
The Nativity
The Toy Store
The Christmas Café
Love at The Christmas Con

Beach House Mysteries
Trouble on Treasure Island
A Caper on Carolina Beach
Peril on Palm Beach (2025)

Other Titles
Back to Carolina
Penance
Penance: Unredeemable
Penance: Absolution
Dark Chase
Dark Chase: Dead Run
Patriot X
Patriot X: Insurrection
Blood in the Snow
Blood in the Water
Blood in the Sand

Children's Books
Letters from Santa
The Hollow
Cryptid Rangers: The Secret of the Skunk Ape
The Heart of a Reindeer
The(Too) Helpful Little Angel
A Puppy Whisperer Christmas

www.ingramcontent.com/pod-product-compliance
Lightning Source LLC
Chambersburg PA
CBHW030338010826
48973CB00004B/1064